THE
MENDER'S
PARADOX

Thanks Bert
for coming to
my book party!
Peace.
Larry Jr.

L. J. Skocik

THE MENDER'S PARADOX

This is a work of fiction. Any resemblance to real life events
and persons is coincidental.

For further information contact: LJSkocik@gmail.com

Cover design: Sailor Adams
Book Layout: Tim Schoenbachler

Uramado Press

Dedicated to all who suffer from an invisible illness
and especially to those who have M.E.
(myalgic encephalomyelitis)

Special thanks to Sarah and Anna
for their inspiration to persevere with joy
and to my beautiful wife Karin
for putting up with me.

TABLE OF CONTENTS

par·a·dox

/ˈperəˌdäks/

noun

A seemingly absurd or self-contradictory statement or proposition that when investigated or explained may prove to be well founded or true.

Preface

In 2014 I attended a spring training matchup between the Baltimore Orioles and the Detroit Tigers at Joker Marchant Stadium. Seeking shelter from the afternoon Florida sun, I found a good spot in the upper deck near the wheelchair section. A boy sitting perfectly still in a wheelchair watched the game as his mom stood guard next to him. His twisted legs jutted out at obtuse angles. One hand remained positioned straight over his head with the hand turned backwards. My heart went out to this kid. I struggled with my own downhill battle with myalgic encephalomyelitis, little knowing that I would also be in a wheelchair five years later. But this boy looked so much worse off. I wished somebody could fix him. Then a crazy thought popped into my head. What if I could do it? I imagined walking over to him and taking his hands in mine. I also imagined his guard-mom slapping me upside the head and calling security.

In 2017 I sent my family to Ohio for Thanksgiving Day. I stayed home because of ongoing health issues. By then I couldn't do much of anything except lay on the couch with Zoe my rescue dog snoring next to me. Being extra bored, I needed a project. It had to be something I could do laying flat on my back all day. Then another crazy thought materialized. I would write a book. Recalling that day in 2014 at Joker Marchant Stadium and the boy in the wheelchair, I began.

Ninety-nine percent of the process churned in my head with me living my horizontal life. I could only write for five or ten minutes a day because of my illness. Unable to use my eyes, I could not review what I wrote each day. Pecking away at my homemade braille keyboard a little each day, I strung together the pieces of the story that I crafted in my head on the couch.

I presented the first chapter to my daughter Sarah who gave me a few pointers and encouraged me to keep going. By the second chapter my friend Mr. Steve joined the reading list. Every month or two I would provide them with another chapter and get their feedback.

Stephen King said that writing is like telepathy. Because of brain fog and the fact that I couldn't review my own writing, I greatly doubted my telepathic powers. My two subscription readers helped keep me on track with the story's cohesiveness and continued to cheer me on.

After three years of this painstaking process, I finished the manuscript. By this time, a text to speech app on my computer read the manuscript aloud and I heard my story for the first time.

I told my brother Dave that I had written a book. His reply, "Now the magic begins." Both he and my brother Mike volunteered to be my editors. Editors? Who needed editors? It turned out that I did.

Fortunately for me, Dave was a published author and Mike used to be in the copy editing business. Since I couldn't read and could barely speak, I used a text to speech talking keyboard so I could communicate with my editors. Dave and Mike took turns coming over to my house for short editing sessions. They would read a line in the book and then I would discuss changes in a British butler voice that emanated from the talking keyboard. We did this line by line, week after week, for a year. It is a real testament to my brothers' patience and dedication to have hung in there with me on this long editing process. Many a writing session ended with my audio keyboard saying, "Thanks for the writing lesson, governor. Cheerio."

Thank you to my talented niece, Sailor, for creating the book cover; to my daughter, Anna, as the book cover model; and to my proofreaders/editors: my brothers David and Mike, and my cousin Ken. I extend my deep gratitude and love to my book helpers and family for their love and support.

Prologue

June 17, 2017

The Rocky Broad River at Chimney Rock, N.C. is an ideal place to kick back and relax — unless you are being hunted by a psychopath whose sole purpose in life is to kill. Dr. Bill Langley found himself in this exact situation.

For three days, Dr. Langley had holed up in a decrepit motel resembling those found in bleak Hollywood Westerns. Dr. Langley had a thriving practice in his clinic outside Athens, Georgia. The results of his most recent treatment methods had been especially promising. Being on the cutting edge of alternative medicine, he was used to being harassed by the American Medical Association.

Ten days ago a young man who didn't have an appointment visited Langley at his office. Langley looked up from his desk chair at the man who did not take a seat. He wore a black hat, black suit, and coke bottle glasses that covered most of the scar that trickled down by his left eye. He claimed that he had a message for Langley from some very powerful people. The visitor did not say anything else but did hand Langley a business card. Then the mystery man left. The front of the card said:

Last Chance Funeral Services

The back of the card had the hand-written message:

'Retire within 3 days or you will be deleted.'

"Deleted?" Langley said out loud. This was definitely not the A.M.A.'s style. 'Was this guy for real? Who did he represent?' Of course he had no intention of ending his thirty-year career, especially since he was on the verge of his life's work culminating in a substantial medical breakthrough.

Three days later the FDA raided his clinic. It was too big of a coincidence that his practice was closed down right after the doomsday visitor. He did not stick around to see if the threat would be carried out. Instead he hightailed it to Chimney Rock, where he had spent time as a boy on family vacations. The Carolina mountains provided a nostalgic sanctuary where he could get some distance between himself and his clinic.

Now he sat in an uneasy chair staring at a tin can precariously propped on top of his motel room's doorknob. He had heard of the untimely deaths of other alternative medical practitioners, including murders and suicides. Could the rumors be true? Was somebody selectively having doctors whacked? Or was he just being paranoid because of the recent chain of events? Even if they knew where he was, would somebody really take the trouble to drive all the way up here? Still, the death messenger had come to him in person and did not seem to care about being seen. Should he go to the police? At this time, the answer was a big 'No' because it was the authorities that closed down his practice for some unknown reason. He decided to sit tight until he could reach someone who could safely bring him in.

The motel smelled like stale bread. A symphony of croaking frogs and chirping crickets filled the summer night air. It was long after midnight, but he had not really slept, only fitfully dozing the past three days. The more he thought about his predicament, the more the sickening feeling of dread crept down into his gut. Worn down by fear and loathing, a foggy sleep drifted over him.

The 'clink' of the tin can falling off the doorknob and hitting the floor turned his brain over like a car engine. In petrified horror, he watched as the doorknob slowly turned a quarter of an inch to the left and then to the right. Langley jumped up out of the chair, suddenly cured of his paralysis, and bolted into the back bedroom, locking the door behind him. He kept his .38 caliber handgun on the night stand with the safety on so he wouldn't accidentally shoot himself. Grabbing the gun, he heaved his body through the pre-unlocked window. As he landed on the dewy wet grass behind the motel he heard the all too real CRACK of his bedroom door being kicked in. Langley ran for his very life along the back of the motel, which bordered the riverbank. The river sounded like an ocean wave breaking forever on a beach. His black Lexus waited at the other end of the motel, strategically backed into a corner so that it wouldn't be noticed from the road at the front of the motel. He sprinted to his car as the thunderous roar of the river cheered him on.

Langley reached the end of the motel and stopped dead in his tracks. By the pale light of the moon he could see that his black Lexus bogged down too close to the ground. The sight of his slashed tire took the air out of his getaway plan, which was to peel out onto U.S. Highway 74 and speed to Charlotte, NC. Now trapped, the proverbial terror meter hit eleven. He couldn't believe it - this was really happening! Forced into a snap decision, his only chance of escape was to go down into the river.

Langley turned his feet sideways and ambled down the steep bank of the Broad Rocky River, a white water moat between the road and the mountain. It could have easily been named the Boulder River as rocks the size of Volkswagens were strewn up and down the river. Langley scrambled across the rocks to get to the other bank. Fortunately, there was enough moonlight for him to see his feet placement in the shallow water. Once on the other side, he made his way downstream, hugging the river bank closely. This side of the river butted up against the base of the mountain so downstream was the only choice. Long out of shape, he huffed and puffed like a locomotive, but kept his bulk moving. His experience on the rocks as a boy gave him some confidence, although he had never done the river trek at night. After about making it a quarter mile downstream he stopped by a large rock to catch his breath. He tried calling 911 but there was no reception. He peered over the rock, looking upstream and across the bank. There were no flashlights or signs of movement. 'Good, there was nobody there,' he breathed to himself. Maybe he gave them the slip.

Langley continued his flight. His mind raced. How did they find me up here, he wondered. He paid for the room with cash and signed in under the name Joe Smith. He could not underestimate these guys. He had to keep moving. His new plan was to make his way to Bat Cave where there would be a landline and people.

Rock by rock, step by step, Langley worked his way down the river. Sometimes he slipped and fell. Driven by adrenaline and the primal instinct to survive he pushed on, not stopping to rest. He kept a vice-like grip on his gun. Occasionally he scanned upstream and across the bank for signs of being followed.

After about three hours, he encountered a waterfall of about six feet, with a large boulder near the edge. Cold, wet, and exhausted, he leaned his back against the boulder. Searching upstream he could see the dawn starting to break. With no sign of anyone following him, he breathed a sigh of relief. He turned around and hugged the boulder so he could edge around it to see downstream. From there he could make out Bat Cave. The pool below the waterfall led to a couple of frothing whirlpools. It was just him and the river. His chest heaving, his heart leapt for joy. The tightness in his chest faded as he thoroughly enjoyed filling his lungs with the crisp mountain air.

Langley figured he could make it around the waterfall if he stuck close to the bank. But first he needed to rest a few minutes before undertaking such a challenging task. Still hugging the boulder, he carefully made his way around to the upstream side of the huge rock and leaned back against it. What he saw dropped his heart to his toes.

A dark figure stood in front of him — a young man, really almost a kid, silhouetted against the rising sun. Langley's knees buckled. As he went down, the menacing figure deftly grabbed the gun out of Langley's hand in a Kung Fu move and pointed it at him. The backlit sun formed an unholy halo on the kid's head, revealing that it was bereft of hair. The deformed scalp appeared as if molten candle wax had covered it, leaving a trail that dripped over his protruding brow down past his left eye. Mottled blotches of pink and red scarring tattooed the bald dome. The absence of eyebrows and eyelashes added to the alien appearance.

Nobody expects to be hunted down like an animal and executed in the wilderness by a relentless freakazoid. Yet, this reality could not be denied. His brain flailed for answers. Is this how it ends, after dedicating his life to helping people who had no other hope?

Langley managed to blurt out, "REALLY? ARE YOU KIDDING ME?" shouting over the constant wall of sound made by the river.

The kid stood over Langley pointing the gun directly at him. He did not reply. Instead he cocked his head to the side as if he did not understand the rhetorical nature of Langley's question.

"Say something! WHO ARE YOU?" spouted Langley.

KABLAM!

The gunshot rang off the mountain side. Langley's body lay at the bottom of the boulder with a gaping hole in the chest. The blood gushed into the water and over the waterfall.

"They call me Leatherhead," said the kid to no one in particular.

The kid threw Langley's gun over the waterfall. He rifled through Langley's pockets until he found what he was looking for - a memory stick. He grabbed an ankle and a hand, and pivoted like a discus thrower to fling the corpse over the waterfall. The body flew through the air in frisbee fashion, landing in the pool below. Caught in one of the whirlpools, the carcass swirled around and around and around... .

CHAPTER 1

Professor Erlenmeyer

Present Day, August 8, 2047

Lincoln Jade caught her breath, then shot out of the elevator as she switched on her Oxy-Boost Breather. The device worn around her neck behind a Tree of Life pendant separated oxygen from nitrogen in the air, providing her with oxygen-rich breathing air. Lincoln's soft brown eyes peered through mahogany hair. She stood 5'8" in her tennis shoes, a bit on the pale and skinny side, but still was pretty without trying. She headed for the office at the end of the hall, clutching a folder bulging with paper. It was a curious sight for those she passed, as paper by this day and age had gone the way of encyclopedia sets.

She strode down the hallway of the Integrative Media and Production Building at Full Sail University. The students simply called it 'The Station' because it was home to the Full Sail Student Broadcasting Station. The structure took up the entire block off Goldenrod Avenue in Orlando where the original Full Sail recording studio used to be. The efficiently rectangular government building belied the array of state-of-the-art facilities on the inside.

Lincoln burst into Professor Erlenmeyer's office and plopped in the chair across from his desk. She wore a pants suit even though it was mid-August. He wore a tie as usual, this one with the Full Sail logo on it. His extra large frame bulged against his too-small, button down shirt, his hairy, meaty arms protruding from the short sleeves. Erlenmeyer's office was known for two things: an oversized American flag dominating one corner, and rocks and minerals everywhere. Some lay loose on the bookshelves in the spaces not occupied by books, and some made their home on his large metal desk. The stone specimens, each labeled, hailed from all over the world. Erlenmeyer was not only the Professor of Investigative Reporting, but a die-hard rock hound as well.

She slapped down the folder stuffed with old newspaper and magazine clippings on his desk.

"And good morning to you, Lincoln. What's this?" asked Professor Erlenmeyer.

"It's going to be my project for my senior final," she replied.

Professor Erlenmeyer picked up the folder. It contained clippings with screaming headlines like:

'A REAL LIFE X-MAN?'

and

'BLUE GENES COULD MAKE A HUMAN DYNAMO'.

"We don't deal with tabloid news," said Professor Erlenmeyer.

"Boss, it's not just tabloid. These are clippings from the Orlando Sentinel, Scientific American, and Discovery magazines," shot back Lincoln.

"Where in the world did you get these anyway?" inquired Professor Erlenmeyer. "These clippings date from 2016."

"A good investigative reporter doesn't reveal her source," Lincoln answered.

Professor Erlenmeyer smiled. "Your source must be a huge fan of this guy to have collected all these articles and kept them for so long."

"I guess so," said Lincoln, wondering herself. She let out a deep sigh. "I...I really need this to matter. I want to make a name for myself while I still can. The world owes it to me."

He stopped going through the folder of papers and looked at his protege. "I know, Lincoln, I know," he said with heart-felt warmth. "I take it you are hoping for a huge story."

"Yep, I'm talking big-time stuff, like blow up a conspiracy, expose corruption, solve a mystery."

This time Professor Erlenmeyer tilted his head down and looked over his glasses at Lincoln. "Be careful what you wish for, intrepid reporter."

He ran his fingers over the clippings, skimming the articles for information. It had been a long time since he had felt newsprint in his hands. "I see the historic part here. So, what does this flash-in-the pan recluse from over thirty years ago have to do with our present-day lives?"

"That's going to be the investigative part," said Lincoln.

"I hope you have more to go on than this," counseled Professor Erlenmeyer.

"I will soon; I have an appointment with Barry Blue Hawkins tomorrow," she replied. "His first interview in 30 years."

CHAPTER 2

The Bee Hive

The next day Lincoln Jade's Tesla Mini-Limo drove her to the appointment with Mr. Hawkins. He lived in Fern Park, a small town a short distance from Full Sail. She hoped that she had not been too abrupt with Professor Erlenmeyer. He knew her well enough by now to know she was not a 'Chatty Cathy.' She referred to him as 'boss' not to be flippant but because he oversaw her work study program. All students bright enough to earn a spot in a public university had a work study grant as part of their college expenses being fully paid by the government.

During the ride, Lincoln rummaged through the folder of newspaper and magazine clippings. She pulled out two articles that were stuck together face-to-face, which is why she hadn't noticed them before. She carefully peeled apart the papers. The headlines read:

'FLORIDA DOCTOR FOUND DEAD AT CHIMNEY ROCK, NC WITH GUNSHOT WOUND TO CHEST'

and

'BONITA SPRINGS PHYSICIAN BLUDGEONED TO DEATH'.

"What the hey!" Lincoln said out loud. She skimmed the articles. Both deaths took place in June, 2017, the same time period of the other articles in the folder. And both physicians practiced alternative medicine with Florida medical licenses. Investigators ruled the Chimney Rock case a suicide. A fisherman found the doctor's body in the Rocky Broad River shot in the chest with his own gun. During his career, this doctor had treated over 11,000 patients with a compound called GcMAF, Globulin component Macrophage Activating Factor, which improves immune system function by binding with vitamin D. The doctor in Bonita Springs also died violently, struck 17 times with a hammer. Authorities pinned it on her husband. An outspoken proponent of natural healing, this doctor boasted a huge following on YouTube. Lincoln's eyebrows twitched up and down as she processed this information. 'What could two dead doctors have to do with Mr. Hawkins? Were these articles included in the folder by mistake?'

She put them back in the folder, leaving the answer to that question for another time, because Barry Hawkins was the main event. The words of her trusted source echoed in her head. 'Meeting this guy will be life changing for you.' Man, how she hoped an exclusive with this urban legend would lead to her breakthrough story. Her anticipation snowballed as her ride navigated the narrow back streets of serene Fern Park.

Lincoln's car pulled into a tree-lined, townhouse community. The Apple Co-Pilot embedded into the car's windshield indicated the location of the house. She arrived at 10:00 a.m. sharp, right on time as was her habit. As she walked up to the front door she could hear a dog barking ferociously. The door opened and a smiling woman in her 70s said, "Hey, come on out of this heat. We've been expecting you." At the same time she deftly blocked the pitbull, scolding, "Moondog, settle down!" Then to Lincoln, "Just let her smell you." After vetting the stranger, Moondog stepped aside and allowed Lincoln to enter the townhome.

The nice lady gave Lincoln a hug like she was a long lost relative. "I'm Jenny, and you must be Lincoln."

Caught off guard, Lincoln stammered, "Nice to meet you. Thank you for letting me talk to your husband."

"No prob Lincoln. Hey Bear, she's here!" hollered Jenny.

No answer.

"Go down the hall, he's in the back," coaxed Jenny.

Lincoln walked cautiously to the back of the house. The first thing she noticed was a six foot tall, fully decorated artificial Christmas tree. Wrapped with lights, the entire tree glowed except for the oversized angel on top. "Geez. Old people," she muttered to herself. "It's summer and they're still celebrating Christmas." The entire back of the house featured large windows furnished with white plantation blinds. Two couches dominated the space, perpendicular to each other. A long elderly man with a shaved head and trimmed white beard lay on the big red couch against the back wall, with a mobility scooter parked next to it. Upon seeing Lincoln, his face looked like he had seen a ghost. But only for an instant. Recovering, he showed a smile with clenched teeth. Barry sat up on the couch. "So it's Lincoln, eh?" he said hoarsely.

It always irritated Lincoln when she felt like she had to explain her given name. "Yes, he was my dad's favorite president." She put one hand on her hip and said, "What's with the 'Blue' in Barry Blue Hawkins?"

Barry lay back down on his couch. "Fair enough. In another life I played sax and bass in bands on weekends. A bandmate started calling me Barry Blue and it stuck."

Barry grinned and motioned for her to sit down on the other couch. Moondog jumped beside him to form a protective canine barrier between her master and this interloper.

"Do you two need anything to drink?" hollered Jenny.

Barry stuck his arm out as she peered down the hallway and signed, "No thanks."

Lincoln took a seat on the other couch. She pulled out her notepad and her 360 degree holorecorder. As she did so, she scanned the room again. Framed photos covered the walls, some of family and some of Barry in his younger years with different bands. A few chemistry patents mounted on wooden plaques also hung on the wall. An antique electric bass leaned on its stand in the corner. "You have a lovely wife."

"Yes, she's the best," beamed Barry. "She's definitely my better half!"

Lincoln gave up a small smile, then got down to business. "Jenny has filled you in that I am a student at Full Sail and that I work at the media station — correct?"

Barry nodded.

"A trusted source has told me to see you…that you could help."

Barry's eyebrows sprang up, as if he were waiting for the other shoe to drop.

"This person has given me a stash of written articles from your days of, shall we say… claim to fame. I'm here to do a piece on it for my senior project. It's supposed to be an investigative piece on a historical topic that is relevant today," explained Lincoln. "Is it all right with you if I record this?"

Barry began to sign, then stopped. He angled a square black device on the coffee table until its raven eye lens pointed at him half-lying, half-sitting on the couch. His hands started to move again.

"OK, shoot," came a robotic voice from the device's speaker. "I'm sure you have a list of the usual reporter questions. You may proceed, carbon-based life form."

Lincoln pointed at the device. "What's going on here?"

Jenny entered at that moment, with two bottles of water and two glasses. "Barry's voice is especially weak today. It happens. So he is going to use his Audio Signer, unfortunately for you."

"Blimey, woman, you're always busting me porridge," came the voice, this time in cockney British.

"Audio Signer," Lincoln repeated. "But why… ."

"-Does Barry need to sign?" finished Jenny. "He's been signing for decades. One of Barry's health issues is that his voice becomes hoarse and painful. He lost his voice for five weeks once, so he started learning American Sign Language. This translator here is a Godsend. It takes Barry's signing and converts it to audio, so he can communicate with people who don't know sign language."

"How may I assist you, young person?" came the voice of a British butler as Barry signed in front of the screen.

"Bear, turn it to American please," Jenny said.

"If Stephen Hawkings' machine had to speak in an American accent, mine will speak in British," came the clipped response.

Jenny rolled her eyes.

"Uh, I just want to hear your story," said Lincoln. She glanced at the wallet-sized device, not quite sure if she should address the audio signer or Barry.

"My story? Where do I start?" Barry held up a waggling index finger.

"How about at the beginning," said Lincoln, switching the camcorder on.

"I'm glad you said that, Miss Jade, because the very beginning is the only place to start."

Barry propped his head on a pillow, only his hands moving. "The first time it happened that I remember, I was eight years old. We lived in Ohio on the end of a dead-end street surrounded by woods. My boyhood pal, Dale 'Bucksty Boy' Buckston, was the Daniel Boone of our neighborhood. He taught me such survival skills like how to catch a snake and how to make a tunnel into the side of a creek bed. We explored the woods every day. One summer day we happened upon a large stump with bees buzzing all around it. Everyone knows that where there are bees, there is honey. Well, being eight years old, we determined the best course of action was to throw a smoke bomb into the tree stump and when the bees left we would grab the honey."

Lincoln sat with her arms crossed wondering where this was going.

"So the next day we crafted a smoke bomb out of common garage stuff like oil rags and lighter fluid. We grabbed a string of firecrackers for good measure. Bees hate firecrackers. We fashioned the smoke bomb by tying the oil rags together with the firecrackers. We returned to the tree stump. The bees had no idea what was going to hit them. Bucksty Boy lit the secret weapon and I tossed it into the stump. Smoke billowed out followed by the rapid fire sound of the fire crackers. To our astonishment, the bees came roaring out of the stump directly at us. Bucksty Boy's survival skills kicked in and he yelled 'run for the swamp!' I ran like heck, dodging trees and getting stung by bees. I hit the swamp and stayed under water the best I could until the bees were gone."

Barry's hands paused and went limp. After an uncomfortable minute, he flexed his fingers and signed, "Hands needed a rest. Anyhow, that was the nostalgic part. I have told only a few people about what happened next. I'm eighty-seven, so what the heck."

He pointed one finger at himself and then two fingers outward. "I looked up and down the swamp and didn't see Bucksty Boy. So I started walking back the way we came. I heard whimpering. It was Bucksty Boy lying face down, caught in the clutches of rusty barbed wire. I turned him over and jumped back in horror. His face was so grotesquely swollen that it was unrecognizable. He looked like a mad-scientist experiment gone terribly wrong, covered and swollen with hundreds of red bee sting welts. Then my kid-mind was hit by panic, knowing that I would get in big time trouble for this. As I untangled him from the snarl of wire, it cut into his exposed skin. He was screaming his head off by now. I grabbed him by his bare arms and yelled 'Dale, Dale, you have to get up. We have to go!' Bucksty boy stopped screaming and I pulled him up. We made our way back home through the woods. Bucksty Boy was limping along with his arm around my shoulders. We made it to his house. It was dark by then. I rang the doorbell and ran."

Barry paused, his hand movements duller. "When I got home my Mom eyed the several bee-sting welts on my crew-cut noggin. 'What happened to you?' I replied, 'I fell down'. To my surprise, that worked. No more questions. I used this tactic many times throughout my formative years. Expecting certain death at the hands of Dale's parents and my parents, I figured I would lie low for a while. Bucksty Boy came over a couple of days later and to my amazement, he looked just fine! I could barely see the welts that were so gross a couple of days ago."

Barry stopped signing and sat up. He spoke aloud what he had hidden for so long. "In fact, he looked better than I did."

Lincoln's eyebrows furrowed.

"So what are you saying?" she asked. "Your friend was miraculously cured?"

Barry shrugged. "This is what you asked for."

"Mr. Hawkins...," started Lincoln.

"Barry," Barry cut in.

"Barry," Lincoln began, choosing her words carefully. "I think maybe there's been a misunderstanding. I'm here looking for actual proof of the incidents reported on about you 30 years ago. With all due respect, sir… um, I mean, Barry, childhood anecdotes won't help me."

"You want the truth, you have to know the whole story. MY whole story," Barry replied.

Lincoln's heart sank as she realized her mentor was right. The Barry Blue phenomenon was just the product of tabloid journalism from a time when people couldn't get enough of fake news. She mentally rifled through the folder of articles and remembered the two stuck together. Maybe her source included them for a reason, not by accident. "What about the murders?" she asked. "The doctors were killed about the same time as when you dropped off the map."

"Yeah, I've heard about those dead doctor cases," said Barry with a sudden edge in his voice, his hands clenching and unclenching. "But I thought you were here to do *my* story."

"So you don't want to talk about the dead doctors or you don't know anything," said Lincoln. "Which is it?"

"My story, my way," said Barry. "I'm wiped out right now. Come back in a couple of days. You'll be glad you did." Barry lay back on the couch, closed his eyes, and put his arm across his face.

Lincoln got up and briskly walked out, waving a curt goodbye to Jenny on her way. 'Life changing?' What was her source thinking? So far this interview was the exact opposite of life changing. Geez! She did not know whether she would return, unsure whether to abandon this project and come up with another, which could end up with her missing milestone deadlines. She bristled at the notion of wasting a good chunk of time with this yarnspinner, possibly derailing her senior project completely. But her source must have pointed here for a good reason. She hoped.

CHAPTER 3

Jamie and Windy

Lincoln's car drove her to her unit in school housing. It backed into her parking space, complete with an induction charging plate. The Student Accessibility Program gave her a first floor unit with up-front parking, but she couldn't help but lament how far she still had to walk from her parking space to her room. As she entered, the lights popped on. The compact student units borrowed from the design of a camper, in which the tables, chairs, and beds folded out from the walls to maximize living space. The walls could change color electrochemically and Lincoln had hers set on aquamarine. The unit contained no cooking appliances for lack of space, and for that reason the students ate most meals at the Student Canteen. The men and women on her floor shared the community bathrooms down the hall, complete with privacy doors. She couldn't really complain, as the government paid for student room and board.

Lincoln's stark room decor consisted of a few pictures — some of her dad and her dad and mom together, one picture of her mother holding her when she was an infant, and one of just Lincoln and her dad together at her high school graduation. Lincoln shoved her dark brown hair back, styled in a bob just like in the pictures of her mother, one of which showed her with the Tree of Life pendant that Lincoln now wore herself.

Lincoln did not have any memories of her mother. She died in a bizarre traffic accident only a few weeks after Lincoln's birth. But it did no good to dwell on it any more than she already had.

Lincoln grabbed a protein bar and took her digestive enzymes. Then she put on her sonic shaker vest and gave herself a one minute treatment to loosen up mucus in her lungs. Finally, she slid her bed out from the wall and took a nap.

When Lincoln got up, she felt refreshed enough to join the living. She ventured down the hall to her friend Jamie's unit. She smelled cinnamon incense wafting out of the room through the open door. 'Purple Haze' pulsed through the hall, filling the space with a retro vibe. The table, seats, and bed were all folded into the walls. This left a rectangular floor space covered by box springs and mattresses, making this truly a one-bedroom unit. The walls were set for 'Deep Purple'.

Jamie and his girlfriend, Windy, lounged on oversized pillows. They were not only her friends and colleagues, but also her emotional support. Jamie Rodriguez sported a surfer look, complete with dyed white hair and a large shark tooth hanging from a leather cord around his neck. Despite his hip persona, this die-hard techno geek sat with his disemboweled holopad and other unidentifiable parts on his lap.

Windy Summers, of American-Asian descent, hailed from New Jersey. To her, Florida was a paradise, an absolute haven for progressive environmental programs and activists. She proudly sported starch-based, biodegradable sandals and a "Humans are the Problem" Sierra Club t-shirt.

Lincoln flopped down beside Windy. "What's Inspector Gadget working on?"

Windy pushed her long jet black hair back and laughed. "He'll know when it's finished."

"So. L.J., what's shakin'?" asked Jamie, flashing his charismatic smile.

"My sonic shaker vest," quipped Lincoln.

"Good one Linc," said Windy.

"Actually, I've started on my pass-fail project for finals," said Lincoln.

Jamie sat up. "Already? I don't even have mine picked out yet."

"Well, you know I need longer to get things done," she replied. "What about you Windy?"

"Oh, I haven't settled on anything yet, but you know I keep my ear to the ground."

"Why don't you do a story on climate change, or better yet, climate control?" said Lincoln.

"It's been done to death already," said Windy.

"How 'bout a story on why there are monsoons in central Florida for nine months out of the year and they still call it the Sunshine State?" said Jamie.

Windy laughed. "Now that's climate change for you. There's a river in the sky," she said, waving her hands and wiggling her fingers above her head.

"Well, the Windy Summers I know always has a cause in mind," said Lincoln.

"Funny you should say. I *have* been following this story unfolding back home in Jersey. Many people from the same housing community have this mysterious illness."

"What kind of symptoms?" asked Lincoln.

Windy shifted on her pillow and made a face. "Nasty stuff like bleeding gums and teeth falling out. Bleeding sores on their bodies."

"Man that's gross!" said Jamie.

"What city in New Jersey?" asked Lincoln.

"Orange," answered Windy. "The authorities are going on the premise that it is a very contagious virus, similar to ebola."

"Orange, New Jersey?" Lincoln's eyebrows moved up and down, resembling the jumping line on an EKG monitor. They did this whenever Lincoln's brain popped into high gear. "It may not be a virus."

"What makes you say that?" asked Windy. "Wait — what holopod series have you just finished?"

Lincoln laughed. "Forget it. It's just a longshot, nothing worth getting into now."

"Yeah, right," said Windy. "I'd rather find a topic that is an environmental issue." She paused a beat. "What's your topic, Lincoln?"

"Well, since you asked, I'm interviewing this living relic who was some kind of media sensation thirty years ago. He lives right here in central Florida. So far he's only told me an embellished story from his boyhood."

"What's his name?" asked Jamie.

"Barry Blue Hawkins," said Lincoln, "but I don't know if this guy is going to give me anything useful."

"Barry Blue Hawkins, Barry Blue Hawkins... ." Windy slapped her knee. "Oh my gosh! He was in the footnotes of our genetics class textbook."

"You're kidding!" said Lincoln.

"No, I'm not." Windy's eyes were wide open. "Something about his DNA having a totally unique quality. But I don't recall what the upshot of that was."

"Whoa L.J.!" said Jamie. "That's pretty chill that you've hooked up with this guy in person."

"Yeah," said Windy. "How did you get the interview?"

"I just called his home number and talked to his wife. I told her who I was and I wanted to interview her husband for a school project. She got back to me the next day and said fine as long as the sessions were short." Lincoln perked up. "Now that you mention it, he never did grant an interview to the media. I guess I have an exclusive."

"There you go," said Windy.

Lincoln got up. "Thanks guys. I'm seeing the old geezer in a couple of days. I'll keep you posted. Oh, and I have a doctor appointment first thing tomorrow so I won't see you at breakfast."

CHAPTER 4

Dr. Walker

Lincoln sat on the examination table in a room hardly bigger than a walk-in closet. The nurse, having taken Lincoln's vitals, left her alone in the stark, white room. White walls, white floor, white ceiling. Silence permeated the room, broken only by the sound of her own breathing.

She was at the University of Central Florida Medical Center. As part of the public university system, Full Sail students received free medical treatment. The government assigned doctors to the patients. Fortunately for Lincoln, her doctor was passionate about her work. Doctors didn't do it for the modest paycheck, but for their zeal for practicing medicine.

Prinity Walker, M.D., Ph.D, entered the tiny room. Five years out of her internship, Dr. Walker was a pulmonologist of Indian descent who saw patients and also did medical research at UCF. Her hand was unencumbered by a wedding band, as she was married to her work.

Dr. Walker managed Lincoln's cystic fibrosis for the past seven years, ever since she started attending Full Sail. A genetic disorder, cystic fibrosis affects the lungs and pancreas and is generally diagnosed in infancy. Lincoln learned early on that abnormally thick mucus build-up caused her chronic lung infections. She did treatments three times a day to keep her lung passages clear. Lincoln also took digestive enzymes with every meal, otherwise her food would go right through her because of pancreas damage. Some CF patients only make it to their 20s, while others can live into their 50s.

Dr. Walker wore an all-white lab coat and carried a tricorder-like holo-chart. She only had ten minutes with each patient so she got right to the point.

"Lincoln, are you paying attention to your shaker vest? You're running a low-grade fever"

"Sorry, doc," Lincoln replied. "I haven't been checking my vitals lately. I've been kinda focused on school."

Dr. Walker sighed. "Well, from now on check regularly. Now I've got to start you on an antibiotics cocktail to fight the infection in your lungs."

"Okay, doc, geez! It's not the first time I've gotten an infection."

Dr. Walker flipped through images using the holochart. "It's different now. I have the results of your lung blow test and the micro-CAT scan of your lungs. Listen, Lincoln, it's not good. I'm sorry to have to tell you this but you are going to need a lung transplant within six months. Your life-time of lung infections have significantly reduced your lung capacity. I have you on the transplant list already. The synthetic lung is at least a few years off, but hopefully that will be an option for you down the road."

This news stunned Lincoln as if she had been given a death sentence. She remained stoic on the exterior, but panicked on the inside. Lincoln barely registered Dr. Walker's voice as she elaborated on the prognosis. Knowing this day was coming and actually hearing it from her doctor were not the same.

"Are you taking your digestive enzymes?" Dr. Walker's voice interrupted her thoughts. "You really could use a few pounds."

"Yes, and I know, I know," Lincoln replied.

"Are you using your sonic shaker?" asked Dr. Walker.

"Yes."

"How is your oxy-boost performing?"

"It's working fine." She wore the oxy-boost gizmo, about the size of a quarter, around her neck and behind her Tree of Life pendant. An almost imperceptible tube ran from the back of her chain, then over her ear and into her nostril. Lincoln ran her fingers over the pendant. Her dad retrieved the piece from her mom's jewelry box when Lincoln was twelve, and it adorned Lincoln's neck ever since. Not only did the pendant hide the oxy-boost device, but it reminded Lincoln that she once had a mom.

"Good," replied Dr. Walker. "Are you pacing yourself? You know you always push too hard."

Lincoln did push too hard. It was a balancing act between getting her school work done without exhausting herself. She took two classes at a time instead of four, putting her on the seven-year plan. "I'm only taking one class this semester," she said.

"Anything interesting?" said Dr. Walker as she sat at her desk updating her digital notes.

"It's my senior project. I'm interviewing this guy, Barry Blue Hawkins."

Dr. Walker stopped what she was doing and spun around on her stool to face Lincoln. "I'm going to check your breathing again." Leaning into Lincoln with her stethoscope, she spoke in a tone that Lincoln could hardly hear. "Barry Blue Hawkins! You know Barry Blue Hawkins? What's he like?"

"He's like a hundred. Possibly senile," Lincoln whispered back. 'Did this appointment just get weird or what?' thought Lincoln. She glanced at the small but conspicuous white camera in the corner ceiling. All rooms had them for both the doctor's and the patient's protection.

"I know he won't talk to outsiders, but can you introduce me to him? I need to talk to him." Dr. Walker's hushed tone conveyed a startling level of drive and urgency.

"I only met him once, so I don't know. I don't feel comfortable with that just now." Lincoln thought, 'What could Dr. Walker possibly have to discuss with him?'

Dr. Walker stepped away and resumed in her normal conversational volume. "I'm refilling your prescriptions and here are some instructions for the new meds." She handed Lincoln a folded scrip. "Also I want you to keep these on you at all times." She handed Lincoln two tubes each in a plastic wrapper. "They are adrenaline boosters – use only in case of emergency, if you're spiralling too quickly. It'll keep you going until you can get to a hospital. And never use both in the same day. They are very potent."

Three musical dings signaled the end of the ten-minute appointment.

"Keep up on your regime of meds, sonic shaker, and your oxy-boost. And don't overdo it! You are on borrowed time, Miss Jade."

Dr. Walker swished out of the room. Lincoln cupped her hand and unfolded the scrip. Instead of instructions, it contained a note:

Call me when you are ready for proof
111-555-629-0880
Prinity

Lincoln shoved the note into her pocket. 'Proof? Call her when I am ready?' She scrunched her nose. 'Yep, things definitely got weird.'

CHAPTER 5

Take Out the Trash

A garbage truck idled in park on Wolf Creek Trail in Hilton Head Island, South Carolina. The man sitting in the driver's seat of the truck sipped his black coffee from a white styrofoam cup. SeaPines plantation was not only a nature preserve, it also hosted the most exclusive neighborhoods on the island. Sprawling homes nestled in pine stands far back from the road. An amber blanket of pine needles covered the expansive front yards.

A big buck stepped out of the woods across the street from the garbage truck. The deer's movement in the predawn darkness did not escape the eye of the man in the garbage truck. The sight of the magnificent beast brought him back to his boyhood when he made his first kill. Yes sir, that moment gave him the deeply satisfying feeling of ultimate control.

The man in the garbage truck took another sip of the hot dark liquid as he reminisced. Everyday after school he would hurry up and do his chores so that he could rove the forest surrounding the farm. The mom-parent ran a crazy tight ship. She made sure the chores were done. 'Bobby! Take out the trash! It's full of germs, you know.' Even though he had taken out the trash, he took it out again. 'There's a banana peel at the bottom of this trash can, Bobby. Take out the trash! Next thing you know, we'll have roaches!' The woman was relentless. Man, how he was always glad to finish his chores and immerse himself in the solitude of the woods.

Even as a boy, he chafed at the mom-parent's cleanliness compulsion. At the same time, he understood what it was like to have an overriding compulsion, a compulsion that he kept bottled up as long as he could.

The mom-parent wanted to rescue the boy like he was a dog from the animal shelter. The dad-parent would say, 'that boy needs to be socialized.' The thing was, some dogs can be socialized and some cannot. He fell into the category of dogs that cannot.

His teachers recommended that he jump ahead two grade levels. The parent people wanted him to stay with kids his own age in the hope he would learn to fit in. But he never did. For one thing, he looked different. 'Don't touch the freak. All your hair will fall out!'

In middle school this loudmouth kid bullied him everyday. One day Loudmouth and his cronies jumped him at the back of the school yard. They dragged him behind the dumpster and piled on. A loud snap. Searing pain around his neck. Hands tugging at his clothes. They inked across his chest that name, that awful nickname Loudmouth called him. Naked and branded, he staggered alone across the school yard, down the halls, and to the principal's office. Loudmouth was trash. Loudmouth was a problem.

Not long afterwards, an opportunity to solve his Loudmouth problem coincided with the unleashing of his secret compulsion. He made Loudmouth disappear. 'Take out the trash, Bobby! Take out the trash.' Yes sir, he took out the trash, all right. Who knew it would be so easy to solve a problem like Loudmouth?

He couldn't stay there anymore. Loudmouth's disappearance apparently upset a lot of people, including the cops. The designated parents shipped him to military boarding school. He expected a new guy initiation. Because of the dumpster incident, nobody would ever get the drop on him again. Yes sir, he was always ready. When his new classmates came for him that night, he allowed them to blindfold and take him to the woods. After all, he was lord of the jungle. The next day those cadets were found tied to trees, their clothes stuffed with poison ivy. Nobody at the boarding school messed with him again.

He made it into the Big Show of military academies. School was easy. He left his classmates in the dust. Of course someone had to make a big deal about his unique appearance. Put him in his place. Humiliate him.

Sure enough, somebody soon took that responsibility upon himself. It happened in the dormitory shower.

'Hey freak. Who says you can be here?' The bellowing inquiry came from an upperclassman, a serious bodybuilder who stood a whole head taller than the rest of the students. This perfectly sculpted human specimen, Mr. Wonderful, was quite the raging 'roider.

'You think this place is gonna' make you a man? Look at you. You don't have a fleck of hair on your entire body, especially where it counts.' Mr. Wonderful stood toe-to-toe with him. By now a small group of toweled and untoweled men had congealed around the confrontation. Mr. Wonderful played to his audience.

'I'm gonna give you to the count of three before I kick your ass. One—'

That was as far as Mr. Wonderful got. The impact of fist hitting cartilage sounded like stepping on an empty milk carton.

Mr. Wonderful writhed on the hard tile floor while clutching his Adam's apple, his mouth silently opening and closing like a fish on a boat deck. Mr. Wonderful didn't look so wonderful anymore.

'Take out the trash, Bobby. We don't want maggots squirming around. Take it out now.' Yes sir, he took out Mr. Wonderful. Problem solved.

Two years into his training at the military academy, he was recruited by government spooks. He excelled in his training at Quantico, setting the all-time record for the obstacle course. No one could touch him when it came to marksmanship. He shadowed field agents doing surveillance.

Soon he was in charge of his own surveillance mission. The agency wanted to take down a slimy bigshot executive. His team tracked Bigshot and his associates both in the real world and in the holosphere. He worked grueling hours in the shadows while Bigshot operated scot-free. Spying on Bigshot's operation was a drag. He began to doubt his future with the agency.

Just when he didn't think he could take the mind-numbing tedium of stakeout work any longer, he received an intriguing invitation from Bigshot. A sawed-off version of Bigshot escorted him to the high-rise corner office where Bigshot himself awaited.

Bigshot said: "Welcome, my boy. We are so glad that you accepted our humble invite."

Sawed-off said: "We know you've been watching us. Don't be surprised, agent. You're rowing in a leaky boat."

Bigshot said: "Your talent is being wasted on the Feds. We want you to work for us."

Sawed-off said: "We'll make it worth your while. Think about it, kid."

He did more than think about it. In his new position he worked alone, answering only to Sawed-off and Bigshot. He got to explore his creative side and do jobs his way. Best of all, each completed job fed his insatiable compulsion. Yes sir, he had found his purpose.

Thirty years later, he sat in a garbage truck observing the deer. Last week's meeting set today's job into motion.

Bigshot said: "Class action lawsuit - not happening."

Sawed-off said: "Bob, you make this shyster disappear."

Bigshot said: "Who's gonna miss another lawyer?"

Sawed-off said: "Nobody – that's who."

The deer across the street twitched its ears and then slipped into the woods. Through his driver's side window, he saw a jogger in a flashy yellow sweatsuit plodding along the sidewalk. Flashy rich guy all yellow. Old Yeller would soon be yellin' his head off.

The sidewalk intersected the street where the garbage truck idled. Old Yeller's path headed straight towards him. He set his coffee down and checked his watch. 'Right on time.' He climbed down from the truck and started towards the rear. He clutched his chest and went down.

Old Yeller was quickly upon him. 'Are you all right mister? I'll call for help.'

He thrust out his arm and tasered Old Yeller's chest. Stunned, Old Yeller collapsed. 'Take out the trash, Bobby. It's your job to take out the trash.' He dragged Old Yeller to the back of the truck and dropped him to the pavement. Old Yeller had soiled himself. Sweat and piss. What a smelly job.

He pressed a button on a remote control and the back of the truck yawned open like the mouth of a mechanical Tyrannosaurus Rex. "Wha...what... what are you d-doing?" said the quaking jogger, starting to recover from the electric shock. "Do you know who I am?"

Grabbing Old Yeller by the belt buckle and collar, he slung him into the back of the truck with the rest of the trash. He pressed another button and the garbage truck rear gnashed shut. Old Yeller yelled a long 'no.'

He strolled back to the front of the truck, clambered into the driver's seat, and shut the cab door. Old Yeller's yells sounded distant like a hiker at the bottom of a canyon. He took a sip of coffee while pulling on a lever marked 'compactor'.

The mechanical beast came to life as metal scraped the inner walls of the compactor, digesting its contents. Old Yeller's cries for help morphed into shrieks of pure terror. The crushing force on the trash made the sound of a whole lot of empty milk cartons being stepped on.

The man in the truck cab let his gaze drift skywards. He wondered if it would rain later today. The shrieks stopped but he let the compactor finish its cycle.

He put the truck in gear. Job number three-hundred and forty-eight, Old Yeller – completed. Yes sir, he sure took out the trash today.

CHAPTER 6

The Parachute

When Lincoln arrived at the Hawkins house, Jenny stood at the door, with a barking Moondog.

"Come on in out of this heat, Lincoln," greeted Jenny. "You look like you could use some electrolytes. Have a 'Cool Breeze' drink."

She handed Lincoln a sports bottle labeled 'Cool Breeze, Now THC Free!'

"Bear's in the living room, where you met him before," said Jenny, gesturing Lincoln down the hall. Lincoln took the bottle, said her thank you, and headed towards the back of the house.

Barry lay stretched out on the same couch as before, with his audio sign language converter perched on his lap. He forced a clenched smile. He made a slight movement with his hands and then a British voice said, "How are you today, Miss Lincoln?"

"Hanging in there, I guess," answered Lincoln.

He crossed his fingers and moved his hands to his side. "I'm ready!"

"Oh, before I forget, my doctor wants to meet you," said Lincoln.

"No way, Jose!" Barry sternly signed. Lincoln shook her head at the cognitive dissonance of hearing such an american colloquialism spoken with a British accent.

"Why not? You don't even know her. Look, she's been my doc for seven years. I trust her with my life."

"My policy for seeing the press, doctors, and other outsiders has been 'no' for thirty years."

"And what has that gotten you, Barry?"

"I'm still alive."

"Whatever, no skin off my nose." Lincoln shook her head and switched on the holo-recorder. "Let's get back to my project."

Barry bolstered his head with another pillow. He continued signing. "Well nothing happened for a long time. Nothing out of the ordinary that is. Then one day I went out hunting rabbit and quail with my friends... ."

"You had guns?" Lincoln interrupted.

"Sure," Barry signed. "Everyone had guns in the 1970's. It was a different time."

"I guess," she replied.

"So we found a parachute in a field. It was like someone landed and just walked away from it," Barry continued. "We couldn't believe our luck! We took it back home and all agreed it would be perfect for parasailing. My pal Fast Freddy, an excellent water skier, was selected to be the test pilot. We also deemed it prudent to test out the parachute before using a human."

"Trevor, my fishing pal, lived on a lake. Me, Fred, and Stan went over to Trevor's house with the parachute. Trevor was able to borrow the neighbor's speed boat, actually a johnboat with a 20 horsepower outboard motor. For the test object, I selected Trevor's canoe anchor, an eight-pound cement block. We laid out the parachute on the beach and tied the cement block to the parachute harness using a rope. Trevor and I stood on the beach while Freddy and Stan manned the boat. They struck out towards the middle of the lake going full throttle. The parachute jumped up, lifting the cement block high into the sky. 'It works!

It works!' we exclaimed." Barry pumped his hands over his head, reenacting the moment.

"Then the brick seemed to eject itself and plummeted down into the lake. 'My anchor!' cried Trevor. We ignored Trevor's hysterics and congratulated ourselves on a successful test run."

"Lake Catherine was a small round lake, but we figured it was big enough to do the job. We laid the parachute on the beach and strapped Fred into the harness and water skis. I stayed on the beach while Stan piloted the speed boat. Stan hit the throttle and Freddy skimmed on top of the water with the parachute bulging behind him. As the boat raced counter clock-wise around the lake, Fred lifted about 6 feet off the top of the water, sometimes skimming the cattails that bordered the edge of the lake. I jumped up and down on the beach, cheering Fred on as he made it to the opposite side of the lake. The boat had to make a pretty tight circle on account of the small lake size. As he approached the beach, the centrifugal force swung Freddy out so that he was almost at a right angle with the boat." Barry's hands illustrated the relative positions of Freddy and the boat, with the Freddy hand whipping around to come parallel with the boat hand.

"Unfortunately, our NASA calculations did not account for an old wooden pier on the approach run, about six feet above the water held up by 3-inch wide metal pipes. Helplessly, I watched Fred, still in the air, slam into the end of the pier!" Barry smacked one hand into the other. "Fred sank into the water. I had already scrambled off the beach into the water. I reached Fred and pulled him up. His eyes rolled around in his head and blood oozed out of his mouth. A lot of blood." Barry paused and rubbed his bald head. "There was a lot of yelling, mostly mine. I clutched Freddy so tightly by his arms that my hands were throbbing. It felt like I was pulling him out of quicksand as I dragged him over to the beach, leaving a trail of blood on the water."

"As I laid him on the beach, I noticed that he had stopped bleeding from the mouth. A few minutes later, Stan arrived back with the speed boat. He was whooping it up at our apparently successful mission. Fred had come to his senses and was sitting up. 'I'm not doing that again!' was all Fred said. He looked like he had been run over by a Harley Davidson, having severe bruising and swelling on his midsection and a goose-egg on his head."

"Mostly motivated by the fear of getting into trouble, we took Freddy back to my house, snuck him upstairs, and put him to bed. My friends left. My parents were used to Freddy staying over, so I told them he was sick and he stayed overnight. The next day both his eyes had blackened like he just lost a fight to Mohamud Ali. On the second day, Freddy was up and out of bed. He seemed fine except for faint traces of his cuts and bruises. I couldn't believe it! Two days before, we probably should have taken Freddy to the ER. My mom asked what happened to Fred and I said, 'He fell down.'"

Barry stopped signing and rubbed his head some more.

"So…?" inquired Lincoln.

"So I realized that I had something to do with Freddy being OK. When he hit that pier, I thought he was dead," Barry said out loud, in his raspy voice.

"Sure, you saved him from drowning," said Lincoln.

"No. I *saved* him," said Barry quietly.

"Barry, look, I've read the articles, and everything written about you since then, and there seems to be no solid proof that you had anything to do with your friends' recoveries."

"Well, who are you going to believe, me or some old news-papers?" asked Barry. "Trust me, I have something amazing to tell you."

"Can't you tell me anything about the dead doctors?"

"Better that you don't know."

Lincoln took a deep breath. "I can see you're getting tired," she said. "Shall I come back tomorrow?" She was hoping he'd decline.

"No," wheezed Barry. "Make it two days, Friday, same time."

Lincoln got up and strode out, meeting Jenny at the front of the house.

"Thank you for having me into your beautiful home." Then she paused. "Jenny, is Freddy real?"

Jenny laughed. "You're not the first person to ask that, dear. He sure was. Bigger than life! He passed away a few years ago in Utah. He and his wife were dear friends."

As she walked to her car, Lincoln fumed at the prospect of hitching her senior project and hopes of graduation on Barry – not to mention her goal to launch her shortened career with a big splash story. She was wasting her precious time and energy with Barry. Why did her source send her to story hour with Father Time here? Didn't the universe understand? After all she has been through and strived for, she deserved recognition and prestige. This was not turning out to be the kind of story that would give what was due to her. She felt her face get hot as her temper flared.

CHAPTER 7

Epiphany

The next day Lincoln paced the floor of Professor Erlenmeyer's office as she vented. "Boss, I'm way stressed over this project. My interview subject is a crackpot. I've seen him twice and he just tells me tall tales. Right now the only scoop I have is

'BARRY BLUE AND HIS BOYHOOD FRIENDS WERE MORONS'.

She put her hands up in front of her gesturing quotation marks and moaned, "I'll never hit it big with this guy."

Professor Erlenmeyer let her rant to blow off some steam. He had known Lincoln for nearly seven years and had become a mentor for her. He genuinely cared about his students and was especially accommodating to Lincoln's particular needs.

Professor Erlenmeyer straightened in his chair and folded his meaty hands on his desk. "Lincoln, you know getting a great story isn't easy. Remember our mantra: 'Adapt and persevere'."

Gasping for air, she turned on her oxyboost and settled into the chair across from her mentor. Adapt and persevere. Living with cystic fibrosis had taught Lincoln how to adapt and persevere. She earned top marks in her classes despite constant setbacks, including many hospital stays. She struggled with her health her entire school career, always one step forward, two steps back. Now, after seven long years, the only requirement standing between her and her degree was her thesis on Barry Blue.

Erlenmeyer picked up a gray, oval-shaped rock from his desk. "What do you think of my latest acquisition?"

"Congrats," said Lincoln, "it's a rock."

Professor Erlenmeyer pulled apart the stone that was neatly cut in half, revealing shimmering flat crystals. "Sure, it's a plain old rock on the outside, but when you open it up it's a beautiful formation of Ethiopian opal crystals. This geode is quite rare. So you see, even a rock... ."

"-has a story to tell," said Lincoln, finishing his sentence. She dropped her head into her hands. "I get it, but I feel like Barry Blue Hawkins is wasting my time and my talents, and I don't feel like wasting either! Help me pick out a new project. I'm sure you have ideas, contacts in high places... ."

Professor Erlenmeyer leaned forward. "Look Lincoln, I understand your frustration and that it's been very difficult for you to get this far. And I understand that you want to make your mark on the world. But have you ever stopped to think that other people have problems too? Everyone is fighting their own hidden battles."

"Yeah, I guess," said Lincoln.

"You guess? You need to get out of your own head, man! If you really want to make a difference...If you really want to help yourself, then help someone else. To quote Ben Franklin: 'Do well by doing good'."

Lincoln was taken aback. Nobody had ever talked to her like this! Had she been so wrapped up in her own day to day health struggles that she was blind to other people's problems? She certainly didn't want to be remembered as a prima donna. "OK, I hear you, but I don't really get it. How did Ben Franklin 'do well by doing good'?"

Professor Erlenmeyer leaned back, his hands moving as if he were juggling. "Well, for example, Franklin invented the lightning rod. Instead of patenting it and reaping the rewards for himself, he gave it to every country for free. Of course, it worked and buildings stopped getting burned up by lightning. Because of this, he became world famous and was welcome anywhere. In fact, he served as ambassador to France."

"Good for Ben, said Lincoln." "Do I have to invent something now?"

Erlenmeyer leaned forward and propped his hairy arms on the desk. "Start by helping Barry Blue Hawkins instead of only thinking of yourself."

Pow! This suggestion hit her right between the eyes. It was true. She had never considered helping the Barry Blue Hawkins's of the world, unless it directly benefited her. What an epiphany! She had always been too busy fighting her own battles to notice other people's problems. Should she put more time into Barry? It would surely be a selfless project since there is nothing for her to gain, other than a grade. She didn't see how things could work out for her like it did for Ben Franklin. Maybe if she helped Barry it would at least take her mind off her own problems for a while. She steadied herself after such a self-realization. "Okay, I'm game. But how can I help him?"

"You tell me, Lincoln."

Lincoln closed her eyes. "I'm not sure what Barry's deal is, but after all these years he wants to tell his bizarre story. Although he and his wife seem to have reservations about what the fallout would be."

"So get Barry's story and share it with the world. Make an old man happy – maybe even get him some peace," said Professor Erlenmeyer. "Put aside your notions of grandeur and *investigate his story*. I bet it will take you where you didn't expect, and you'll probably come out with something very interesting to tell the world."

Lincoln didn't say anything for a minute, her eyebrows working overtime. "I have a lot of material already and there is plenty more where that came from. I've got it! I'll produce and host a holopodcast on Barry Blue Hawkins."

"Hmmm, actually, the student station could use a fresh new show. How many episodes do you have so far?"

"I'll have material for four after tomorrow's interview."

"Great! Let's launch the first episode Friday."

Lincoln threw her hands in the air. "What? So soon? There's so much to do! What's the rush, Boss?"

"Welcome to the real world of crunch time and deadlines," he said. "It'll be a good experience for you. Make sure you bring some help. We'll meet Friday at 6 p.m. at the Station."

"Yeah, sure. I know just the people to help," replied Lincoln.

"Don't worry, it'll be fine Lincoln."

"I guess. I'm just not sure where Barry is headed with his story. We'll be drifting into uncharted territory."

"You know, there is an air of mystery to this thing between you and Barry Blue Hawkins."

"Mystery? Such as?"

"Such as, why hasn't Mr. Hawkins ever given an interview, even during his fifteen minutes of fame? And why is he now talking, and why to you?"

Lincoln sat up straight. Professor Erlenmeyer may have a point. Her eyebrows did a couple of leaps as other thoughts stumbled in to join the brain rave. Why in the world does Prinity Walker need to see Barry? And what about the two clippings about dead doctors?

Professor Erlenmeyer and Lincoln enjoyed a comfortable silence. She could tell that the professor was very satisfied with himself on a mentoring job well done. Lincoln's mind blazed with her new mission: to help Barry Blue Hawkins by getting his story told to Joe Public.

BEEP BEEP BEEEEEP!

The phone interrupted the brief stillness of thought.

"Excuse me a minute, Lincoln," said Professor Erlenmeyer. He picked up the hand-sized, antique desk phone from its beige cradle.

"Hello."

Silence. Lincoln watched the color drain from the professor's face.

CHAPTER 8

The Phone Call

"Yes, this is he," Erlenmeyer said in his telephone voice, visibly straining to regain his composure.

More silence.

"It's been a while. You people aren't big on communicating." Silence.

His voice turned firm. "I'm a patriot! My bond is my word." Silence.

Professor Erlenmeyer's face grew red. "Is that supposed to be some kind of threat?"

Silence.

"No, no, no. You, you leave my son out of this. He is an innocent." Professor Erlenmeyer's words trailed off to a whimper. "I'll do whatever you want. Just stay away from my boy." Although the conversation was apparently over, his trembling hands still held the phone for a moment.

"Boss, are you OK?"

He looked intensely at Lincoln. "Lincoln, your Dad…Does he still work for Homeland?"

"No. He retired last year."

"His number…Give it to me."

"Boss, what's going on?"

He raised his voice slightly. "The phone number…I need to talk to your Dad."

Lincoln's mind raced. Her dad greatly appreciated Professor Erlenmeyer's support for Lincoln over the years. She and her dad had many conversations about Professor Erlenmeyer, and she knew her dad would be glad to help him. But the kind of help that her dad gave was for people that were in trouble. Like big time trouble. What could her professor possibly be mixed up in that required her dad's expertise?

"Yeah, sure Boss." She typed into her holoband. "I just sent you my dad's number."

No response.

"Boss. Talk to me."

He stared past Lincoln and softly said to no one in particular, "I've made a huge mistake."

CHAPTER 9

The Best Day Ever

Jenny met Lincoln at the door, with Moondog barking as if facing down a bear. "So good to see you Lincoln. Come on in."

"Thank you," said Lincoln.

"Would you mind if I joined you for this session?" asked Jenny.

"Not at all," replied Lincoln. "Maybe he'll behave with you back there."

"I doubt it," chuckled Jenny. "I have some ice tea for us."

Lincoln could not stop thinking about the Professor's phone call two days earlier. He sounded scared for his life and she wanted to know what was going on. But now she had to turn her focus to Barry. Professor Erlenmeyer's story would have to wait.

They joined Barry at the back of the house. He reclined on the couch and Moondog trotted over to lay down on the floor next to him. Lincoln switched on her recorder. "Okay, Barry. Dazzle me."

Barry silently mouthed as the audio signer translated out loud, in the usual British accent. "Jolly good. Prepare to be dazzled, then."

Lincoln turned to Jenny with a puzzled look on her face. "We just got an upgrade to his audio signer. It reads lips now when he's too tired to show off his signing," Jenny explained.

Barry continued. "I attended college at Emory University in Atlanta. In my junior year, I worked a summer job as a handyman in a huge apartment complex. I didn't really know what I was doing, but the other handymen took me under their wing and showed me how to fix things. So I would walk around the complex with my tool belt working from my punch list. One day this kid in a motorized wheelchair started following me around. He caught up to me and he struck up a conversation. His name was Josh. He had this big smile on his face, a face that was flat as a pan. I didn't ask him what his deal was, I just treated him like any other kid, as I had three younger brothers and knew how to horse around with a kid."

"Every day I would shoot the hay for a little while with Brenda, the secretary that worked up front. After a week of Josh following me around, I found out he was her son. Soon she invited me to dinner after work at their place in the apartment complex. When I arrived Josh greeted me with 'Hi Mr. Barry' and the usual big smile. I reached down and gave him a low-five as he could not raise his hands more than a few inches off his arm rests. I sat at the kitchen table with Josh and his younger sister as they did their homework, while Brenda got dinner ready. After finishing the best meal I've had all week, we all hung out until the kids went to bed. Brenda filled me in on Josh. She said that she knew when he was two years old that something was wrong, although the doctors didn't think so. The diagnosis of muscular dystrophy at age five confirmed her worst fear. The dad couldn't handle it and he left. I thanked her for dinner and went home."

Barry rubbed his head for a minute. "As I drove home, I pondered how could that kid be so happy all the time. Stuck in a wheelchair, this eleven-year old boy was living out a death sentence. Surely he had some understanding of his situation. I just didn't get it."

"Josh and I did some weekend outings. Once we saw the Harlem Globetrotters and got to sit right up front. I kind of became like a big brother to him, often having dinner at their place after work. On another weekend we saw the premier of Star Wars Episode V, The Empire Strikes Back. This was 1980 and Josh was a huge fan. After the movie we made our way to the very far side of the lobby to get out of people's way and to wait for his mom to pick us up in their wheelchair van. Josh looked up at me and said, 'Mr. Barry, this is the best day ever!' His expression of joy hit me like a two by four over the head. Josh was a natural at the Art of Gratitude! The kid live-streamed thankfulness for everything good that came into his life. From then on I carried that lesson in my heart. Little did I know that decades later, I too would become a practitioner in the Art of Gratitude as I coped with my own debilitating illness."

"I got down on one knee to hug him. What an awesome kid! After our hug I gave him a double 'low five' and just hung on to his hands, my eyes closed. My pulse sped up and my hands began to sweat. I could feel a connection between our hands, a little bit like static electricity. After a couple of minutes, I let go and looked at Josh. 'Good, I thought, the kid's not freaking out.' In fact, he was beaming with a big smile across that flat face of his. His mom arrived and we loaded Josh into the van. On the ride home, Josh just talked about how great the movie was. I don't think he gave our hand-clasp a second thought. That was on a Friday."

"Monday at work Brenda cornered me and in a hushed tone said, 'Barry, there is something going on with Josh. He's doing little things he hasn't done in years. I don't know what to do. I want you to come over after work.' When I got there, I stooped low to give Josh a 'low-five' as usual, but he stuck his hand up to shoulder height. 'High-five Mr. Barry,' he said with a smile on a face that didn't seem so flat and featureless. At dinner, he was able to lift his glass with both hands to drink, and even cut his own food."

The Audio Signer paused as Barry rubbed his bald scalp and rested for a minute. Lincoln realized that she was sitting on the edge of her chair. "After dinner the kids went into the other room to watch TV and left us alone in the kitchen. Brenda looked weary, yet excited at the same time. She put her hands to her face and told me she wondered whether she was going crazy and imagining things. He seemed to be getting better, but she didn't want to get their hopes up. I told her to just see how it goes. I tried to sound reassuring, but at the same time I felt the way she did — excited yet cautious."

Closing his eyes, Barry stopped to rest. He seemed to be sleeping. Eyes still closed, he continued mouthing the words to his story. "As the last few weeks of summer went by, Josh steadily improved to where he could get out of his wheelchair and bear his own weight. At this point Brenda took him to his doc and eventually got Josh into physical therapy. I had to go back to school to finish up my last year. I was very busy working and doing my Master's thesis in chemistry, so consequently I only saw Josh one more time. I could tell he would be fine. Brenda swore it was a miracle and that their prayers had been answered. I had never felt so good about myself. It was the best thing I had ever done in my life. At that point, I made a most fateful decision."

Barry signed "peace out" and rolled over on his side, facing the couch. Ten seconds later his snores confirmed the end of that day's interview, with Moondog beside him joining the log-sawing chorus. Lincoln looked at Jenny, palms upraised, with 'What the heck' etched all over her face. Jenny chuckled. "He does that sometimes."

Lincoln says, "He can't just drop a cliff-hanger like that and then go to sleep."

Jenny shrugged. "When he's tired, he's tired. He doesn't really have a choice."

Instead of hustling out of there, Lincoln turned off the holorecorder and sat quietly. Her eyebrows scrunched up as she processed Barry's latest story. Clearly this tale was deeply personal for Barry. That boy gave Barry this gift of gratitude that meant so much to him. Barry believed his stories as true and not just tall tales. He really thinks he healed Josh and those other people. He doesn't seem crazy. Eccentric, but not crazy. So why is he compelled to tell his personal life journey after all this time? And what, she mused for the umpteenth time, does this have to do with the murdered doctors?

CHAPTER 10

Invisible Illness

Lincoln leaned towards Jenny and said in a hushed tone, "Will it disturb him if we talk?"

Jenny let go a little laugh. "He's already disturbed. Just kidding. We won't bother him. He'll be out cold for at least an hour."

"In that case, may I ask what's going on with him? You know, his voice, his head," inquired Lincoln.

Jenny let out a sigh. "Barry has severe M.E."

Lincoln put both hands to her face. "Geez. I'm...I'm so sorry Jenny." Lincoln had heard of M.E., myalgic en-cephalomyelitis, a chronic neuro-immune disease that affects millions. "He rubs his head a lot. What's the deal with that?"

"He has a neuropathy that makes his brain feel like it's burn-ing. And he can barely talk, which is why he learned American Sign Language decades ago. It's all part of the M.E. package deal," explained Jenny.

Lincoln had never met anyone with M.E. Jenny's descrip-tion of Barry's condition intrigued her much more than listening to him ruminate about his delusional childhood. She pointed to the patents on the wall. "I don't take Barry for a lazy person considering his science career. But I can't help but notice that he spends most of his time laid out flat on the couch."

"Well, Barry is a horizontal person living in a vertical world. He can only be on his feet for a few seconds at a time. That's why we have the mobility scooter in the house. He can sit up for about half an hour with the help of his homemade 'neck-thing-in-a-pant-leg'. It helps him hold his head up without drawing attention in public." Jenny gave a nod towards the black pant leg with a brace poking out of the top. "And on top of all that, it's painful for him to focus or track with his eyes. So he doesn't use a computer, read, or watch TV."

"But what about the new medicines?" asked Lincoln. "I've heard that it's made a difference for many people with M.E."

Jenny nodded. "You mean the ones developed at the Lake Nona M.E. Center? Oh yes, they have helped some people. But that line of treatment didn't work on Barry. He's a special case."

"Geez, Jenny, I can't imagine how hard it's been for both of you dealing with M.E. for so long." Lincoln paused for a long moment. "How bad is the fatigue part?"

"He has exhausting fatigue every minute of every day. He wakes up that way. He's like a battery that winds down as the day goes on," Jenny said matter-of-factly.

Lincoln clasped her hand over her mouth. "So that's why he'll only see me in the morning, and not on consecutive days. I see now, Jenny. Barry is going through a lot of effort to work with me."

"Hmmm...Lincoln, you seem to have some insight into what it's like to have an invisible illness."

Lincoln nodded. She knew all too well what it was like to be judged by people who didn't understand that she had limitations caused by her disease. She couldn't keep up with the world and the world did not care.

"I figured you have some lung issue going on," continued Jenny. "Is that what that little tube is for?" Lincoln absentmindedly let her hand go to her Tree of Life pendant.

"Yes, I have CF, and this helps me breathe." Lincoln caressed the oxy-boost device that seemed like a natural part of her.

"Don't get me wrong," said Jenny. "You look lovely. But I've been around Barry long enough to be able to recognize those suffering from an invisible illness."

"Yes, but most people don't," said Lincoln. "To friends, doctors, and other students I look fine, so they expect me to be able to do anything a healthy person can do. People don't get it."

Jenny smiled. "Like we've always said, 'When it comes to an invisible illness, you don't get it until you get it.' Or until a loved one gets it."

For a moment, there was no sound other than Moondog and Barry snoring.

Lincoln's single-minded drive brought her back to her project. Barry's fantastic stories still puzzled her. Switching gears, she measured her words. "Jenny, Barry seems sincere about what he is telling me. But is he like, you know, with it?"

"You mean has he lost his marbles?" Jenny swatted her hand through the air in a dismissive fashion. "Oh, the old codger is with it, all right. He gets real forgetful and loses things all over the house, which drives me nuts. And he gets brain-fog if he pushes too hard. But his long-term memory is spot on."

Lincoln leaned her head back on the couch. Though running on empty, she pushed on. "So why is Barry opening up now? And why me?"

Jenny took a long drink of iced tea. "After you called asking for the interview, Barry and I talked for a long time. Barry isn't getting any younger. He wants to tell his story before it's too late. We both agree that you should be the one to do it. Been over 30 years since all the fuss, so we're hoping there won't be any... issues."

"Issues?" asked Lincoln, her eyebrows arching up.

"It's complicated," said Jenny.

Lincoln grimaced. "I have no idea where all this is going, but my source said I should see Barry. And I trust my source."

"I bet you do," said Jenny with a knowing look.

CHAPTER 11

Detective Rick Jade

Rick 'Ricochet' Jade dedicated himself to serving and protecting his country. He was so dubbed due to a bullet glancing off an iron grating and nicking him in the neck. He was lucky to be alive today and he darn well knew it. A dad first, his life consisted of taking care of his daughter in addition to his job, although his job kept him away more than he liked. After his wife died, his extended family took care of little Lincoln when he had to be away. A good dad never stops being a parent. Even now, he thought of Lincoln all the time, but he knew that she needed room to become her own person. Always a phone call away, he visited her in Orlando frequently.

Right after Lincoln's last breathing treatment for the day, her holoband buzzed. It projected her dad's tiny hologram image with crystal clear resolution. He sported a crew cut with ray bans sitting on top of his head. "Hey superstar! How is life in the big city?"

"It's super, of course," she replied. "Are you working?" Silly question — her dad always worked.

"A little," said her dad. At age sixty-one he still worked, but under the radar. Mandatory retirement for U.S. citizens arrives at age sixty, instituted years earlier to ensure job openings for young people entering the workforce. With the government paying for education, medical expenses for life, and a retirement wage, most people didn't need to hoard money or work full-time in their twilight years. However, many of them engaged in some type of free-lance under-the-table work to fully make ends meet or aspire to a higher standard of living. Rick fell into the first category and now worked as a private investigator.

Rick started out as a Navy pilot but a congenital eye defect ended his flying days. Eager to serve his country nonetheless, he obtained a transfer to Homeland Security where he excelled at information analysis and became a special agent. His job focused on identifying and protecting U.S. assets. Human assets, to be precise.

"How are you feeling?" asked Rick. "What were the results of your latest CAT scans?"

Normally Lincoln kept her dad in the loop on her health, but she didn't want him to sideline her from this case if he knew the doctor's orders were for her to completely rest. "I'm fine. I saw Dr. Walker this week. My CAT scans and blow test showed I am maintaining lung capacity," she lied.

"Good." As a dad, Rick did his best to check regularly on her health without getting on her nerves, so he moved on. Dealing with the ongoing medical journey and their everyday lives at the same time was their 'normal'. "How's school?"

"Ehhh. I guess the big news is I started my senior production project. Remember when you gave me your file with all of those articles on Barry Blue Hawkins? I'm interviewing him."

"School project? Hm! Well, I'm glad you're seeing him. How is Mr. Hawkins?"

"One fry short of a happy meal, if you ask me. And he has M.E. He's pretty jacked up," replied Lincoln.

"Yeah, I've heard that about him. How's the interview going?"

"Oh, fantastic! So far he's told me tall tales about his juvenile delinquent days. And get this — he claims he cured a kid who was in a wheelchair," said Lincoln.

No response.

"Dad? Did you hear what I said?" asked Lincoln. "He's cuckcoo for Cocoa Puffs!"

"I heard you. You need to get to know him. He can help you."

Lincoln huffed. "Dad, haven't you been listening to me? What makes you think he can help me?"

"Because Mr. Hawkins and I have a history going back over thirty years."

"Whaaat? You mean you know him?" asked Lincoln. "How?"

"Barry Blue Hawkins saved my life," came the answer.

Lincoln peered intently at the image of her dad on her holoband. "Dad, what do you mean 'he saved your life'?"

"I can't talk about that over the phone."

"Why not?" Then Lincoln smacked her forehead with her palm. "Wait a minute! So if you know Barry Blue Hawkins, why have Jenny and Barry acted like they didn't recognize my last name? Surely they made the connection between you and me right away."

"They did that out of respect for my wishes," he said. "They're protecting you."

"Dad, this is nuts. I don't understand."

"Star, I will explain when I see you in person. I have something that you need to see. Now let's get off this line."

"Wait, Dad, where are you?"

"Orange, New Jersey."

This town name struck a dissonant chord with Lincoln. It's where Windy said all of those residents were hit by some strange illness. She managed to get out, "Be safe, Dad."

"Good night, Star. Dad loves you."

CHAPTER 12

Radium Girls

The three friends hung out in Jamie's all-bed unit the following day watching their favorite show, 'The Newest Sherlock Holmes Chronicles'. A box the size of a brick projected the image onto a floating hologram screen. A news flash icon appeared on the screen entitled "National News Flash, Orange NJ."

Windy pointed at it. "Hey, this is that story I was telling you guys about. TV, play news flash!" The television paused the show, and B-roll footage of a quiet street expanded to fill the screen.

Breaking news from Orange, New Jersey...Viewers are warned that this report contains disturbing content! People that live at the upscale Chetola Housing Community have been experiencing a strange illness. The seemingly unrelated symptoms range from bleeding gums to sarcoma cancer. One teenage girl recently had to have her lower jaw removed. The number of people affected is now 469, which is almost the entire Phase I community. Previously thought to be a virus, officials are investigating the possibility –

"TV Pause!" said Lincoln and the broadcast stopped.

"It's radiation sickness, most likely caused by radium. Geez, you guys — my *dad* is up there!"

Jamie and Windy looked at her in astonishment but said nothing.

"TV Play," said Lincoln and the show resumed.

- that the bizarre symptoms could be caused by radiation sickness, blared the TV.

"TV Pause!" said Windy. "All right sista-gal, what in the world is going on?"

"I recently read a book called 'Radium Girls'. I *knew* I had read something about Orange before but I didn't put it together until just now."

"Well, of course!" said Jamie. "Why am I not surprised that you read a book on this exact same subject?"

Lincoln wagged a finger at Jamie and grinned. "Hey boy genius, reading is an endless joy - you should try it sometime."

"Welcome to today's episode of 'Roasting Jamie," said Windy, laughing and nudging him teasingly.

Lincoln exhaled with a whoosh. "Dad better be super careful. A virus you can treat, but radiation poisoning is forever! Geez, I hope he knows his history."

Jaime said, "Oh, good. I was hoping for a history lesson. Can't get enough of those!"

Lincoln made a point to ignore Jamie and faced Windy.

"As I was saying, it's the true story that took place back in the 1920's — wait for it — in Orange, New Jersey. The U.S. Radium Company hired young women to paint watch dials that glowed in the dark, mostly for soldiers during World War I. The ingredient that made the paint glow in the dark was radium, which is highly radioactive. The girls had no protection from the radioactive paint, and to make matters worse, they were instructed to keep the tip of the paint brush pointed by wetting it in their mouths. Most of the four thousand girls and young women employed died horrible deaths from radiation poisoning."

"Yeah, but how did you know it was radiation sickness?" asked Jamie.

"First of all, because it took place in Orange, New Jersey where the U.S. Radium headquarters was located. That's a big red flag. And secondly, because the sickness manifests itself in a wide array of seemingly unrelated symptoms," said Lincoln.

"So that's why you didn't buy the virus theory at all the other day," said Windy.

"That's right," answered Lincoln. "It seemed like too much of a coincidence for a localized mystery illness to be located in a town where radium was handled with little regard for environmental safety. And I don't believe in coincidence."

"So how are they getting sick from radium after over a hundred years?" asked Jamie.

Lincoln smirked. "Look who's all into today's history lesson! Okay, radium has a half-life of sixteen hundred years, so it's still very radioactive. The U.S Radium Company had a second production facility in ...oh, where was it?... oh yeah, Ottawa, Illinois. That factory was shut down around 1930, but in the following decades people continued to work in those buildings and live in that area. Many of them died of cancer. If this Chetola Community was built on a former radium contaminated worksite or waste-dump, they would suffer the fate of the Ottawa residents."

"That's awful! And to think it's happening again!" said Windy.

Lincoln clenched her fists. "The real tragedy is that it didn't have to happen. U.S. Radium knew about the dangers of radium but didn't tell the employees. The company provided no protection or chemical hygiene. Four of the workers took U.S Radium to court. The company used underhanded tactics, mainly stalling the court dates until the plaintiffs died. Three of the women survived long enough to win the case. They received a paltry sum of money for their medical bills. But the ruling closed down U.S. Radium. Because of this case, the government established the U.S. Department of Labor to protect all workers, including the thousands of people that worked on the Manhattan project."

"Wow," said Windy. "So these women made a huge difference! Add them to my list of heroes."

"I know. I can't imagine being sick and dying and having to fight a corporate behemoth!" said Lincoln.

"Heavy, man," said Jamie.

"They eventually built a monument to the Radium Girls, as they were called in Ottawa," said Lincoln. She paused a beat. "TV play!"

The Phase I Chetola Houses have been evacuated and the patients are under quarantine. The situation is dire for Phase I residents since there is no cure for radiation sickness.

Three-dimensional images of swanky brownstone houses made in the style of old New York City brownstones appeared on the screen.

So far residents in Phase II of the Chetola community are unaffected by any symptoms. Authorities believe that the situation is isolated to the Phase I community.

The TV cameras panned one block over to show phase II brownstones. An authoritative voice droned on.

The city of Orange has a dark history involving radium used in factories for painting watch dials. Authorities are investigating the possibility that the radiation sickness is coming from an old factory or waste disposal site involving radium.

The investigation has found radium in soil samples taken from Phase I.

"TV pause!" said Jamie. The screen froze on the mirror images of Phase I and Phase II with a barricaded city street between them. "Man, something here is whack. On one side you have people sick and dying and the other side is unscathed!"

"Hon, you're brilliant," said Windy.

"I am?" asked Jamie.

"Yeah. What are the odds that one side of the street is radioactive and the other isn't," said Windy. "Omigawd Guys! I have to investigate this mystery for my senior project."

"Go for it!" said Jamie.

"Yeah," said Lincoln. We'll help you."

"But where to begin?" asked Windy. "It's so overwhelming!"

"The first thing to do is to gather all the intel you can on Phase I and Phase II," said Lincoln.

"I guess I could download the blueprints," said Windy. "And get diagrams of the Chetola water system."

"Then you'll need to take a trip up there on the bullet train and talk to people," said Jamie.

"Look for patterns and outliers in the radiation cases," said Lincoln. "My dad might also uncover something related to your angle."

"Yeah," said Windy. "I can stay with my parents when I am up there. Thanks guys, I'm on it!"

"This Chetola business is right up your alley," said Lincoln, leveling her gaze at Windy.

"You betcha, girlfriend. Windy's my name, saving Mother Earth is my game."

"I love your passion, babe," said Jamie. "Perfect senior project for you."

"Yeah, I feel like my whole life has been leading up to this," said Windy. "When my mom used to take us camping she would always say, 'Leave the campground cleaner than we found it.' From that point on, I have not been able to stop noticing all the ways we abuse the environment. This isn't just our campground — this is our home, y'all. Wouldn't it be awesome if everyone decided to leave this planet better than we found it."

"Nice rant Babe," said Jamie.

"Speaking of investigative projects, can we listen to your interviews with Mr. Hawkins?" said Jamie.

Lincoln said, "In fact, I need a big fave from you guys. I'm doing a holopodcast on Barry Blue Hawkins and we launch this Friday. Can you be on my podcast team?"

"Absolutely!" said Windy. We'll hold it down for you!"

"Oh yeah, perfect!" said Jamie. "I'll be your wingman L.J. Just leave the audiovisual to me. I'd like to be on this for my senior project too."

"No prob, tinker boy," said Lincoln.

"So this is quite the one-eighty for you and this Barry Blue Hawkins thing," said Windy. "What the heck happened?"

"Let's just say that Professor Erlenmeyer got my mind right and challenged me. By the way, have you guys noticed the Boss acting kind of weird lately?"

"What makes you say that?" asked Windy.

"I was in his office when he got a phone call that seemed like a threat," said Lincoln.

"Maybe it was just a prank," said Jamie.

"I don't know," said Lincoln. "He seemed pretty upset, like he knew the person on the other end of that phone call."

"Weird," said Jamie.

"I wonder what he's gotten himself into," said Windy.

"I don't know," said Lincoln, "but surely it has nothing to do with our holopod."

CHAPTER 13

A Coward Dies a Thousand Deaths

The next day Lincoln returned to the Hawkins' residence and joined Jenny and Barry in the back room. Rain rattled the tin roof of the adjacent closed-in porch. Her last conversation with Rick left her full of questions. She let loose. "Do you guys know what I found out? That you people know my dad from back in the day! Why didn't you tell me that you knew who I was all along?"

Jenny remained calm. "Lincoln, it was clear to us that you didn't know anything about our history with your dad. He asked us not to tell anybody about what happened thirty years ago. It was for everyone's protection, including your own."

"Protection? Protection from what?"

"Not what, but whom," said Barry. He mouthed his input into the audio signer. The British voice rang out, "My fame caught the attention of some very bad people. We were in danger. Your dad saved the day, by Jove."

Lincoln hunched her shoulders and raised her hands. "Clearly I have no idea what you are talking about. Why don't you just tell me what happened back then?"

Barry looked at Lincoln intensely as if peering into a microscope. "I am telling you, through the interview. I have to tell you my entire story so that you will understand. I need you to believe what I am telling you." His right hand slapped hard into his open left hand.

"My dad said that you saved his life, which I find very hard to believe," said Lincoln.

"See!" Barry growled aloud. "That's what I'm talking about!"

"Point taken," replied Lincoln. "Tell me Barry, why haven't you ever given an interview? Thirty years is a long time to keep quiet about whatever happened to you."

Barry looked at Jenny, then locked eyes with Lincoln. "Because they threatened to kill our two daughters if we went public. Our kids were about your age when all this went down."

"The bad people," Lincoln said flatly.

No response.

"Okay, so why now?" asked Lincoln. "What's changed?"

"Because I'm tired of living in fear!" said Barry in his own voice, as loudly as he could.

Barry returned to the audio signer. "I intend to send up a big enough flare so if the bad guys are still out there, they'll come after me and not my kids."

Lincoln raised her voice over the sound of the downpour, now hammering the tin roof. "If you say so," said Lincoln. "Well, if you want to send up a flare, what would you say to a holopodcast on your story? We can launch it as soon as Friday night."

Jenny answered for him. "Oh, that sounds exciting, but Barry and I are going to have to discuss it first. I'm not sure that is a good idea for any of us."

Barry sat up. The rain pounded the tin roof, making it hard to hear him. "Jen, there is no need to discuss it. We've been keeping a lid on this thing for decades. My dad told me when I was a boy that 'a coward dies a thousand deaths; a brave man only one.' It's time to be brave! I'm ready for a showdown if it comes to it!"

Jenny set her jaw. The tension in her face resolved into determination. "Okay, let's do this holopodcast thing. We've played duck and cover long enough."

Barry looked a little surprised. Then he whispered, "All right Lincoln, we're in."

The rain stopped. The room was quiet.

Lincoln wasn't sure what to make of their exchange, but at least they agreed on the Podcast. She figured her dad would explain the rest since he was part of the story himself. "Are you up for another session, Barry?"

Barry held the Audio Signer and gave a firm thumbs-up. "You bet!"

CHAPTER 14

Saving the World

Lincoln switched on the holo-recorder and settled back into the couch. "I have a couple main things I want to cover today. When we last spoke, you shared some stories in which you claim to have healed people with serious injuries and muscular dystrophy. And then you said, and I quote," Lincoln referred to her screenpad for the transcription of their last interview, 'At that point, I made a most fateful decision. Zzzzzzzzz.' That 'Zzzzz' part is you snoring as you fell asleep right after dropping that line on me. And second, I found a couple articles about dead doctors that I thought my source included by accident. But I did some digging and it turns out there weren't just a couple of suspicious doctor deaths back in your heyday, but dozens! And that's just the ones I've been able to find. What was going on back then? I want to find out!"

Barry began signing and the Audio Signer took over. "I catch your drift, old girl. You aren't the only idealist that wants to make a difference. I had that fire, too! When I was young, I wanted to save the world! I took it as my mission to help people suffering with illness and pain. What I meant by 'I made a most fateful decision' was due to two things. One, my experience with Josh. The second was an experience just after that which still haunts me."

"My Grandpa owned a bar called the Seven Mile Inn. On Sundays it was closed to the public, but was a gathering place for family. While sipping my rootbeer and sitting at a table with my Grandma, a ghostly thin boy entered the bar, escorted by his mother. The veins and blood vessels pulsed across his translucent skin of his exposed arms, neck, and face. He looked like a living anatomical model of the circulatory system. As the kid took a seat at the bar, I learned from my Grandma that he was a distant cousin of mine. I asked her what was wrong with him. She told me that he was born missing some of his skin layers. This blew my boy mind. How could such a thing happen? I wondered if I could help him. But I didn't dare try. I just stared at that kid like he was a wax museum freak show. Afterwards, I pounded myself for my inability to act. After all, my success with Josh taught me that I can help people like that. So I resolved to figure out a way to help people that were really messed up, without being found out. Because let's face it, you can't just go up and grab people. It's too bad I never saw that kid again."

"Before I knew it I was twenty-one years old and in my last year of college at Emory University. I was determined to help people without getting arrested. I participated as a volunteer in the Ministry of the Sick for the Newman Center at the university. That's where you visit people in a nursing home or sometimes their home. We gave them Holy Communion and prayed together. You can hold hands while saying a prayer. So that was my plan. Have the Newman Center send me out into the world to see sick people. However, I would have to be careful about people putting two and two together. I would never visit the same person twice."

Barry stopped signing to stretch his hands and arms. He rubbed his head. Sunlight streamed through the back window and onto the floor behind his couch.

Barry continued signing. "The first person I helped with my new plan was this guy Travis at one of the nursing homes. This particular nursing home smelled like mothballs. I didn't sign into the visitor book. I had a list of Catholic people that were in this nursing home. When I got to Travis's room I saw this little old man listening to a video tape of an old western TV show *Gunsmoke*. He mouthed the words as the tape played. The red-tipped cane leaning against his bed told me that Travis was blind. When I knocked, he motioned for me to take a seat. I asked him if he would pray the Lord's Prayer with me. Travis drawled a 'sure'. I clasped his hands and we started saying the prayer. Immediately I could feel my heart working hard and my hands break out in a sweat. My arms tingled as though electricity flowed through them. Drawing in deep breaths I tried to appear calm. After the prayer, I let go of his hands. He didn't speak for a moment and then said 'Thanks'. I said 'Good luck' and headed down the hall.

"The next guy on my list was JoJo. His door was open, so I knocked and asked if he wanted some company. Though scrunched up in bed, he said he was up to it. This young man of about thirty had long hair and a beard. His scrawny arms and clenched hands poked out from a white t-shirt and folded across his belly. A wheelchair equipped with an oxygen canister rested at the foot of the bed. He volunteered that he had Guillain-Barre syndrome for the past nine years. He used to be a bluegrass guitar player. Now his arms and legs were completely useless. After chatting, we said the 'Our Father' together, his hands in mine. The physical connection with JoJo felt the same as with Travis. After we finished, hunger rumbled my belly and I felt wrung out. I left the nursing home, mission accomplished."

"The Newman Center rotated me through six nursing homes on a weekly basis. It had been six weeks since I visited the first nursing home. As I wandered down the green hall lined with patient rooms, I saw Travis slowly walking towards me without his red-tipped cane. I wondered whether he could see me. As he walked past me, my question was answered. I smiled at him and he smiled back, not knowing who I was. I kept going until I got to JoJo's room. I sneaked a peek inside, but another patient occupied his bed. I wondered whether he moved to another room. I asked the charge nurse about JoJo, and she told me that he had a remarkable recovery and had been discharged from the nursing home. I wanted to jump and shout at the news! The people I connected with were becoming well with no one the wiser about me."

"I did my best to make my rounds through the nursing homes, never visiting with the same person twice. 'Saving the world one person at a time' became my mantra. I rode the wave through my senior year. Engaging with these patients left me drained, but I ignored this side effect because I always bounced back the next day."

Lincoln rested her chin on her hands and peered into Barry's eyes. When he told his stories, his sincerity drew her in. She decided to suspend her disbelief and interview him as if he was for real. After all, Barry believed this stuff was real, and she had to admit the material possessed entertainment value.

"Barry, I would like to understand how you see yourself, for the record," said Lincoln tapping the holo recorder. "So let me get this straight. Throughout your life you've basically gone around laying hands on sick people and healing them."

Barry held his hands up. "Whoa, it's not like that. First of all, I have to grip a sick or injured person with both hands and hang on." He half-held his thin arms out with balled fists. "When I grip the sick person I feel like I am making some kind of biochemical connection with them."

"What makes you say that?"

"Well, my hands get sweaty with the grip, my arms get warm, and I feel the energy going out of me," he said while his arms slightly shook.

"So it's your grip that heals them," said Lincoln, pressing him further.

"I believe that I am passing something on to the person that I am helping. It's something that their body needs for whatever is ailing them. Their body does the rest. It usually takes a couple of days for the person to really recover," said Barry, his eyes wide open. "So I don't consider myself to be a healer. I just put them on the mend."

Lincoln's eyebrows arched. "If you put them on the mend, that makes you a mender!"

"Yeah, I reckon so," Barry whispered. "A mender."

Lincoln calculated her next question and spoke softly so as not to sound obnoxious. "Isn't it ironic that you can mend others, but not yourself?"

"Yeah, I know it sounds absurd, but that's the way it is," said Barry.

The idea for the name of the podcast popped into Lincoln's thoughts. She put the idea into her mental file cabinet for later.

"So, back to your story. What happened after college?"

Barry rubbed his face before signing. "Well, I graduated and started my first chemistry job, which was at Research Triangle Institute near Durham, North Carolina. Everything had gone according to plan. And then my world took a U-turn."

CHAPTER 15

U-Turn

"What do you mean by your world took a U-turn?" she asked without thinking.

Barry answered with his speaking voice, "I became one of the broken people."

Lincoln's mind spun. This might have something to do with Barry's M.E.. "Are you okay to go on?" she asked.

Barry's head sank into his shoulders. "Yes, I want to get through this next part."

He switched to mouthing what he said as the Audio Signer read his lips. "Shortly after graduation, I woke up with a crick in my neck. You know, the kind of muscle pain that stays with you all day and really gets on your nerves. Well, the muscle pain quickly spread to my shoulders, then my entire back. It got so bad that I had to leave my job after only three months. I moved back in with my parents. It spread to my arms and legs until I was a mass of constant pain twenty-four seven. We went to all kinds of doctors. They had no diagnosis for me. In fact, since nothing irregular was showing up on my blood tests, I was labeled a hypochondriac by many docs. One doc said that I was an overachiever and this was my way of taking a rest! I can tell you that a hypochondriac is treated with total disdain. I even had a couple docs laugh in my face. Others yelled at me. My parents stood by me and took care of me, God bless 'em. I stayed mostly in my room, living day by day. Sometimes hour by hour as my condition grew worse. After about three years, my legs hurt so bad that I could only walk to the end of the driveway. My brother had to shave me as I couldn't use my arms. My parents hauled me up to Emory University Research Hospital. Tests, including a muscle biopsy, showed that I had some kind of muscle myopathy but still no diagnosis."

"My mom took me to see a doc in Winter Park, Florida. He looked ancient, like the Crypt Keeper. I told him my sad story. I was so beaten down that he couldn't even look me in the eye. I expected him to tell me I was lazy and crazy. But he didn't. He just said, 'My boy, something you are eating is triggering your myopathy.' He told me to go on the caveman diet of tuna and potatoes. I figured, what did I have to lose? Two days after being on the caveman diet, I felt great. Soon I got my old chemist job back and returned to North Carolina. Eventually I figured out that dairy products were not my friend."

Barry rubbed his head and closed his eyes momentarily.

Lincoln paused the recording and mused on Barry's words. She had her own experiences navigating endless doctor visits and hospital stays. "Barry, knowing that you have M.E. now, it sounds like you had severe fibromyalgia, part of the M.E. package."

"Yep, you're right," Barry said with his speaking voice. "I know that now."

"It's unbelievable that a doctor would dismiss someone with your symptoms as a head case," she said.

"You have to remember that this was the early 1980's." He switched to his Audio Signer, mouthing, "Few doctors had heard of M.E. The few that knew about it called it CFS for Chronic Fatigue Syndrome. There was no blood test for it back then. The NIH didn't classify it as a disease until about 2015. The CDC classified it as a psychological disorder until about 2010."

"Sounds like living in the dark ages for people with M.E," Lincoln said. "What would you say got you through those three-and-a-half years?"

"I was mad, really mad. I was determined to prove that I had a real physical illness and that I wasn't crazy. The only way to prove that was to persevere and get better somehow."

"What did you get out of this horrible experience?" asked Lincoln.

"Nothing. At least for a long time. I didn't look at getting better as a miracle or anything like that. I just wanted to get back to my life."

Lincoln decided to ask one more question, even though it was on the fantasy side of the fence. "What about your crusade to help broken people?"

Closing his eyes he rasped, "I walked away from it. This nightmare was a side effect that I couldn't handle again." His eyes stayed closed.

It had never occurred to Lincoln that there was a time when many diseases were not even recognized by medical doctors and that patients suffered the consequences. At least her docs knew what CF was and could treat it. "That's quite an ordeal, Barry."

"You haven't heard nothin' yet," he croaked.

Picking up the cue, she turned on the recorder. "Barry, you say you mended lots of people. What would you do if you woke up tomorrow morning and *you* were mended?"

Barry propped himself up on one elbow. In his own voice he said, "I would swim in the ocean. You know, ride some waves and get back to nature." He layed back down.

Lincoln cocked her head, a little surprised at this answer. She was expecting something more spectacular like taking a round trip to the moon or fixing climate change. Without his hypothetical mending powers, he was just a regular person. Lincoln replied, "That sounds like fun, Barry. Maybe if that dream doesn't come true for you, it will for somebody else."

She watched him lying limp on the couch, eyes closed, a slight smile. Perhaps he was picturing himself taking that swim.

CHAPTER 16

A Holopod is Born

As the theme song 'Heroes' faded, a pair of shiny dolphins splashed towards the sun melting into the sea.

"Sweet take, L.J. That's a keeper!" said Jamie from the Station's audio-holographic control room. Everyone called it the Fishbowl because the front and two sides were enclosed in glass. Jamie wore an earpiece and stood at a control panel that wrapped around the inside of the control room in large U-shape. He had been at the station all day preparing the equipment for the podcast work.

Lincoln sat outside the Fishbowl at a news desk wearing her navy blue business dress. An image of the Orlando skyline at dusk provided the background. New buildings dwarfed the old buildings. The SpaceX launch pad simulation building loomed in the skyline, celebrating the colonization of Mars. She gave a thumbs up to Jamie and unclipped her microphone.

Inside the Fishbowl a holo-pad projected Lincoln's holographic image. Windy and Professor Erlenmeyer stood by beaming. "The camera loves you, girl!" said Windy.

Professor Erlenmeyer removed his headphones. "That's a wrap. Nice job!"

Lincoln stepped off her desk platform and walked past the robotic cameras to the control room and entered using the back door. Switching on her oxy-boost, she sat down and relaxed. She gazed upon the darkness of the studio, the black floors, walls, and ceiling. The vibrant news desk appeared tame and contained without the city skyline projected on the greenscreen behind it.

Jamie's hands worked the audio-holo board in a blur of quick motions. "Hey everyone, I took the liberty of making the introduction for the podcast using the headline and song that L.J gave me. We can watch it after I mix in her part."

"I'm sure it will be fine," said Professor Erlenmeyer. "Let's view it and then launch this baby!"

"Okay, ready," said Jamie.

The holographic image of the beach and ocean came to life on the holo-pad. The 1977 David Bowie hit 'Heroes' filled the space.

"Why did you pick this for the theme song, Lincoln?" asked Professor Erlenmeyer.

"Because I know Barry will like it."

The holograph showed the sun rising over the ocean and dolphins frolicking, images evoked by the lyrics, as Bowie's warbling baritone accompanied.

Then Jamie's head swirled out of the holographic image of the ocean with his voice-over introduction:

'Welcome fellow hipsters to *The Mender's Paradox*. This is Jamie "J-Rod" Rodriguez coming to you on a cool breeze from Full Sail University's Student Station. And now, here's our hostess with the mostest…Lincoln Jade.'

Windy whispered "Hon, you sound like a game show host!"

Lincoln's image of her at the news desk blossomed on the holo-pad.

'Hi, I'm Lincoln Jade. This holopod is the story of biological phenom, Barry Blue Hawkins. Mr. Hawkins has been silent for thirty years, but now we are bringing to you this exclusive interview. To set the stage for our first episode, we'd like to bring you a segment from the year 2017 of the Larry

King television show that will enlighten us on what makes Mr. Hawkins so special.'

The image brought up Larry King at his desk with another gentleman sitting in the guest chair. The guest looked like Thomas Jefferson with his high forehead and red hair. Larry King began:

My esteemed guest tonight is Dr. Shawn O'Malley, PhD. M.D. and professor of cell biology at Stanford University. Dr. O'Malley is touting his new book, Blue Genes: The Barry Blue Hawkins Biology. *Dr. O'Malley, tell us about your findings. What is it about Barry Blue Hawkins that has scientists so excited?*

Dr. O'Malley: *Well, Larry, a routine DNA test showed that Barry Blue Hawkins has extraordinary DNA mutations that are unprecedented in humans. Let me explain. Human DNA is made of four amino acids: adenine, thymine, guanine, and cytosine. These amino acids pair up forming codons that make the DNA double helix that we are all familiar with. Barry has this normal DNA. However, in his junk region of DNA, we found that the amino acid uracil has replaced thymine and tyrosine has replaced adenine. It's like this new set of DNA was dropped in along with his normal DNA. Genetic mutations are usually very slight and may or may not manifest itself in the phenotype, or body.*

Larry King: *Did your team find anything different about Barry's physical makeup?*

Dr. O'Malley: *Yes. The one amazing difference we did find was that Barry has twice the amount of mitochondria on average in his cells. The mitochondria are, of course, the organelles responsible for energy production within the cell. Basically, it's what makes us go at our most fundamental biological level.*

Larry King: *Wow, twice as many! So, uh… does Barry have any, you know, super powers?*

Dr. O'Malley: *No. You'd think he would be stronger or faster with all that extra mitochondria. I can tell you, he isn't The Flash.*

Larry King chuckles: *An interesting facet of your book is that you personally know Barry.*

Dr. O'Malley: *Yep. We were roommates our first year of college.*

Larry King: *And what can you tell us about Barry as a person?*

Dr. O'Malley: *I can tell you that he is a regular guy; a normal human being. We became very good friends. I contacted him when his DNA news became public. He was very receptive to my request to sample his blood, body fluids, and even do tissue biopsies.*

Larry King: *What do you know about rumors that Mr. Hawkins has the ability to heal people of disease? In particular, a woman severely deformed by arthritis claimed that he healed her.*

Dr. O'Malley: *Ha! You mean the Crab Lady? That was proven to be a hoax. All of these people claiming to have been healed have been discredited. Barry is no miracle worker. In fact, Barry has a debilitating disease and cannot even heal himself!*

Larry King: *So if he doesn't have super powers because of his extra mitochondria, why the big fuss? Sounds as useful as a second appendix.*

Dr. O'Malley: *Barry might not be a miracle worker, but the study of his DNA very likely will help us unlock some extraordinary mysteries. Only time will tell what discoveries it will lead to!*

Larry King: *I understand Mr. Hawkins has children. Has their DNA been tested for... abnormalities?*

Dr. O'Malley: *Oh, yes. We've thought of that, but extensive testing has shown they have DNA no more interesting than yours or mine. It appears to be something unique to Barry.*

Larry King: *Fascinating! Dr. O'Malley, one more thing before we wrap up here. There seems to be all kinds of hysteria surrounding the Blue Genes news. Isn't it a fact that Mr. Hawkins has been shot at?*

Dr. O'Malley: *Yes, unfortunately. There are crackpots out there that believe Barry is an alien. Or that he is a super evolved human that is a threat to mankind. I can't believe I have to say this, but these are absolutely untrue.*

Larry King: *Wow! It sounds like it's tough being Barry Blue Hawkins. This has been a most fascinating interview. We'll have you back to share the discoveries that I'm sure you'll make. Thank you for your time, Dr. O'Malley.*

The image of Lincoln at the new desk returned to the holo-pad. 'Urban Legend or government cover-up? As we dig deeper into facts and eyewitness accounts, you may find yourself a true believer. We welcome feedback and questions. You can message us at the Student Station. Our engineering is done by Jamie Rodriguez and production design by Windy Summers.'

The holo-pad projected an image of the ocean at sunset, while the theme song 'Heroes' faded in:

" - and out," said Jamie.

"Yes!" exclaimed Professor Erlenmeyer. "I have a great feeling about this holopod!"

"Yeah," said Jamie. "Like the moment you catch the perfect wave!"

Clapping and high fives went all around in the fishbowl control room.

Though she was hitting the wall with fatigue, Lincoln felt a charge of excitement go through her. Maybe this holopod series would launch her into the spotlight after all.

It was 9:15 p.m. Professor Erlenmeyer seemed very anxious to wrap things up for the evening. "Jamie, launch the next two episodes this weekend. We want this podcast to gain traction and build a fanbase fast. Lincoln, continue those interviews and news desk commentaries. It's a great format for your content. And I love the intro and outro segments of the ocean and dolphins — it fits the lyrics of the theme song perfectly. Windy, keep track of listener feedback. And guys, keep this podcast going no matter what." Professor Erlenmeyer paused to sniff and wipe a tear from his eye. "And... always know that I'm so proud to be your teacher. Now let's call it a night."

The students shot each other confused looks. It was strange to see the professor get so emotional over a school project. But Lincoln had no energy to dwell on it. A wave of relief swept over her knowing the evening had come to a close, as she was ready to hit the hay. The three friends exited the building to start for home. Professor Erlenmeyer walked around to the side of the Student Station Building where his car was parked. Lincoln and her friends laughed as they walked and made plans for upcoming holopods. Lincoln heard the slam of Professor Erlenmeyer's car door.

Five seconds later...POP POP WHUMP! An ear-piercing sound like a transformer exploding made the three friends stop dead in their tracks. A blinding flash of white light lit up the parking lot followed by the sounds of crackling electricity and sizzling raw meat. Lincoln dashed to the corner of the building to see Professor Erlenmeyer's car burst into flames.

CHAPTER 17

Professor Erlenmeyer's Folly

Flames engulfed the interior of Professor Erlenmeyer's car. The charred figure in the driver's seat crumpled like a burning marshmallow. She started running towards the car but fell to the ground out of breath. "Boss! Boss!" she gasped.

"We can't help him, Lincoln!" said Windy. "He's gone!"

Jamie picked up Lincoln and carried her to a nearby bench. The three friends huddled under the sound of sirens.

A police officer approached them as firemen dealt with the inferno of a car. "Did you three see anything?" he asked.

"No, we were sorta on the other side of the building," Windy answered. "What caused this?"

"Yeah," said Jamie. "What the hell?"

The police officer looked down at the three friends still clumped together on the bench. "This is police business. You need to move along, there's nothing more you can do here," said the officer.

"Was this an accident or some sort of sabotage?" asked Windy.

"There will be a complete investigation."

"What about Professor Erlenmeyer?" asked Lincoln. "Can we see?"

The police officer hemmed and hawed. "There is nothing to see. Technically, your teacher has been cremated in his car. Sorry."

He took down their names and contact information in his padbook as the interior of the car smoldered, even with the flames extinguished. The putrid stench of barbecue and burnt rubber overpowered Lincoln. She vomited, some of it getting on the police officer's shoes.

"I think we're done here," dead-panned the officer and he walked away.

Windy said, "Jamie, Lincoln is wiped. Let's take her to your place, it's the closest. I'll spend the night helping you watch her. Could you please call her dad and have him come in the morning."

"Roger that," said Jamie.

The next morning Lincoln woke up from a bad dream. Except it wasn't a dream. It dawned on her that her teacher and mentor had died horribly last night.

"Star, are you all right?" She opened her eyes to find her dad hunkered next to her on the wall-to-wall bed in Jamie's unit. Jamie and Windy sat Indian style in the doorway. "We're all here," said Rick. "Jamie called me and told me what happened."

"I'm all right, Dad," said Lincoln, her eyes glassy with tears. But she was not one to wallow in grief with unanswered questions. "Guys. What happened last night?" she asked. "People just don't explode!"

Jamie looked up from his laptop. "Near as I can figure, it appears that the car failed to disengage from the charger station. You know that "classic" hybrid he loved to drive? We joked with him that it was a death trap and he should upgrade to something that hadn't been recalled by the manufacturer, but I never thought... ." He paused.

Windy put a hand on his arm. "Do you think the batteries got overloaded and started a fire?"

Jamie shook his head. "Could be. The boss's car had a plug-in charger. It didn't use induction plates like modern cars. That set of charge stations are all connected so there may have been a malfunction that involved a high voltage current from multiple chargers. And once that upholstery catches fire, I imagine that stuff burns pretty hot."

"Dad, did Professor Erlenmeyer call you? I was with him when he received a phone call that really upset him."

Rick's head jerked back as if he had received an electric shock himself. "Well, since you asked, yes he did call me last week."

"Was he in trouble? What did he say?"

Rick glanced at Jamie and Windy. "It would be best if your friends went to breakfast."

Lincoln came back at him without hesitation. "Dad, whatever you have to say to me, you can say to Jamie and Windy. I totally trust them."

Rick wiped his face from top to bottom. "So it's like that."

"Yeah, Dad, it's like that."

"He was our teacher, too," said Windy.

Rick looked around at them and then looked up for a couple of seconds, thinking. "Okay, but know that once you're in it, you're in it."

"Man, I got a feeling that we're already in it," said Jamie.

"What does that mean?" asked Windy.

"It means that if you want to be a part of this investigation, there's no turning back," said Lincoln.

Rick nodded.

"We're in, Mr. Jade, I mean Detective Jade," said Jamie.

Rick looked around the room. "Criminy! Is there not a chair in here? Never mind. Close the door."

Jamie shut the door.

"To answer your question, Star, yes, your teacher was in trouble. A world of trouble."

"But Dad, why couldn't you save him?"

"What I need all of you to know is that I did everything that I could to help him. Knowing Professor Erlenmeyer, he would want us to carry on."

"Then tell us what happened," said Lincoln.

"I'll tell you what you need to know right now. When Professor Erlenmeyer called me he was very distraught. He said that three years ago he entered a contest in one of his nerd-rock magazines. The contest not only tested the contestants on their mineralogy knowledge but also on their ability to procure rare minerals. You've probably seen some exotic rocks displayed in his office."

"Yeah," said Windy. "I bet that he had a few rock formations that belonged in a museum."

"Or were from a museum," said Jamie.

"Right," said Rick. "It turns out that the geek contest wasn't a contest at all, but a ruse to find someone like your teacher. Someone who had connections to procure hard-to-get rock stuff."

Rick shifted, his old bones clearly not comfortable sitting on the mattress. "A couple of weeks after the so-called contest, an agent from the CIA approached him. They told him they had an anti-terrorist initiative to determine if radioactive materials could be collected by someone with his expert skills and network. They said the goal was to test the CIA intelligence system and to develop ways to block the wrong people from getting hold of radioactive materials."

"Holy cow!" said Jamie. "Who would have thought Professor Erlenmeyer was working for the CIA!"

"That's the problem," said Rick. "The people recruiting him were not the CIA! They were very dangerous people who convinced Professor Erlenmeyer that he would be helping to thwart a terrorist attack on U.S. soil. In his mind he was a patriot doing his country a tremendous service. Your teacher's venture was a very foolhardy and dangerous endeavor."

"Oh man, that's bad," groaned Jamie.

"It gets worse. The agent asked him to obtain one gram of radium. It was to be completely top secret, so he couldn't tell anyone, not even me."

"One gram! '' said Jamie. "That doesn't sound like anything to worry about."

"Radium is like the most radioactive substance in the world," said Windy. "One gram of radium can go a long ways."

Jamie looked at Windy, surprised.

"What?" said Windy. "I've been doing research for my project."

"Like... enough to poison a housing community?" asked Lincoln.

"Way more than enough," said Windy.

"Your Professor found a source of radium and arranged for the pickup and the drop," said Rick. "The CIA imposters bankrolled it."

"It seems more than coincidental that radium illegally enters the country, and a couple years later a housing community comes down with radiation sickness," said Windy.

"Right," said Rick. "And I don't believe in coincidences."

"I see that line of thinking runs in the family," said Jamie.

"Geez," said Lincoln. "If someone poisoned that housing community with radium, then they could make it look like it was contamination from an old U.S. Radium Company's waste disposal site."

"Why would someone want to poison innocent people with radiation and then make it look like it was an accident?" asked Jamie.

"I don't know," said Windy, "but I'm going to find out. I smell a Pulitzer at the end of this story. And a very bad ending for whoever took out the Boss." Tracks from Windy's eyeliner streaked her cheeks. She sniffled. Jamie put a lanky arm around her.

"So since Professor Erlenmeyer was naively involved in this radium plot, his death was probably not an accident," said Rick. "He was a loose end. The Chetola Housing Community radiation poisoning from radium was getting to be big news. The upsetting phone call that he received was a death threat to keep his mouth shut."

"I was there for that, Dad. When Professor Erlenmeyer received that phone call his face went completely pale. How did he know that this threat was legit?"

"Because they put his five-year old son on the phone to say 'hi'," said Rick. "They called him from his own house. The boy is okay, but it put the fear of death in him right then and there. That's when he realized he was in deep and he called me."

Lincoln grabbed her dad's arm. "Dad, is this the case that you were working on in Orange, New Jersey?"

"Negative," said Rick. "I've been working on another case and that's where it took me."

"So what do we do now?" asked Windy.

Detective Jade took in a deep breath and let it out through gritted teeth. "First of all, trust no one. Professor Erlenmeyer's folly stays in this room."

Windy, always proactive, said, "Like I said, I have already done research on the radioactive poisoning at Chetola. But the holosphere can only provide so much. You know what the Boss always said," Windy intoned. Lincoln joined her in unison to complete the sentence. "Dig in the mine if you want the gold."

"He also said the holosphere is mostly crap," Jamie added.

Windy nodded. "It's my senior project. I'm taking The Bullet to Orange to see what gold I can dig up."

Rick pointed a stern finger at Windy. "Windy, you need to keep a low profile when you go. The Chetola victims are all in quarantine. Your best bet is to talk to relatives and neighbors."

"Professor Erlenmeyer told me to launch the holopods that we have been working on," said Jaime. "I can at least honor his wishes, so I'm headed back to the Station."

"What about me and you, Dad?" asked Lincoln.

"Road trip to St. Pete," said her dad. "I need to follow up on a lead for the case I've been working on. It would be good for you to get away."

"Dad! What about solving Professor Erlenmeyer's case? Whoever did this has to pay!"

"I'm already working on it," said Rick.

CHAPTER 18

The Case of the Dead Doctors

Lincoln and her dad headed to St. Petersburg, Florida in his gasoline-powered Dodge micro-van. For Lincoln, it was the Roach Coach, filthy brown with half a million miles and a couple hundred bobby pins holding up the roof liner. The faded brown paint of the old van disguised its stock of surveillance equipment.

Lincoln, though grief-stricken over the death of her teacher and mentor, focused on her dad's case. "So about that lead you said you were following up in Orange, what is this case about?" Lincoln asked.

"Would you believe it's the same case I've been working on for the past thirty years," said Rick as he pulled onto the interstate.

"What? Thirty years on the same case?"

Rick slid into the upper right lane of the I-4 multi-level highway and engaged the cruise control. "It's about dead doctors."

Lincoln jerked. "Dead doctors! You know about the dead doctor cases?"

"You know, Star, I've done my best to shield you from what I do. In my line of work, I see the underbelly of society."

"Dad, hello! I've just seen my mentor of seven years fried in his own car. I think I can handle it. I mean, what could possibly be worse?"

No response. Then Rick said, "You're right. You're an adult and an investigative reporter. Here goes."

"When I was recruited by Homeland Security, I started as an information analyst. One of my first assignments was to look for correlations between the untimely deaths of medical practitioners in the U.S. Some doctors met with untimely deaths."

"Why would Homeland get involved in that?"

"Part of Homeland's mission statement evolved into protecting human assets. A wave of doctors being put down didn't bode well for the country. Granted, it was unlikely any correlation would be discovered, which is why they gave it to an entry level analyst, but it raised enough of a red flag for Homeland to look into it."

Lincoln laughed. "So your first big case as a Homeland Security agent was investigating a conspiracy theory?"

"Laugh it up, smart aleck. We have to check out everything, because terrorists are always looking for different ways to mess with us. At first, I couldn't find any correlation between the murders. I looked at gender, age, specialty – all kinds of parameters. I spoke to the families of these murdered doctors. A couple doctors received death threats that demanded they close down their practice. Most of the victims were on the cutting edge of holistic and alternative medicine. These docs usually didn't practice allopathic medicine. Instead, they advocated helping the body to heal itself."

"But that's not really evidence that the murders were connected," said Lincoln.

"Maybe. But my gut felt that they were. I expanded my analysis of the murders to include doctor suicides and doctors that died before age sixty."

"Let me guess," said Lincoln. "You found that a high percentage of the doctor suicides and early deaths were doctors that were front runners of alternative medicine."

Rick smacked the steering wheel. "Yes! Family members of the suicide doctors didn't believe that it was suicide. They told me that these docs were successful and happy. Others died in suspicious accidents."

"Hmmm…so you had a scenario where alternative medicine docs were being whacked. Some were outright murders but others were made to look like accidents or suicide."

"Yeah, but I didn't have enough evidence to make a federal case. There was no smoking bullet."

"Dad, don't you mean 'smoking gun'?"

"Guns don't kill people. Bullets do," said Rick.

Lincoln closed her eyes and decided not to argue with her dad's gun philosophy. "Okay, so you knew that you were onto something. What happened next?"

Rick rubbed his chin. "Most of the cases flew under the media radar. But in June 2017, two murders involving Florida docs got a lot of attention."

"How so?" asked Lincoln.

"The media loves two things," growled Rick. "Sensationalism and gore. The cases of these two doctors had plenty of both."

CHAPTER 19

Sending a Message

Rick sipped on his coffee while driving the Roach Coach. "A lady doctor in Miami was bludgeoned to death with a hammer in her own kitchen, hit seventeen times in the head. They ruled out robbery since nothing was stolen. Hey, Star, reach down in my attaché case and grab the first folder."

Lincoln retrieved the folder. It contained a photo of the doctor. "She was a looker, I'll tell ya," said Rick. "Brace yourself, Star, for the murder scene pics." The pictures of her dead body in the kitchen showed her head smashed open like a pumpkin. Rick shook his head at the memory. "Blood splattered the floor, cabinets, and ceiling."

"The district attorney pinned the murder on the husband, even though at the time of the murder he was thirty-seven thousand feet in the air on a 747. The prosecutor said the husband hired someone to kill his wife while he was out of town. A recent four-million-dollar life insurance policy on his wife provided a motive. The husband swore he had not taken out this extra insurance and had never seen the insurance contract. And why would he? They were already loaded, so they didn't need the money. And his wife had a lucrative practice."

"You would think that if the husband hired someone to murder his wife that they would make it look like a robbery," said Lincoln. "This looks more like a hate crime."

"Agreed," said Rick. "It's like whoever killed her, really had it in for her. My theory is, whoever killed her meant to send a message."

"Send a message? To whom?" asked Lincoln.

"I don't know for sure. But get this—this lady doctor practiced alternative medicine. Her gorgeous looks and charismatic personality helped her build a huge following on her holosphere channel. She crusaded for a paradigm shift in how doctors treat patients. She happened to be a big fan of another alternative medicine guru, one Dr. Langley, and taught his methods on her channel. Her last video promoting research for self-healing mechanisms went viral. She was about to be picked up by one of the TV networks for her own show."

Lincoln's eyebrows pumped. "Maybe the message was meant for other alternative medicine practitioners. Like, 'This could happen to you too, if you buck the medical status quo.'"

Rick nodded. "The murder and trial were well publicized, so I bet other doctors took note. The media ate it up and pooped it out."

"Since everyone assumed the husband was the perp, there was no real investigative reporting. The media found him guilty. The case went to trial very quickly and the husband was convicted and sentenced to life in prison. They had the murder weapon, which was the hammer, and the motive, which was the insurance policy. It was a slam dunk for the prosecuting attorney."

"Are you saying that the husband was framed?" asked Lincoln.

"Yes!" Rick pounded the steering wheel. "The murder weapon had no fingerprints on it. The insurance policy on his wife could have been forged. Besides, taking out a four million-dollar insurance policy on her would lead the police straight back to him. It's too moronic. And he didn't need the money. Plus, the prosecuting attorney never produced his theoretical hit-man, so there was no witness to tie the husband to the hit."

"Could the trial have been rigged, like people bribed or coerced?" asked Lincoln.

"Affirmative," said Rick.

"Hmmmm. If the husband didn't do it, then who did?"

"Someone who has done this before. Someone who had no qualms about killing a person like he was slaughtering a pig."

"What about the other dead doctor case you mentioned?" asked Lincoln.

"Okay, but this next one's not exactly a bedtime story."

CHAPTER 20

Murder In Disguise

Uncharacteristically light traffic allowed the Roach Coach to make good time to St. Petersburg. A small black screen on the dashboard lit up with green circles. "What's the tiny TV for, Dad?"

"That's a drone detector. It works like radar and tells me if I'm being tailed."

"Uh, aren't you being kind of paranoid?" asked Lincoln.

"In my line of work, it pays to be paranoid. Star, pull out the green folder with 'Dr. Langley' on the tab."

Lincoln flipped open the folder. It contained 8X10 photos of a body in a river. Another photo depicted a closeup of the body that was too big for its clothes, probably because of bloating. The ugly gunshot wound through the chest signaled this guy didn't die of natural causes.

"That's Dr. Bill Langley, or rather *was* Dr. Bill Langley. A fisherman discovered his body in the Broad Creek River at Chimney Rock, North Carolina in June 2017 – three days after the murder of the doctor in Miami."

"So you think her murder is linked with Dr. Langley's?" asked Lincoln.

"I don't believe in coincidence," said Rick. "I arrived at Chimney Rock the day after they found Dr. Langley's body. The sheriff told me that they classified it a suicide."

Lincoln shuffled through the photos. "I take it that you disagreed with that assessment."

"You know it! The local authorities said he was shot at close range with his own gun, which they found in the river near the body. Langley had been staying at a motel along the river bank about three miles upstream. The river has too many rocks and shallow areas for his body to have floated downstream all this way. So that means he walked here. Now why would he have gone through all that trouble to hike three miles downstream in the middle of the night to shoot himself?"

"Maybe something was driving him downstream," said Lincoln. "Maybe somebody was chasing him."

"That's what I think happened. Check out the autopsy pictures."

Lincoln looked at the photos of the pale corpse. Closeups captured the gunshot wound from many angles including the exit wound from the back.

"I saw the body myself," said Rick. "The pathologist showed me how the exit wound in the back was an inch lower than the bullet wound to the chest, suggesting that the gun was shot at a downward angle. The doc also told me the gun was not held up against the chest as you would expect for a self-inflicted gunshot, but fired from a few feet away."

Lincoln's eyebrows twisted. "Hmmm, interesting. That paints a scenario of Langley shooting himself by holding the gun out in front of him and up over his head. That doesn't make much sense."

"Or," Rick interjected, "someone shot him!"

"Were there any physical signs of somebody chasing him?" asked Lincoln.

"Look at the photos of Langley's motel room."

Yellow police tape blocked the motel room door. A tin can on the floor inside the front door seemed out of place. Everything else looked normal. The bed was turned down ready for a guest. Bath towels lay folded and stacked in the bathroom. "I don't see anything out of the ordinary here."

"Exactly, the motel room looks too normal. Check out the pic of his bedroom door."

Lincoln inspected the photo of the door. "The door looks fine."

"It's better than fine," said Rick. "It's brand new! The rest of the place is pretty beat up. There is nothing else new in that room."

"So what are you saying, Dad?"

"I'm saying that somebody kicked in that bedroom door. And then somebody replaced that door to make it look like nothing happened in the motel room."

"Anything else?"

"Oh yeah. Check out my pics of Langley's car."

The first car picture showed a black Lexus parked out front of the motel. The car looked fine. Then she looked at the close-up pictures of the four tires. "I don't see anything wrong. Tires look fine."

"Except that three of the tires are nearly bald and the front left is brand new. I think someone slashed his tire to prevent his getaway," said her dad. "See how Langley's car is parked in front of his motel room? I seriously doubt he parked it there."

"Oh yeah? Why's that?" asked Lincoln.

"Because Langley paid with cash and didn't use his real name when he registered with the front desk. Traveling incognito, he'd have parked his car out of sight."

Lincoln sifted through the Langley photos again. "That would mean that somebody slashed Langley's tire, and then put on the spare and parked his car out front."

"That's what I'm thinking," said Rick.

"And no one heard or saw anything." Lincoln looked at Rick with eyebrows raised.

Rick shrugged. "Yeah, seems unlikely, unless the killer bribed or threatened potential witnesses. That's a trend I've found in these cases."

"Did Langley leave a note?" asked Lincoln.

"Nope. No note. Oh yeah, one more thing…When the FDA raided his office they found a stash of narcotics."

"Drugs?" asked Lincoln. "He was selling illegal drugs?"

"Maybe. More likely planted to discredit him as a legitimate doctor. And being caught with illegal drugs makes the suicide story easier to swallow."

Lincoln closed her eyes as she worked to stitch all this information together. "Let me get this straight. The authorities' official take on what happened is that Langley saw his office was being raided and he knew he was busted for drug possession. He drives up to Chimney Rock and checks into a motel under an alias to hide out. Then he decides in the middle of the night to hike three miles downstream and shoot himself by holding his handgun out in the most awkward and unlikely position possible?"

It began to rain. Rick turned on the wipers. "That's the official version. There wasn't any solid evidence to support anything else."

Lincoln ran her fingers through her mop of hair. "But your version is that Langley holed up in a motel in Chimney Rock but someone found him, forcing him to leave his motel room in the middle of the night. He ran to his car, saw it was out of commission, and fled on foot. He made it three miles down the river before his pursuer shot him with his own gun. Did I miss anything?"

Rick nodded. "That's pretty good, Star. Don't forget the new door and new tire. Everything had to look normal for the suicide conclusion to stand. I estimate the killer had enough time to hike back and put on the spare tire and replace the door before the body was found and the cops arrived."

Lincoln said, "One guy did all this?"

Rick grimaced. "Yep. Remember, I've been following this guy for thirty years and I know two things for sure: he works alone, and he's very good at what he does."

"The murder is a more plausible theory than suicide," said Lincoln. "Did the local authorities entertain your idea?"

"Nope. Not at all. It could have been sloppy police work on their part, but my gut tells me that somebody paid off the cops. It shouldn't have been an open-and-shut case."

"A murder disguised as a suicide," said Lincoln softly. "Why would the assailant go through the trouble and risk to make Langley's murder look like a suicide?"

"A murder would have brought unwanted attention. Someone wanted to disgrace him and discredit his work."

Lincoln's eyebrows zigged and zagged. "I would be curious as to what Langley's patients had to say about him."

"I was curious about that, too," said Rick. "I went to the clinic and I was able to track down several of his patients. They all had chronic conditions like asthma and M.E. These patients could not find any treatment to help them until they found Dr. Langley."

"Were they getting better?" asked Lincoln.

"They told me that they were."

"Awesome! What was Langley doing to help them?" asked Lincoln.

"The interesting common thread is that he did not prescribe prescription medicine or even over-the-counter meds. Instead,

Langley's patients say he gave them a home-made remedy that he prepared. Essentially, he did his own clinical trials without FDA knowledge."

"That's illegal," said Lincoln. "Why would he be doing patient trials in secret?"

"Probably because he didn't want to become a target for whoever was killing doctors like him."

"What happened to Langley's remedies?" asked Lincoln.

"Gone. I didn't find anything in his clinic that looked like homemade medicine."

Lincoln threw her hands up. "What happened to Dr. Langley's research?"

Rick shook his head. "His computer had been wiped clean. He took his treatment formula to the grave."

For a moment, Lincoln did not speak. She drummed her fingers on the dashboard. "You've told me that thirty years ago you had this string of dead doctor cases. This last one was especially suspicious. That can't be the end of it. What became of these cases?"

No response.

"Dad?"

Rick slid the Roach Coach onto an exit lane. "I'll tell you what happened, but I'm going to have to pull over."

CHAPTER 21

Chasing a Demon

Rick pulled the Roach Coach into the back parking lot of a McDonald's. A sign said 'Way over a trillion served'. He parked the vehicle under an oak tree that overhung the back fence. The light rain had progressed to a thunderstorm. He turned off the car but left the AC on.

"What gives, Dad?" asked Lincoln. "I have a feeling there is something you're not telling me."

Rick looked straight out the windshield, his hands still gripping the steering wheel. Lincoln looked at her dad's profile. Other than the hard lines around his eyes, you'd never guess he was sixty-one. Finally, Rick said "I do have something to tell you. I was waiting for the right time, but there is no such thing."

Light and shadow swept around them as the branches above swayed back and forth. Rain enveloped the Roach Coach, making their conversation seem even more private.

Rick continued, "I pursued the last two cases that I just told you about. Remember the husband who was convicted of murdering his wife in South Florida? And how I thought that was a load of crapola? Well I proved that the incriminating four-million-dollar life insurance policy on his wife was a forgery. The insurance agent who supposedly signed the policy didn't exist. Ha! Five years after being convicted the husband was exonerated of murdering his wife and set free. Of course, this begged the question 'Who wanted her dead and why?' The media had a field day with it. It was even eventually made into a Lifetime movie."

"As for the so-called suicide of Dr. Langley at Chimney Rock, I succeeded in reopening the case in 2022. This was also around the time that the south Florida murder conviction was overturned."

"2022!" said Lincoln. "That's the year I was born." She paused. "And the year Mom died."

Rick turned and gazed at Lincoln. "Yes, it was the best year and worst year of my life. You and your mom were so beautiful. I never wanted it to end."

"I know, Dad," said Lincoln.

"I received death threats demanding that I stop pursuing these cases. Of course, I don't negotiate with criminals. I was so obsessed, so stupid. I… I never realized that they might go after my family."

"Dad?" said Lincoln, her voice wavering up a pitch.

Rick reached over and put his arm around Lincoln. He turned on her oxy-boost. "Star, your mom's death was not an accident."

"What do you mean it wasn't an accident?" asked Lincoln. She closed her eyes, bracing for the answer to her question.

"Someone murdered your mom. It was made to look like a traffic accident," said Rick in a steady voice.

"But why?" asked Lincoln. "She never hurt anybody."

"It was to send a message to me," said Rick. "They wanted to punish me for exposing the deaths as murders. It was also their way of saying 'drop the whole thing'."

"But you didn't drop the whole thing."

Rick set his teeth. "I was more determined than ever to catch the killer."

Lincoln's breathing became fast and shallow. Rick let her absorb what she had just heard. "Dad, not a day goes by that I don't think about her and wish I had grown up with her in my life. I never even knew her," she whispered, "but I *miss* her, every day."

Rick hugged her with both arms. "After you were born, you spent your first few months at the hospital because of your cystic fibrosis. You were a miracle to us. Mom was with you the whole way. She loved you so much – she practically lived at the hospital. You two formed an unbreakable bond. That's why she's with you every day."

Lincoln rested her head on Rick's shoulder. "It's so…so unfair. She didn't have to die. Why do bad things happen to good people?"

Rick hugged her a little tighter. "This ain't heaven, Star."

Lincoln sobbed, hanging on to her dad.

"Breathe, Star, breathe," said Rick. "I know it hurts."

Lincoln strived to take deeper breaths. Rain pelted the tinny roof of the van. She focused on her breathing. All these years her dad had been carrying by himself the terrible burden of her Mom's murder. Lincoln lifted her head off her dad's shoulder. Tears streamed down her face like the rain on the windshield. "Dad, why didn't you tell me that Mom was murdered?"

"It was hard enough explaining to a little girl that her mom was in heaven," Rick answered. "As you got older, I knew that stress really affected your CF illness. I didn't want to put it on you. I'm sorry, Star."

Rick gently pushed her back by the shoulders, just enough to look her in the eyes. "Star, I don't think this is the time to get into details about your mom's death."

Lincoln wiped her face. "This is the perfect time to talk about Mom. So how do you know it wasn't an accident?"

"All right, then," said Rick. "Your mom had spent the day with you at the hospital. She was stopped at a traffic light coming out of the parking garage. While she was waiting, a Mack flat-bed truck carrying a forklift swerved over a lane and skidded to stop next to your mom's car. The forklift fell off the flatbed onto her car. The driver, dressed head to toe in black and wearing a hood, jumped out of the truck and fled the scene. We had been talking on the phone when the line went dead. Uh, should I keep going?"

"Dad, I can handle it," said Lincoln.

Rick leaned his head back in his car seat. "When I arrived at the scene the police were already there. I drove my car up the side of the road to get around the ensuing traffic jam. I ran up to the truck to see a forklift on its side on the road. A car was under it, smashed so flat that I could not tell the make and model. I flashed my Homeland badge and the police told me what happened. The bad feeling turned into a titanic sinking feeling when I saw that the color of the car was orange, the color of Mom's car. There was no way to tell who was in the crushed car under the forklift. But I knew it was her."

Rick stopped for a moment and stared up at the cluster of straight pins holding the Roach Coach headliner in place. Lincoln held his hand.

"When it hit me that your Mom was in that mass of mangled metal, I fell to my knees. I crawled over the wreckage and pushed on the forklift like a crazy man. An officer pulled me off the wreck and put me in his car. He gave me ten minutes in the back seat, and I did my best to beat the car to death and beat myself to death with the car. I never did get the chance to thank him or to apologize for what I did to his cruiser."

"I watched the police work the scene. A crane heaved the forklift off the wreckage of her orange Prius. The flatbed truck was still next to it. The hydraulic clamps on the flatbed meant to secure the forklift were unused, still down in their slots."

"So what are you saying, Dad," said Lincoln.

"It was rigged," said Rick. "It would be quite a coincidence for me to be getting death threats and then for an unsecured forklift to fall directly onto Mom's car as she was leaving the hospital. You know how I feel about coincidences."

"Yeah, I know," said Lincoln. "You don't believe in them. Yet, Mom's death was ruled a traffic accident."

Rick wiped his face from forehead to chin. "Officially it was ruled manslaughter due to an improperly secured forklift."

"Did they ever find the driver?" asked Lincoln.

"Negative," said Rick. "It was like he disappeared from the face of the earth. The police assumed that it was the company truck driver who fled the scene, but they never could track him down for questioning. I figure that Mom's murderer hijacked the truck, killed the original driver, then made sure the driver's body would never be found."

Lincoln pressed on. "What about videos? Did anyone get the fleeing driver on their cell phone?"

"Oh yeah! He ran past a woman who was videoing the fork-lift. Also, the traffic light camera shot a frame of the driver as he leapt out of the truck."

"I take it you couldn't ID the perp or else you would have locked him up by now," said Lincoln.

"Affirmative," said Rick. "Using comparative digital analysis on the traffic camera pic, we were able to determine that he was five foot eleven inches tall, about 180 pounds, and in his mid-twenties. The woman taking the video did zoom in on the driver, but a hood and ball cap covered most of his face. The only feature visible was what looked like a scar by the left eye."

"Well, that narrows it down to about a billion people," said Lincoln.

"Yeah. The perp got away. I found it very suspicious that the local authorities ruled this an accident, not a murder."

"Dad, from what you have been telling me it sounds like somebody is manipulating these cases to be swept under the judicial carpet. It would have to be someone very powerful to pull that off."

"Yeah," said Rick. "Someone who had a lot to lose if they were found out."

"That makes your investigation all the more dangerous," said Lincoln.

"I was so furious that I didn't care about the danger anymore. Rage fueled my mission to catch this guy. At first, I wanted to kill him with my bare hands." Rick smacked his fist into his hand. Thunder claps punctuated his words.

Lincoln knew that her dad's threat was not just bravado. Still powerfully built, he looked like he could carry out his vengeance as promised. Lincoln didn't speak, letting her dad release feelings he had carried for decades.

Rick continued, his eyes locked into a squint. "Your mom was the love of my life. I would have traded my life for hers, but it doesn't work that way. I grieved not only for myself but for you not having your mom. I put the blame squarely on myself. If I hadn't pursued those dead doctor cases, then your mom would still be alive. The one thing that kept me going was that I had you to take care of. The self-loathing oppressed me for years."

Lincoln clasped his hands in hers. "Dad, look at me. It's not your fault. I'm so sorry you've had to carry this burden for so long."

Rick looked at Lincoln and nodded. "Thanks, Star. I've worked through it and I don't blame myself anymore for Mom's death. But I never stopped working her case. I vowed to bring the perp to justice, and I've been hunting him ever since."

"Man, I've heard of people facing their demons, but you are literally chasing yours," said Lincoln.

"This perp is a demon!" said Rick. "He's gotten away with so many hideous crimes. The guy is like a ghost. He never leaves any fingerprints or hairs at the crime scenes. I'm sure he lives off the grid."

"Dad, I'm glad you've told me all of this. It sure explains a lot. All the times you were away....Phone calls in the middle of the night....You were so driven. I thought you were just dedicated to your job, but it's more than that. It's personal. You are on a mission."

"Yeah, that about sums it up. I can't let it go. I have to find this guy."

"So how are we going to do that?" asked Lincoln.

"We?" said Rick. "Are you sure about that?"

"Absolutely," said Lincoln. "You've worked this case alone too long. So what's the plan?"

"I changed my tactics a long time ago," said Rick. "My boss took me off the dead doctor cases for our protection, but I never stopped working on them. I'm very careful where I place my trust. I keep a low profile. I learned to bend and even break the rules."

"I had no idea, Dad. You told me that you were a desk jockey."

"Not really, Star. In the field is where you find the dirt!" said Rick.

Rick shifted in his captain's chair towards Lincoln. "After the dust settled on your mom's case, I visited the nurse that used to work in Dr. Langley's clinic a second time. I first spoke with her while investigating Langley's death in 2017, but she was a total clam. Five years later she admitted that she had been too afraid to come forward with any info regarding Dr. Langley's death. She told me that a few days before Langley was killed at Chimney Rock, a young man in his early twenties came to the clinic without an appointment. He pushed past the nurse and barged into Langley's office. She couldn't hear any of the conversation but noted that Langley was very shaken afterwards. I asked for a description of the man and the nurse described him as being just shy of six feet and having a medium build. He wore a black suit, a hat, and thick glasses. Then she told me one more thing. The young intruder had alopecia."

"Alo-what?" said Lincoln.

"Alopecia," said Rick. "It means he has no hair. The nurse said when he pushed past her she could see through the side of his glasses that he had no eyelashes or eyebrows. Oh, and that he had skin disfigurement over his left eye."

Lincoln pumped her fist. "So do we have a way to track this guy!"

"Yeah," said Rick. "The first thing I did was to reexamine the traffic light picture of the perp at Mom's crime scene. Using micro-enhancing digital technology the shot revealed that this guy had no hair anywhere on his face. It could not see his left eye because of the angle."

"Same build and height. No hair. A few years older. This could have been the same guy that killed Langley," said Lincoln.

"Agreed!" said Rick. "And he could have been the same guy that killed the south Florida doctor, because she was a big fan and promotor of Langley. And who knows how many other doctor deaths he's responsible for. I've catalogued hundreds of suspicious deaths in their field."

"This guy is the key to the case of the dead doctors!" said Lincoln.

"Affirmative! My strategy was to look for a male Caucasian with alopecia and disfigurement on his head. Since he murdered

Langley in 2017 and was in his early twenties according to the nurse, I searched for someone born in the years around 1995. Homeland has access to all medical records, including births, so I methodically looked for a person that fit these parameters."

"Then you had to investigate each person to determine if they could be the killer," said Lincoln.

"Right," said Rick. "I compiled this huge list of possible suspects. It took years to investigate each one. Some of them were dead. Some did not fit the physical description... too short, too tall, too fat...I was sure that I would find our killer by the process of elimination."

"But obviously that didn't work out," said Lincoln.

Rick clenched his fists. "I even worked with Interpol to search other countries for a person matching the description that immigrated to the U.S. I kept at it for years and years. Nothing panned out."

"I don't get it, '' said Lincoln. "There must have been something missing in the killer's profile."

"Then it struck me. WHAM — he could have been born in another country and adopted by someone in this country."

"Why didn't Interpol find him?" asked Lincoln.

"Because apparently his records had been lost very early in his life. But I found him on the U.S. adoption registry. It took a court order to get access to that info. Turns out he was adopted in 1998 and born in 1995 in Bavaria, making him twenty-two years old at the time of the Langley Murder."

Lincoln did the math. "Then he was twenty-seven at the time of Mom's death. Now he is... fifty-two years old. Do you know if he's still alive and in this country?"

Rick pivoted in his seat to face Lincoln. "He's still out there. I got a tip from one of my snitches that he was seen in New Jersey at the Chetola housing community disaster."

"So that's why you've been working in New Jersey." said Lincoln.

"I investigate wherever this guy surfaces and whenever there is a suspicious dead doctor situation," said Rick.

"So how does St. Pete tie into all this?" asked Lincoln.

Rick looked straight through the windshield. "I thought we could have a chat with his parents."

CHAPTER 22

Leatherhead

"His *parents?*" Lincoln's eyes bugged out.

"Yep. Mr. and Mrs. Harris T. Kuby adopted the boy and named him Robert. They were horse farmers in Kentucky and then retired in St. Pete."

"Dad, if you know who he is, then why can't you find him?"

"Robert Kuby has no known address, driver's license, bank account, or place of employment. We don't have a good eye-witness because people that have seen him up close usually are his victims. We don't even have a decent photograph of him."

Lincoln rubbed her eyes. "Do we know anything about this Robert Kuby?"

Rick cranked the Roach Coach engine and put it in gear. "We will shortly."

Lincoln and Rick spent the night in a St. Petersburg motel and slept in. After a short drive and a brief, stiff introduction, they found themselves with the Kuby's in their condo. The Mr. and Mrs. occupied matching large lazy-boy recliners while Lincoln and Rick sat on the black leather couch. The large windows revealed a cloudy day on the intercoastal waterway.

"The truth is, we have not seen hide nor hair of the boy in over thirty years," said Mr. Kuby.

"Do you really think you can find our Bobby?" asked Mrs. Kuby.

"That's been my goal for a long time," said Rick. He leaned forward. "As I had explained on the phone, I formerly worked for Homeland and I'm now a private eye. My daughter, Lincoln, is along for the experience. She's getting a degree in investigative journalism."

Lincoln placed her holo-recorder on the coffee table. "Mind if I record the interview for my school project?" asked Lincoln.

The Kubys looked at each other and nodded.

Rick continued, "I am interviewing you because I am tracking a person who is suspected of multiple homicides. Now I'm not saying that your son, Robert is -"

"- Bobby. His name is Bobby," said Mrs. Kuby.

"But I called him Bobcat on the account that we might as well have adopted a wild cat!" said Mr. Kuby.

Rick looked at Mr. Kuby and raised an eyebrow.

Mr. Kuby continued. "The boy must have been sedated when we saw him at the orphanage, because once we got him home he tore up the dang house."

Mrs. Kuby nodded. "Bobby didn't want to be cuddled or held. He didn't want anyone to touch him. I tried so hard to be a good mother to him. We just couldn't bond."

Lincoln could hear the heartache in her voice.

Rick said gently, "Could you tell me about where you found Bobby?"

"We couldn't have children of our own," said Mr. Kuby. "The adoption agency pointed us to a Bavarian orphanage that we could afford. When we got there, it was plain to see that the staff was completely overwhelmed with taking care of babies."

Mrs. Kuby cut in. "We had built up so much hope and anticipation for adopting a boy from Bavaria, home of world famous castles. We fancied that our adopted boy would be our little Bavarian Prince."

That's when Lincoln took a closer look at the oversized, hardcover book on their coffee table: Fairy Tale Castles of the

World. The one on the cover looked awfully familiar, but she couldn't quite place it.

"The actual orphanage was in a far west alpine village. Believe me, the only part of that place that looked like a castle would have been a dungeon," said Mr. Kuby.

"The living conditions were pretty bleak," said Mrs. Kuby. "The orphanage was run by the Missionaries of Charity, founded by St. Mother Teresa. The Sisters worked around the clock feeding babies and changing diapers. Our hearts went out to these orphans. We asked them to give us the child that was most in need. They brought us to a little boy sleeping alone in a room. He was completely hairless… no eyebrows or even eyelashes."

"The baby's head was burned in a fire at the orphanage," said Mrs. Kuby with a wipe of her eye. "It left extensive scarring on his little head."

"Let me put it this way," said Mr. Kuby. "I took one look at that poor boy and knew he wouldn't have to dress up for Halloween."

Lincoln looked over at her dad. His expression had not changed upon hearing about the boy's physical appearance. She decided she wouldn't want to ever play in a poker game against her dad.

"We left and then came back after the boy was awake," said Mrs. Kuby. "He was very shy and wouldn't let us get near him. We figured that was normal considering we were two strangers to him. The Sisters said that he had been passed over for adoption many times, because of his unusual appearance. We knew right then and there that this was our chance to do something really good. We decided to adopt him."

"Then we found out that we had the boy with no name," said Mr. Kuby. "At least there was no legal name. The same fire that burned the baby boy also destroyed the storage area and his legal papers were lost. Apparently, before the fire, nobody spent any time with him to even get to know his real name. But eventually they got things sorted out and we brought him home. He was two-and-a-half to three years old at that time."

"Could you tell us about Bobby's boyhood once he arrived in the U.S.?" asked Rick.

Mr. Kuby stretched his arms and then put his hands behind his head. "We bred horses in Kentucky. The Pine Hill State Forest was our backyard. 'Bobcat' loved the outdoors. He was always trying to escape the house to the woods. Eventually he settled down when he figured out that we were providing him three squares and a cot."

"Bobby was a good boy," said Mrs. Kuby. "He did his chores every day. He learned English very fast, though he never had much to say. Strange thing was, Bobby called us Mr. and Mrs. 'K', not Mom and Dad. And that was rare – he barely acknowledged us. We tried including him in all family activities, but he clearly wanted to be left to himself."

Lincoln couldn't hold back. "I hope I don't come across as prying…but you had this boy, your son, who doesn't seem to connect with anyone. Did his doctor have any ideas on this behavior?"

Mrs. Kuby paused. Lincoln could tell this was getting hard for her. "We took Bobby to all kinds of doctors. He was eventually diagnosed with reactive attachment disorder. RAD for short. It was explained to us that babies that didn't have maternal bonding or human physical contact within their first two years of life often had this disorder to some degree. We told the docs that Bobby was from an orphanage that was extremely overcrowded and understaffed. They said it wasn't uncommon for these children to have RAD." Mrs. Kuby ran out of words at this point.

"What was the prognosis for him?" asked Rick.

Mr. Kuby fielded this one. "At the time they told us that most children come along quite well and are able to adapt to society. However, some do not. 'Early intervention,' Lord, how we heard those words tossed around! The Bobcat was at least four years old before we got him diagnosed and into family therapy."

Rick nodded thoughtfully. "Did the therapy help?"

"Heck no!" came the reply from Mr. Kuby. "We tried therapy treatments for years and it didn't help a dang bit. The boy made a Tibetan Monk look like a social butterfly!"

Rick pressed on. "Sorry about this question, but I need to ask how your son was with animals on your farm. Did he ever hurt any animals?"

"Heavens no!" said Mrs. Kuby. "Bobby did fine with the farm animals. In fact, he was especially good with the horses. Taking care of the horses gave him purpose. It was the best therapy he ever had."

"Was there an activity or hobby that your son took to?" asked Lincoln.

Mr. Kuby's face brightened. "Bobcat took to riding them horses. He'd ride off into the sunset if I let him. I taught him how to shoot, hunt, and field dress a deer. After his chores were done, he'd spend the rest of the day in the woods of Pine Mountain."

Mr. Kuby put his feet back on the floor and let his elbows rest on his legs. "I also taught him how to survive in the wild. Man oh man, he was a quick study! By the time he was twelve he was camping overnight in the woods by himself. Sometimes a week or two at a time. He would bow-hunt wild boar. One time he took one of those mean, ugly beasts down with just a spear. A spear, I kid you not! Yeah, no doubt, he was a natural outdoorsman."

"It seems like camping was classic father-son bonding time," said Rick. "Did this help form a relationship between you and your son?"

Mr. Kuby let out a long sigh and stood. He walked over to the big picture window and looked out at the grayness. With his back to Rick and Lincoln, he said, "No. At first it was very gratifying to have him hanging on every word I said and picking it up so fast. But when he was done with me that was it. It was like an alien had come to learn our ways."

Rick cleared his throat. "I'm sorry if things are stirring up personal memories. Are you all right to continue?"

"I don't mind tellin' it," said Mr. Kuby. "No one else wants to hear it, that's for sure."

"We just want to know what happened to Bobby," said Mrs. Kuby.

"Can you tell me about how Bobby did in school?" asked Rick.

This time Mrs. Kuby got bubbly. "Oh yes. Bobby did very well in school. He was way ahead of the other students, so they did an IQ test. His scores were so high that the local school couldn't meet his potential. They said he'd be better off at the School of Science and Math in Durham, NC. We didn't want to send him away. I mean, what's the point of going all the way to Europe to find a child and then sending 'em away? We decided to send Bobby to the local school and not skip any grades, so that he could be with kids his own age. We were hoping he would develop some social skills," said Mrs. Kuby.

"How did he get along with his classmates?" asked Rick.

"Oh, just fine," said Mrs. Kuby. "He was picked on because of his appearance, but he never said anything about it."

"Fine and dandy my big, hairy butt!" said Mr. Kuby. "Shall we tell them about the mattress incident when he was thirteen, Sugar?"

"Mattress incident?" asked Lincoln.

Mrs. Kuby sunk back into the couch and covered her eyes.

Mr. Kuby returned to the couch. "As you can imagine, the Bobcat was bullied by his classmates. A lot. One day when he was thirteen years old, a bunch of boys jumped him out on the school track. There was a dumpster there and someone had deposited a box spring and mattress. Up to now it had been name calling and light scuffles. But what they did next was deplorable."

Mrs. Kuby took Mr. Kuby's hand. "It's okay, Poppa."

Mr. Kuby continued. "The boys stripped him naked, I guess to see if he was hairless everywhere. They wrote 'Leatherhead' across his chest in permanent marker. Then they threw him down on the box spring and put the mattress on top of him. They commenced to piling on the mattress and jumping on it until they busted Bobcat's collar bone. Then they scattered like cockroaches. He had to walk naked with the word 'Leatherhead' on his chest to the school office with a broken collar bone during school recess. When I found out, I was madder than a nest of hornets in a plough field!"

"It makes me mad just hearing about it!" said Lincoln. "What did the school do about it?"

"They suspended the ringleader for two weeks. There was an investigation and apparently this bully had been harassing Bobcat for a long time."

"Was your son able to go back to school?" asked Lincoln.

"Oh yeah, he returned to school like nothing ever happened," said Mr. Kuby. "He never said a word about the whole incident."

"And that was the end of it?" said Rick.

"Not buy a longshot, pardner," said Mr. Kuby. "This is something you need to hear."

Lincoln and Rick looked at each other and then back at Mr. Kuby.

"A few months after the Bobcat's humiliation at the school, the ringleader bully disappeared. The last time that kid was seen alive was walking home from school."

"Did they ever find this missing kid?" asked Rick.

"Oh yeah, they found him all right," said Mr. Kuby. "In about a thousand pieces."

Mrs. Kuby garbled like a chicken and flew out of the room.

"Sorry, Sugar!" hollered Mr. Kuby after her. He turned back to Rick and Lincoln. "She'll be all right."

"Um, what do you mean the bully was found in a thousand pieces?" asked Rick.

"Mr. Ringleader went through a wood-chipper," said Mr. Kuby. "You know, one of those log grinding machines."

"Witnesses?" asked Rick.

"None," answered Mr. Kuby. "There were two trimmers working high in the trees and a groundsman fetching water for their cooler. Obviously something horrible had happened when the groundsman came around to the back end of the truck and saw the chipper chute spattered with blood. The police found pieces of the kid's shredded clothes in the back of the truck. The identification of human flesh in the truck was confirmed by DNA testing."

Lincoln made a face like she just smelled a wet fart. She noticed that her dad's tone had not changed. He had probably heard all kinds of terrible things in his line of work.

"How did your son react to all this?" asked Rick.

"Bobcat was completely indifferent. It was just another day to him. The police questioned all of us. They knew about the mattress incident and the bullying of Bobcat by the victim at school. And somebody pushed that kid into the chipper chute, he didn't fall in. There were no witnesses and no video capturing the incident. Bobcat was their prime suspect. But he had nothing to say to them – the police did not faze him."

Mrs. Kuby returned to the room and sat in her lazyboy. Mr. Kuby patted her hand saying, "It's okay, Sugar."

"I have to ask," said Rick. "Did a psychiatrist see your boy after all this trauma?"

"Oh yes," said Mrs. Kuby. "Many doctors talked to him, tested him. Taking into account his case history from the orphanage, they told us that Bobby was technically in the sociopathic category. But they explained it wasn't like he didn't know right from wrong. It was more like his mind was so dissociated from humanity that killing a person was like killing a wild boar. It's not his fault that he's that way, it's really not."

Lincoln studied the Kubys's faces as an uneasy silence fell upon the room. Mr. Kuby patted his wife's hand some more.

"What was the upshot of this tragedy?" said Rick.

"Bobcat had to leave," said Mr. Kuby. "The newspapers and TV were all over it. The gossip spread through the town like wildfire. The bully's parents brought a lawsuit against us, which they lost. We received death threats and there were protests in front of our house. We sent him to a military boarding school for his own protection, hoping it would help him join the human race."

"And after boarding school?" asked Rick.

"After boarding school Bobcat went to West Point," said Mr. Kuby.

"West Point? Geez!" said Lincoln.

"Yep," said Mr. Kuby. "But he only stayed there for two years."

Mrs. Kuby cupped her hand to the side of her mouth as if she were telling a secret. "The CIA recruited Bobby right out of West Point." She put her hand down, nodding knowingly. "Bobcat spent some time at Quantico and then Langley. After two years with the CIA we got a call from them. The CIA people wanted to know if we knew where he was or if we had heard from him. We had no idea what they were talking about. Apparently, he left the CIA. Even with their resources, they could not locate him. That's the God's-honest truth."

"I believe you," said Rick. "He's still living off the grid after all these years. Do you have any pictures of him?"

"We figured you'd want pictures," said Mrs. Kuby. "We don't have many of him as a grownup – he was so skittish about having his picture taken."

"He behaved like the camera would steal his soul," said Mr. Kuby. "You know, like what the Indians believed?"

Mrs. Kuby handed Rick a picture of their son in his dress uniform at West Point. And then another photo of him taken at home. Lincoln looked at the home photo. A young man dressed in camouflage held a rifle with a buck knife in his belt. Bald with no eyebrows, his scalp resembled an overcooked pepperoni pizza. His expressionless face stared back at her, shielding whatever was going on behind his eyelashless eyes.

"I'd like to borrow these pictures," said Rick.

"Dad, they have these new things called 'electronic photographs'," Lincoln said as she snapped a picture with her holoband.

Rick ignored her.

"Take 'em," said Mr. Kuby. "If he's the one responsible for your murder cases, then we want you to stop him."

"Bobby already broke our hearts a long time ago," said Mrs. Kuby. "Ya' can't break what's already broke."

Rick switched off Lincoln's holo-recorder. "You people have been straight with me, so here's the reality of the situation. I'm looking for someone with the skillset to hunt down and kill a man in the middle of the night in the woods. Your son has that skillset. Someone savagely bludgeoned a woman with a hammer. Your son has been diagnosed as a sociopath. Someone living off the grid for thirty years, reportedly hairless and with a burn scar covering his head. You get my drift. It all points to your son."

Mrs. Kuby looked at Rick with weary eyes. "Please don't hurt him, detective."

Rick stood up. "That's going to be up to him."

CHAPTER 23

Dots in the Sky

Rick plopped into the driver's seat of the surveillance van. He rubbed his temples and groaned, his countenance like an Easter Island statue.

Lincoln slammed her passenger door. "Okay, Dad — what's bothering you?"

Rick blew out a long breath. "During my undercover days I heard of this phantom assassin...went by the street name Leatherhead. Until today, I figured he was a crime world urban legend."

"Holy cow!" said Lincoln. "It's not a legend at all! AND, we got his real name and picture! Leatherhead. Wow! This is a giant step forward in solving the dead doctors' case."

Rick grinned for a moment, then went back to his serious face. "Yes but.. we've got the 'Who', now we just need the 'Why'."

They were going back to O-town. Rick cranked the Roach Coach engine. Lincoln muffled a cough and then turned on her oxy-boost. Then she reached over and turned on the drone detector.

"Now who's paranoid?" said Rick.

"Hey, after that intense interview with Leatherhead's parents, I've come around to your way of thinking."

When they got on I-4, it started to rain. A comfortable silence settled between them, with just the rhythm of the windshield wipers to listen to.

After a while, Lincoln switched on her holo-pad to check if Jamie had launched all of the podcasts they made. She found 'The Mender's Paradox' and the episodes so far:

'The Beehive'

'The Parachute'

'The Best Day Ever'

'Saving the World'

'U-Turn'

'Dots in the Sky'

"Cool!" said Lincoln. "I haven't heard the latest episode yet. Dad, would you mind if I put on a holopod? It's my senior project."

"Yeah, sure, Sta – Hold the phone! I thought your senior project was interviewing Barry Blue Hawkins."

"It is. Barry is telling me his story and we are putting it out as a series of holopodcasts from The Station."

Rick yanked the Roach Coach to the side of the Interstate. He slammed the brakes, almost hydroplaning in the driving rain, until they came to a complete stop under an overpass. Turning to Lincoln he said, "Star, are you telling me that you have already broadcast these podcasts?"

"'Streamed' and 'holopod', but yeah. All the Barry Blue Hawkins interviews that I've done so far are out there. What's the big deal? It's just an old man's fantasy. None of it can be true."

"You have no idea what you've done," said Rick. "Barry hasn't ever talked to a reporter. And now, after thirty years, he decides to spill his guts to you?"

"Take a chill pill, Dad. You're just as uptight as Barry and his wife were when I told them we wanted to stream his story."

"Uptight? What did Barry say about doing the podcast?"

Lincoln scratched her head. "Umm, he said something about how he was tired of being afraid."

Rick clasped his head in his hands. "Tired of being afraid? Now he definitely has something to be afraid of."

Lincoln muffled another cough. "I just don't get what all the drama with you guys is about."

"Star, I thought that you were just going to do a one-time interview with Barry and write it up for your teacher. I wanted you to get to know Barry so that he could help you," said Rick.

Lincoln waved a dismissive hand across her face. "Help me? I'm the one helping him by getting his story out there! It's what he wants."

Leaning his forehead on the steering wheel Rick said out loud, "Think, Rick, think!" Turning to Lincoln he said, "Let me guess, Windy and that Rodriguez kid are involved in this podcast production."

"Yeah, of course," said Lincoln. "And Professor Erlenmeyer really championed the whole thing."

His brow scrunched. "Yeah, and look where that got him. Okay, fine. I need to know how much of Barry's story has been put out into the world. Let's listen to your latest broadcast."

"Holopod, and sure," said Lincoln. She swiped the most recently released episode, 'Dots in the Sky.' Pressing the play button, the hologram of the dolphins playing in the ocean emerged over the holopad. The theme song 'Heroes' filled the Roach Coach with the rocking synthesizer beat over the driving rain. Then Jamie's huge head swirled out of the ocean.

"Welcome back, fellow babies, to the latest edition of The Mender's Paradox. I'm J-Rod, your executive engineer and M.C. And now I'm turning it over to the lovely Lincoln Jade."

Lincoln's holograph appeared at the news desk. "Thank you, Jamie. In our last episode of The Mender's Paradox, Barry had crashed and burned, becoming very ill. His perceived ability to help people mend their bodies has been the undercurrent for the series so far. Let's hear from Barry in his own words what happened next."

Lincoln and Rick huddled around the holopad on the dashboard. The eerie holographic image of Barry Blue Hawkins filled the windshield.

Holographic Lincoln said, "Barry, in your last podcast you said that you walked away from it all. What exactly did you mean by that?"

"It meant I went on with my life and never looked back. Mending all those people took its toll on me to the point that I was a shell of my former self. I wasn't going to let that happen again," said Barry, sounding like a case of laryngitis.

"I can certainly understand that. How did you get on with your life?" asked Lincoln.

Barry rubbed his head and turned on his Audio Signer. The automated voice took over in his favorite British accent as he signed. "I was lucky to be given a second chance. Before I moved out of my parents' house, I worked construction to make sure I was truly well. Then I moved to North Carolina where I was a hard rocking scientist."

"Hard rocking scientist?"

"Yeah, I worked my chemistry job during the week and played sax in a rock n' roll band on weekends. Eventually I met a nice girl, got married, had a couple of kids. Life was good."

"You didn't mend anyone, not even your kids?"

"Mmm, I did mend daughter number one of migraine headaches, and daughter number two of mono. I didn't mend my kids of anything else because they had to build up their natural immunity. But I didn't mend anyone else."

"How did you feel about that?"

"How did you think I felt?" Barry snapped. "Bad, of course. I don't want to talk about the people that I didn't help. I had a family to take care of."

Barry's expression sagged and he paused for a moment.

"Barry? You okay?"

"Yeah, um, where was I?"

"You were saying that life was good."

Barry perked up. "For twenty years. Everything was fine. Then one day at work everything got messed up. It was September 27, 2006. I was working in my lab at American Chalk and Chemical Company. My lab on the back corner of our building gave me a direct line of sight to the plant thirty yards away that manufactured specialty chemicals."

"What happened next happened really fast. It was after lunch when I heard a BOOM like you hear at a fireworks show. A ruptured disk blew out from a reactor. A split second later, a shock wave rocked the labs, making me stagger back into the countertop. My window facing the plant cracked. The one that blew up was our 2,000-gallon reactor, the Big Boy."

Lincoln shook her head. "Geez, sounds bad."

"Okay," said Barry, "for comparison's sake, I once saw the aftermath of a 100-gallon slow add tank that had a runaway re-action. The explosion launched it through the roof, bending two-foot thick steel I-beams like pipe cleaners. The tank took out a distillation tower a quarter mile away! And THIS tank was twenty times bigger."

"Immediately after the blast, I ran outside to the back of my lab. A co-worker, Roy, had joined me. Through the billowing black smoke we could see that the plant was on fire. Roy was looking straight up into the sky and hollered something about dots in the sky. I looked up to see the sky over us filled with tiny black dots hovering over us. Roy and I stared at the dots as time stood still. Then he yanked me back underneath the overhang as the black dots got bigger. Crashing metal and black blurs surrounded us. The dots in the sky were 55-gallon steel drums! Apparently, a couple hundred steel drums had been staged for product pack-out right outside the reactor that had exploded. They crashed into the pavement as if we were under attack. The scene looked like a battlefield."

"Gary, one of the warehouse men, ran towards us to seek shelter from the falling sky. A drum glanced off Gary's stout body and he went down. We dragged him to the lab's overhang. I shouted at Roy to get all the other lab peeps to the conference room and do a head count. I wasn't sure if Gary was dead or just knocked out. I grabbed him by the wrists and hung on until his eyes fluttered open. I looked up and saw Dayna, a plant operator, running through the wall of black smoke surrounding the plant. Flames engulfed her legs. I dashed out to meet her, almost getting nailed by a falling drum. Tackling her, I covered her legs with my lab coat and rolled the fire out. As she screamed and flailed, I sat on her and grabbed her wrists and felt the prickly charge of energy going through my arms."

"After the shock of the explosion and falling drums, it dawned on me that I could hear the wailing of firetrucks in the distance. The fire department had been trained for such an incident and had an eight-minute response time to our plant. Shouts coming from the other side of the black smoke propelled me towards ground zero. The site looked like Chernobyl. The blue sheet metal that was once walls were mostly blown off, leaving the steel skeleton of the building. A burning crater glowed where Big Boy used to be. A hole gaped in the roof as if a Mars V heavy rocket launched through it."

"The radiating heat of several fires inside the structure caused me to recoil. Cries for help came from the far end of the plant. I could see through the smoky mist a figure pinned to the cinder block firewall. Hot reactor product and rubble covered the place. I carefully made my way to the firewall and found Eldon, one of our maintenance guys, trapped by a platform that had fallen across his body. Blood trickled from his mouth – not good. I couldn't budge the metal wreckage, so I held his wrists for the prescribed time. He stopped bleeding. I told him help was on their way."

"And so it went. I mended anyone who was in dire straits, which was plenty. Soon the place swarmed with firemen, so I left the scene."

Holographic Lincoln asked, "What happened to your policy of not mending anyone?"

"Most of those that I mended, we'd worked together for twenty years. I couldn't leave them to die right in front of me. I guess it was an emotionally driven response. I was probably pumped up on adrenaline."

"Were there any you couldn't save?"

"Thankfully no. I got to the few that did get hurt and that was that."

"Amen to that. Did anyone suspect that you had a hand in saving lives?"

"No. Everyone that I helped was either unconscious or in shock."

"What about you? That sounded like an unprecedented mending spree."

Barry turned off his Audio Signer and hoarsely replied, "The next morning I couldn't get out of bed. I had full blown M.E. I was forty-five years old and couldn't work. We ended up moving to Florida for our extended family support. I've been this way ever since."

"Barry, you know I have to ask this next question. Was it worth it?"

Barry looked straight into the camera. The lines in Barry's face mapped his weariness. "All I can say about that is that I wouldn't have been able to live with myself if I let those people die that day."

Lincoln moved on to a classic 'what if' question. "I hope this next question isn't too personal, Barry. Would you trade mending yourself for the power to mend other people? Would you take it all back if it meant healing for you?" Lincoln was struck by the absurdity of asking a hypothetical question to Barry's hypothetical ability.

Barry fiddled with his beard. When his pinky finger brushed his cheek, the Audio Signer spoke up. "If you asked me that question a long time ago, I would have definitely said yes to mending myself instead of others. But after all I've been through and seen the rippling effects on the lives of people I've mended, I wouldn't take any of it back. The ripple has affected me too. For I am a much better person for going through the gauntlet of suffering caused by my predicament."

Barry's head sunk into the ocean. The 'Heroes' theme song cranked up. Jamie's head materialized from the ocean as two dolphins bounded towards the setting sun.

"This is J-Rod With No Bod beaming to you from The Station in sometimes sunny Orlando. We hope you have enjoyed this edition of the 'Mender's Paradox'. And just like you, we can't wait to find out what's going to happen next!"

Jamie's head vanished into the holographic ocean as 'Heroes' faded out.

As soon as the holopodcast was done Lincoln asked her dad, "Well, what did ya think?"

Rick glared through the windshield where the holographic show had played. He turned to Lincoln. "Barry's life is at risk again."

CHAPTER 24

Special Delivery

Wet gusts of wind buffeted the Roach Coach still idling under the highway overpass. Oblivious to the storm outside, Rick flipped open his old Homeland laptop, fired it up, and placed it on the console so that Lincoln could see the screen. "Watch this, Star." He put the car into gear and pulled back onto the highway.

An image of a tall man walked a pit bull away from the camera. "This is a video taken from my Homeland car in 2017 from the dashboard mounted camera. That's Barry walking his dog up to the stop sign from his home in Fern Park, Florida. He did that little walk every day. Homeland assigned Barry to me as a human asset and I was keeping an eye on him. Okay now, check out the U.S. mail truck driving up to the stop sign."

Lincoln observed the white mail truck creeping from the other direction. "What's a mail truck?"

"Oh brother," said Rick. "The United States Postal Service used to hand-deliver our mail on pieces of paper in envelopes to every person, every day, if you can believe that." Rick tapped the screen. "Keep watching."

The mail truck approached the stop sign, made a right-hand turn, and stopped. When Barry and his pit bull reached the stop sign, a masked man dressed like a ninja jumped out of the back and grabbed Barry. The camera zoomed in quickly as Rick punched the gas and sped forward. Barry's pit bull lunged at the would-be kidnapper. With a bite pressure of three hundred pounds per square inch and bred to take down wild boars, it was a formidable force. But the masked man moved in a flash to grab the dog by the collar and fling it off to the side like a stuffed animal. He then threw Barry into the truck.

Thwack! Thwack! Thwack! Shots fired from the mail truck cratered into Rick's bullet proof windshield. Lincoln instinctively jumped. The truck's back door closed and the masked head disappeared inside. Soon the truck sped off with Rick's car in hot pursuit. The kidnapper hung a right onto the boulevard to get out of the neighborhood, narrowly missing being hit by an oncoming Cadillac. The Cadillac swerved to miss the mail truck but smashed into Rick's car.

The dashboard camera view jostled as Rick maneuvered his car to break free of the Cadillac. The camera steadied then ate up the road as Rick's car continued pursuit.

The mail truck disappeared from view for a moment, until the camera field took an abrupt turn behind Bass Central. Suddenly the truck was right in front of the camera, filling up most of the picture. The back door was open, and a man could be seen getting into a dark sedan about ten yards from the mail truck.

In a flash Rick was in the camera view crouched down behind the open door at the back of the mail truck. Gunshots popped as Rick and the masked man exchanged fire.

"Pause the video here, Star." Lincoln tapped the screen to stop the playback. "Here's where I got hit by a shot that ricocheted off the window iron bars on the back of the building. Okay, hit play." Sure enough, when Lincoln restarted the video, she watched him go down and blood gush from his neck. She gasped at her dad bleeding out on the pavement behind the mail truck.

"Pause it again, and zoom in. See how the bullet grazed my carotid artery in my neck? After a couple of seconds there is already a pool of blood."

"Dad, you're freaking me out!" Lincoln could not tear her eyes away from the image of her dad, only a few years older than she is now, on the ground clutching his neck.

"Sorry, Star, but need you to see that this wound is not a scratch."

Rick tapped the screen to restart the video. Immediately, Barry flopped out of the truck onto the ground, almost landing on top of Rick. Barry slapped his hands around Rick's neck and hung on.

Lincoln cringed. "Dad! Why is Barry strangling you?"

Rick looked grimly amused as he gazed through the windshield. "Barry's not strangling me. He's helping me. Mending me."

Finally Barry let go of Rick's neck and rolled onto his back. A syringe dangled from his forearm. Both men lay on the pavement behind the mail truck looking more dead than alive. A pool of blood joined them, however Rick was not bleeding anymore. Sirens indicated that help was on the way. At this point, Rick shut off the video.

Lincoln looked at her dad expecting him to give her a logical explanation for what she just saw on this thirty year old video. "Geez, Dad! What just happened?"

"Star, this is what I wanted to show you. Barry Blue Hawkins saved my life. I would have bled out in under a minute if not for him. He did some kind of biochemical cauterization to stop the bleeding." Rick pulled down his shirt collar, exposing the small scar on his neck.

This was not the logical explanation that Lincoln was hoping for. "Geez, Dad, that ricochet bullet probably just grazed you. And look, you were both unconscious, so you don't really know what happened once you got hit. The paramedics probably patched you up."

"That was the official 'Ricochet Rick' story that I told Homeland. Barry was my asset and I had to protect him from people knowing what he could really do. I lifted this video recording from the evidence room so that nobody would see it." Rick's voice became a little louder with excitement. "But I'm telling you now that Barry has mended lots of people and he can mend you too, Star. Just imagine being healthy and doing all the things that you can't do now!"

Silence overtook Lincoln. Her dad would give anything for her to be rid of C.F. His words were those of desperation, his face so sincere. She took his hand and spoke softly. "Dad, look, I know how badly you want Barry's abilities to be for real. But wanting something to be true doesn't necessarily make it true. Listen to yourself. What you are saying about Barry having this amazing power is impossible."

"Star…"

Lincoln cut off Rick so abruptly that he could not get a word in. Her voice was loud and agitated. "Now after seeing that video I have about a million questions! I mean, what's with the special delivery of Barry Blue Hawkins to the back lot of Bass Central? Why would anyone want to kidnap him? Who was that ninja kidnapper? I…I don't understand any of this."

"That's fair," said Rick. "I'm sure it's mind boggling to take in all of this at once. But I can answer one of those questions right now. Rewind the video and stop it right at the point where the kidnapper threw Barry into the mail truck. Then go frame by frame until you see it."

"See what?" asked Lincoln as she backed the video up. "I don't know what I'm look-"

Something made her stop when the truck doors closed. She clicked back through the frames until the camera caught the kidnapper's eyes head-on, just before he closed the doors. She zoomed in.

Rick glanced over. "I guess you found it. There he is looking right back at us from thirty years ago. Check it out – no eyebrows or eyelashes, the lifeless gaze."

Lincoln leaned in close to the screen. "Where have I seen those eyes?"

Rick pointed to the photos in the console between them. "Would you believe, a couple hours ago?"

Lincoln gasped. She recoiled from the pale blue eyes outlined by the ninja mask and picked up the photos. It was the same soulless stare in the photograph of Robert Kuby.

CHAPTER 25

The Crab Lady

"Leatherhead tried to kidnap Barry? But why?" asked Lincoln.

Rick looked at her. "That'll take a little history lesson."

"Okay, but I'm recording this."

Rick put his hands up to show that he gave in to this request. "Go ahead and record what I have to say, but you might think twice about releasing it in one of your shows."

Lincoln turned on the holo-recorder. "I guess that'll depend on what you have to tell me."

Rick screwed up his face into a pensive grimace. "It all started two years before the attempted kidnapping, back in 2015 when Barry had his DNA examined as part of his search for the root cause and treatment of M.E. Remember, back then they knew very little about how and what to do about M.E. After about a year, the director of the National Institute of Health visited Barry. He told him his extraordinary DNA had sequences of amino acids not found in any DNA. The NIH wanted to do further testing on him. The testing was intensely thorough. Barry cooperated completely."

Lincoln was in full interview mode. "What exactly was the NIH testing for?"

"They searched for any physical manifestations of his DNA that were different from those found in ordinary humans," Rick answered.

Lincoln felt the old familiar fatigue creep over her, but she pressed on. "And what did they find?"

"They did find that he had a double dose of mitochondria in his cells," said Rick, "in which case you would expect him to have super-human energy output. However, Barry had M.E. so his energy levels were a fraction of that of an ordinary person."

"If Barry's crazy DNA didn't do anything for him, then why all the newspaper headlines?" asked Lincoln.

"During the government study, news of Barry's DNA leaked," said Rick. "Tabloids, then mainstream newspapers, picked up the story. Remember, Barry's so-called junk DNA is unique to not only humans, but the animal kingdom in general. People were afraid, and the media preyed on the public's fears."

"You've got to be kidding! Who would be afraid of Barry?"

Rick let go of the steering wheel momentarily to put up his hands in exasperation. "Oh, man. Fringe religious groups thought Barry was the devil. Other zealots thought he was the second coming of Christ. Then you had your freaks that were convinced that this was the start of an alien invasion. In all cases, the forecast for these crazies was that the end of the world had started."

"Geez," said Lincoln. All that fuss because of Barry, the most harmless person she had ever met. "But didn't they know that the government studies showed that Barry had no special abilities?"

"We're talking about conspiracy theorists, people who had gone down the holo-sphere rabbit hole." Rick stared through the windshield of the Roach Coach and down the long stretch of highway as if he was looking back in time. "They only listen to what fits their warped worldview and discard the rest. So of course they didn't believe it when the government finally reported that Barry had no physical manifestations of his DNA. In fact, many of these groups thought that the government report was a big cover-up!"

"But the government thought there was nothing special about Barry. So how did he rate as an asset to anyone, let alone the U.S. government?" asked Lincoln.

"Because he was a one-of-a-kind genetic anomaly." A shadow of confusion crept over Lincoln's face. Rick continued. "Look at it this way. Barry Blue Hawkins is a unicorn for mankind. And when a unicorn comes along, ya take care of it."

"Why Homeland?" asked Lincoln. "Why not put Barry under the witness protection program?"

"Good question," said Rick. "Barry didn't want to be cut off from his extended family. Fortunately Homeland had a Human Assets program. An added bonus to having Barry under Homeland's jurisdiction is that it really messed with our foreign enemies. We picked up chatter from North Korea wondering if Barry was the blueprint for a race of superhumans for our national defense."

"Okay, like Barry was your secret weapon or something." Lincoln could see that this story had multiple layers. And she was determined to get to whatever lay hidden in the middle of this mystery. "You and Mom were already living in Orlando, right around then. It makes sense that Barry was assigned to you for protection."

"Exactly," said Rick. "It became evident that things were getting out of hand when protesters clogged up the streets near where Barry lived. So many people were fearful of Barry. Meanwhile, lots of college students were pro-Barry. These opposing groups hacked at each other with their protest signs. The media broadcasted ambulances hauling away bloodied protestors and police clearing people out of the streets. Talk radio and social media fanned the flames of this snowballing news story."

"Geez!" said Lincoln. "But how does all that get us to Barry being jumped by Leatherhead in the mail truck?"

Rick rubbed the back of his neck as if this next memory was bringing back a tension headache. "The *Orlando Sentinel* newspaper broke a story about a woman who claimed Barry had cured her of crippling arthritis. The story included documentation such as pictures of her X-rays before and after. The media dubbed her the 'Crab Lady'." Rick put his fingers up to make air quotes.

"Okay, I'll bite. Why did they call her the Crab Lady?" asked Lincoln.

"Because she was scrunched and hunched like a crab. She could have been in a circus sideshow. Pull out the news clipping from my folders."

Lincoln found the 2017 news story and the photographs of the so-called Crab Lady. The 'before' picture depicted a young woman bent over at a 45-degree angle with a head that looked like it had been pushed down into her body. Her elbows were locked so that her crooked arms were bent forward, like a crustacean. In the 'after' picture the same woman stood upright looking quite statuesque. Lincoln questioned Rick. "Surely, this is a hoax!"

Rick paused a beat. "That's what I thought! However, it turns out that it's for real. I recorded Barry's account describing his encounter with the arthritic woman one day when he was at church over in Altamonte Springs. Here, you might as well hear it from Barry himself. Go to the folder labeled 'Crab' on my desktop and play the video file."

Lincoln double clicked the thirty-year-old recording. The video screen on Rick's laptop lit up and there was Barry looking very distraught.

"Yeah, I know the Crab Lady." He sounded as if he had a sore throat. "During Mass at church we have this thing where we offer to each other the 'sign of peace', shaking hands, hugging, or whatever. It's been my observation that many people don't even make eye contact when they are doing this. I don't see how you can make such a wish for someone when you don't even look them in the eye. When the time came for the sign of peace, I looked down into this woman's face and she was able to turn her head up just enough so that we made eye contact. I could tell by her smile that not many people bothered to do this for her. It wasn't pity, but compassion that I felt for this person. We hugged and then I held on for a minute as we clasped hands. I could see her smile give way to a dumbfounded look. Then I let go and left the church quickly. I knew that I had put her on the mend. I never went back to that church."

Rick reached over and turned off the video on his laptop. Rick and Lincoln were both silent for a moment and then Rick said, "Since you've been interviewing him, I'm sure this day in the life of Barry sounds familiar."

"Yeah, it's vintage Barry all right. I'm not buyin' it, but I'll roll with it for now," said Lincoln. "What was John Q. Public's reaction to the newspaper stories?"

"That's when the chocolate tapioca hit the fan," said Rick. "When the New York Times picked it up, the news exploded here and then around the world. The woman that claimed she was the deformed Crab Lady appeared on the biggest talk shows on television including 'Oprah' and 'Ellen'. She told her story of how Barry's touch had transformed her from a deformed suffering invalid into her now healthy self. She came off as very sincere, and her doctor backed her story. TV, radio, and newspapers begged to interview him, but he refused."

Lincoln was rifling through the thick folder containing the faded news clippings from this period. "I can see that there are lots of other people that claimed that Barry restored their health. Let's see... there's polio, cancer, schizophrenia..."

"Barry said those were all copycats and that he had nothing to do with those people. The copycats, of course, made the situation worse. The media, however, was glad to add them to the mix."

Lincoln held out one of the old newspaper articles where Rick could see it while he drove. "These old photographs of Barry here show him with a full head of hair."

"Yeah, he shaved his head and grew a beard to thwart the paparazzi that would sneak around his house. They would sit up in the oak trees hoping to get pics of Barry walking his dog. But the paparazzi were the least of our problems."

"Geez," said Lincoln. "What next?"

"The pilgrims," said Rick. "At least that's what they were dubbed by the media. They came in droves from near and far swarming Barry's neighborhood. They were camped out everywhere. A tent city sprang up in the field behind Lowes. It got so bad that the National Guard was called in."

Lincoln pulled out the Time Magazine from 2018 that Rick had saved along with the other Barry articles. The cover of the magazine read: 'Blue Genes: Hope For Mankind?'

'Professor Erlenmeyer was right,' she thought. Barry Blue Hawkins was world-famous back in the day. The article featured glossy full-page pictures of the pilgrim tent city. A sidebar told about a couple from England who brought their fourteen-year old son with them. Lincoln's heart went out to the boy with sunken eyes and limbs like sticks in a wheelchair. He had stage-4 sarcoma cancer. His mom and dad flanked him. The family photo captured their desperate belief that Barry could save their son. They camped in the tent city in the hope of getting to see Barry. "Geeeeez," Lincoln said. "This is heavy." She pointed to the picture.

Rick shook his head. "Yeah, thousands of people like them clambered to see Barry, hoping for a cure."

"I imagine the scientific community was interested in Barry," said Lincoln.

"Everyone wanted a piece of Barry. And by 'piece of Barry' I mean that quite literally. Universities, research labs – you name it – wanted blood and tissue samples. The only samples and testing Barry had undergone was with the government."

"I gather that Barry didn't want to spend the rest of his life being a human guinea pig," said Lincoln.

"Correct," said Rick. "Then things got crazy."

"Crazy?" exclaimed Lincoln, the inflection of her voice going up. "I thought we were way past crazy!"

Rick adjusted his seat position slightly. "What I mean is that the situation escalated. Like I said, everyone wanted access to Barry. There was one particular firm that wouldn't take 'no' for an answer."

"Which firm was that?" asked Lincoln.

"They wouldn't say," said Rick. "After phone calls and telegrams, they finally sent a representative to Barry's house."

"Tele-what?" asked Lincoln.

"Sorry," Rick said. "Telegrams were a way of sending a letter electronically, which was transcribed onto paper and, uh, delivered in person…to the recipient's house."

"This clearly is the first time you realized how ridiculous that sounds," said Lincoln. She mimed at typing on her holoband. "Look, I'm sending you an electronic telegram."

Rick grunted. "Barry wouldn't see the guy, so they talked through the door. This man said he was authorized to offer Barry one-hundred million dollars for the exclusive rights to his blood. You gotta realize that one-hundred million was a ton of money back in 2017. Anyway, if there were any secrets locked away in his unique DNA, Barry wanted the benefits to be available to everyone for free. He told the guy in his own colorful way 'no' and to leave. The representative for this holding firm told Barry that he had twenty-four hours to change his mind and that it would be in his best interest to do so."

"That sounds doomy," said Lincoln.

"Turns out it was," said Rick. "The next day Barry took his dog for their usual short walk to the stop sign. Nobody else was around as the National Guard kept the streets clear of pilgrims. Homeland had twenty-four-hour protective surveillance on Barry. On my shift I guarded Barry from my cop car when he took his morning walk."

"And that's when Leatherhead grabbed Barry and threw him into the back of the mail truck," said Lincoln.

"Yep," replied Rick. "The rest of what happened is on the video that I showed you taken from my cop car."

Leaning back in her seat, Lincoln's eyes gravitated towards the milky way of bobby pins in the car ceiling, her eyebrows pumping for a moment as she took it all in. "Oh, I see," she said. "Barry wouldn't cooperate with that holding firm, so … they hired Leatherhead to kidnap Barry?"

"Right," said Rick. "Or maybe just to get a sample of his blood. Barry said when he was grabbed, the guy had put a rag over his mouth — probably chloroform to sedate him. He came to as Leatherhead was drawing a vial of blood from his arm, which is when I showed up and broke up the party. When Leatherhead shot me, it hit me harder than the bullet that Barry really was a Human Asset, and he and his secret needed protection! I knew what I had to do."

"Which was?" asked Lincoln.

"First, the Crab Lady had to be discredited. I felt really bad about pulling the trigger on that operation, but it had to be done."

"You mean that the public had to be persuaded that the Crab Lady was an elaborate hoax," said Lincoln.

"Homeland has specialists that handle public opinion," said Rick. "The Orlando Sentinel and New York Times printed a retraction of their original stories. The new story became that the woman who claimed to be the former Crab Lady was a fraud. The media stories were all about the Great Crab Lady Hoax of 2017. Then we went after the copycat stories, which was easy because they really were fake news. And finally, his health condition was released regarding his as an M.E. person. People reasoned that if he couldn't heal himself, then he couldn't possibly heal other people."

"So that was the end of the world's fascination with Barry?" asked Lincoln.

"Mostly," said Rick. "The Pilgrims packed up and went home. So did the National Guard. Homeland set up a surveillance drone to fly over Barry's neighborhood so that we had twenty-four-seven coverage on activity around Barry's house. I had to protect him from government exploitation, Leatherhead, and the public. I never told Barry's secret to anyone except your Mom."

"Mom knew Barry and Jenny?" asked Lincoln.

"Of course," said Rick. "After all, he saved my life. We used to have dinner on occasion with Barry and Jenny."

Lincoln sat in the Roach Coach with her mouth agape. No wonder Barry and Jenny greeted her with such fondness when they first met.

"Okaaay…Let me get this straight. The Crab Lady's claim that she was cured brought unwanted attention to Barry. This caused a guy we think is Leatherhead to try to steal Barry's blood. This is the same guy that has been killing doctors. The same guy that killed Mom and probably the same guy that killed Professor Erlenmeyer."

Rick nodded. "Yeah, that's pretty much it. The question is, why? Why would Leatherhead want to stop the progressive work of Dr. Langley, and yet want the presumable key to healing? It doesn't make sense."

Lincoln turned off her holo-cam. "Dad, from my point of view, how we proceed with investigating the Leatherhead connection with Barry hinges on whether or not Barry is the real deal."

Remembering the card that Dr. Prinity Walker had given her at her last appointment, she pulled it out.

Call me when you are ready for proof.
111-555-629-0880, signed Prinity

"What's that?" asked Rick.

"Proof, I hope," she said as she dialed the number.

CHAPTER 26

Proof

"Barry, this is Dr. Prinity Wal - "

"No!" Barry sprang up and on his feet in front of his red couch. He glared at Lincoln. "I was done being a lab rat a long time ago," he rasped. "I don't see medical people!"

"You also said you don't do interviews, yet here we are doing a holopod series on your life story," said Lincoln.

All Barry could manage to get out was "Bollocks!"

Barry turned towards Jenny and pointed at Prinity. "Ding-dang it, woman! Why did you let this blood sucker into our house?"

Jenny did half an eye roll.

Moondog growled a deep long growl.

Prinity withdrew her outstretched hand. "Mr. Hawkins, if I may - "

Barry spastically waved his arms and said, "That's it! Everybody out!" his shout more of a whisper.

'That went well,' mused Lincoln as she started for the door. She knew Barry would never agree to a meeting with Prinity, so she had given Jenny the heads up that she was bringing her over to see Barry. Looks like they had been stonewalled by the old coot.

Just then Jenny raised her voice and said, "Hold it! Everybody take a seat. Bear, zip it! Prinity is a medical re-searcher and she is Lincoln's assigned physician. You need to hear what she has to say. Detective Rick is keeping guard out-side, so rest easy."

173

Prinity sat down and leaned forward towards Barry. She wore street clothes and had her hair down. She locked her eyes on Barry. "Barry Blue Hawkins, I know the secret to your secret! What I meant is, I know that you really can mend people back to good health and I have a theory how it works. Lucky for you, I have a way to prove it!"

Barry scooted back on his couch a little. "Yeah lucky for me. So, what makes you so sure of my mending ability?"

"Because I am part of an underground-research organization that was founded by Dr. Shawn O'Malley, your old college roommate. Our charter is to discover how to actually cure diseases instead of treating the symptoms. We know about the dead doctors, so we work in secret. Shawn told me everything."

"Uh...everything?" asked Barry.

"Yes, indeed!" said Prinity. "He told me how back in school you saved a kid that overdosed on drugs. You know your friend Shawn is a heavy hitter in the cell biology field. He used his credentials to deny that you had any special abilities when he went on the Larry King show back in 2017. He was protecting you."

"Yeah," said Barry, his gravel voice fading. "People pretty much left me alone after that."

"I also believe that the episodes from your Mender's Paradox holopodcast are all true stories based on real life," said Prinity.

Lincoln tilted her head to one side. Prinity sounded just like her dad when talking about Barry. How could an intelligent medical researcher like Dr. Walker passionately believe that the stories about Barry were true? Lincoln pulled out her holorecorder and switched it on.

Prinity smiled. "Do you want to hear my theory on how you are able to mend people?" asked Prinity.

"Do I have a choice?" said Barry.

"My theory is an extension of Dr. Langley's research. Are you familiar with his work?"

Barry nodded. "As part of my own research to figure out how to cure my M.E., I have studied all I can about Dr. Langley."

Lincoln interjected. "For my listeners in holo-land, Dr. Langley was murdered thirty years ago in Chimney Rock. He was one of several doctors in the alternative medicine field who were killed." Her heart raced. Prinity's theory might shed light on the dead doctor's case.

"Which is why our medical research to cure disease is underground," said Prinity. "You see, Dr. Langley was at the cusp of a medical breakthrough. He treated his patients with vitamin D3 derivatives with much success. However, the compilation of the details of his research was never found."

"So, what's so special about vitamin D?" asked Jenny.

"D3," said Barry with a slight pause, "my favorite vitamin."

He stopped talking long enough to place his auto-signer on his lap and switched it to lip reading mode.

"It's involved in over two-hundred biochemical reactions in our bodies and is key to the function of the immune system." As he mouthed his words, the auto-signer converted it to speech with his favored British accent.

"It was discovered in the search for a cure for a terrible disease called rickets. Children with this disease had very soft bones. Their legs would bow so that they couldn't hardly walk."

"A doctor in nineteenth century England noticed that all of his rickets patients came from the poor children who played in the dark alleys of the ghetto. He observed that well-to-do children played in the open sunlight and did not get rickets. Then he reasoned that sunlight was making the difference. So he prescribed playing in the sun for his rickets patients and voila! The rickets scourge was no longer a problem."

"Quite a revelation back then," said Lincoln. "So what's the connection between sunlight and vitamin D3?"

"Good question, young reporter," said Barry. "Sunlight starts a chain reaction at the surface of our skin. Photons from the sun cause the hydrocholesterol in our skin to be converted to a compound that goes to the liver for further biochemistry, and finally to our kidneys resulting in D3."

Prinity raised an eyebrow. "My, you have done your research! Dr. Langley realized that there are at least a dozen other known photo-reactive compounds in the skin that theoretically take the same biochemical pathway as hydrocholesterol, the starting material for vitamin D3. These photo-reactive chemicals evolved over millions of years, yet nobody knows why they are in our skin. Dr. Langley's theory was that these chemicals are the building blocks to compounds that could heal the body."

"Right," said Barry. "Langley apparently had some success, but his clinical trials data was never recovered."

Prinity contemplated Barry. "And now, Barry Blue Hawkins, we come to my theory…which is that your body produces the missing Eureka Chemical that makes the mending process work!"

"Uh, how's that? said Barry. "My blood has been studied by NIH and there has been no such chemical found."

"Because that Eureka Chemical is only produced when you are grabbing somebody with your hands to mend a real bonafide injury or illness. When you are mending someone, you transdermally pass the Eureka chemical into the person's skin that you are healing. That chemical reacts with the vitamin D precursor and the other photosensitive chemicals in your skin. They follow the same biochemical pathways in the liver and then kidneys to make the compounds that restore the body to health."

"Ah. So that's why it took two days for the people I mended to show results. That's about the timeframe for the vitamin D production," said Barry.

"Interesting," said Lincoln.

"Yeah biochemistry is fascinating," said Barry.

"Yes, indeed!" said Prinity. "This further supports my theory. The process to make the mending chemicals would take two days once Barry has transferred the Eureka compound. I've been following your 'Mender's Paradox' Podcast and that seems to be the case."

"Right-O," said Barry, "but how do you explain the instantaneous mending of wounds like when I saved Rick from that ricochet bullet?"

"Don't forget, Barry Blue Hawkins, that you have twice as much mitochondria in your body as everyone else. Yet it seems you have no use for it. I believe that all that mitochondria energy kicks in when you grab someone and mend them. It facilitates a rapid biochemical cauterization for wounds. It probably also generates the required activation energy for these mending reactions to happen."

Lincoln marvelled at their chemistry over biochemistry — they were clearly kindred spirits. Now their nerd bond was about to be put to the test. "According to your theory, Prinity, sounds to me like the only way to get this Eureka chemical from Barry is to take the blood sample while he is mending someone."

"Bollocks! That would be a hard 'no' for me!" said Barry. "I didn't sign up for this today." He laced his arms across his chest defiantly.

"Barry, you know Lincoln is right," said Prinity. "Once we have blood samples taken while you are mending someone, we can isolate both the Eureka chemical and the compounds formed from it. We will take a quantum leap toward treating every kind of illness. And you will have the added bonus of personally curing Lincoln of her CF!"

Brakes squealed in Lincoln's head. She didn't sign up for this either! Prinity and Barry talked a good science game, but did she dare hope to be cured of her CF? She had been living with this disease day in and day out fighting to keep it from totally defining her life. Prinity had been true to her word, offering her a chance at proof…but she did not believe Barry's mending was possible…especially for a disease so encompassing and damning to her life expectancy. "Uh, you guys, not to sound ungrateful, but I'm not comfortable with this."

At this point Jenny stood in the middle of the room. "Enough from you two! Lincoln, this is what your Dad wants for you – for you to be mended from CF. And Bear, what does the past forty years of misery on the couch add up to if you don't do this? This can be your legacy for the good of all mankind."

"But Jen," said Barry out loud, overriding the auto-signer, "I have maybe one or two mendings left in me. And I've been saving it for you."

Jenny sat next to Barry and took his hand. "I know Bear, you've always put me first. But I'm just one old woman versus millions of lives." She turned to Prinity and said, "Tell us what to do."

"Great!" said Prinity. "Let's all go into the dining room and sit at the table." Prinity grabbed her medical bag and placed it on the table. "I'll need Barry and Lincoln to sit across from each other."

Barry scootered to the dining room. He slipped the neck-thing-in-a-pant-leg brace behind his back as he slid into a chair, positioning the auto-signer on the table in front of him.

Lincoln reluctantly allowed the undertow of this development to drag her into the next room. When she woke up this morning, she didn't think she would be part of a pseudo-science ritual. Lincoln sat at the table under the bright dining room light.

"Vampire," Barry grumbled.

Lincoln looked over at Barry and saw the face of dread. His teeth clenched in a grimace like he was about to be punched in the face. A fit of coughing struck Lincoln as she felt the stress pull her down below her comfort zone. She filled her damaged lungs with air but it was not enough to keep her from gasping for more. Maybe this was really supposed to be a faith healing. Was this all some elaborate plan to psych her out into being healed? Or was Prinity's agenda surely a medical pipe dream? Lincoln shuddered. The thought of Barry's veiny hands on her repulsed her. She pulled her arms off the table. The force of her standing up slammed her chair backwards into the sliding glass doors. "I can't," said Lincoln. "I can't do this!"

"Fine with me!" came back Barry.

"Prinity!" said Jenny. "What do we do now?"

"Plan B!" said Prinity, who had already sat down in Lincoln's chair across from Barry. She had a blood-draw device inserted in her right arm. Proving that the hand was quicker than the eye, she shoved a tiny syringe blood withdrawal unit into Barry's arm. Wielding a scalpel, Prinity made a tiny incision into her left forearm. A needle-thin stream of bright red blood immediately squirted out of her forearm and hit the dining room lamp hanging above the table.

Barry mouthed, "What in the blazes are you doing!"

"I just made a pinhole prick into my ulnar artery. You can see how forceful the positive pressure is." Then Prinity made a one-inch incision where the blood spurted out of her forearm. She muffled her audible rush of pain. The crimson liquid gushed from the cut, pooling on the table. In a wavering tone she said, "I will bleed out in about two minutes if you don't mend me, Barry Blue Hawkins."

The sight of the blood geyser emanating from Prinity's forearm worsened Lincoln's coughing fit. "No Prinity! No!" she coughed.

Prinity sat with her head down with both arms extended on the table towards Barry. The blood pond dripped off the table onto the floor.

Barry pounded his fists on the table. Red faced, he snarled, "You crazy zealot!"

Jenny cut him off with a firm yet calm voice. "Bear! Do it! Do it now!"

"No way!" Barry shot back sharply. "She did this to herself!"

Jenny put her hands on Barry's shoulders and said softly, "Bear, do it for me. Do it for the millions of people."

Barry let out a raspy yell of frustration, willing himself through his anger. "Yaaaaah!"

Lincoln covered her mouth with her hands as Barry grabbed Prinity's outstretched forearms. Barry's hand covered the scalpel wound, the blood running through his fingers.

Prinity slumped further. "Medtronics Units One and Two, begin one-minute blood-draw," she said in a fading whisper. The tiny pumps on the syringe units in Prinity and Barry's arms simultaneously began collecting dark blood into their attached vials.

Blood still trickled between Barry's fingers as he held onto each of Prinity's arms.

"Come on, Bear. You can do this," coaxed Jenny as she held Barry close.

Stunned, Lincoln had the presence of mind to hug Prinity. "Don't die, don't die, Prinity," she chanted.

Lincoln's eyes were glued to Barry's hand gripping Prinity's scalpel wound. "She's bleeding to death!" sobbed Lincoln. Prinity's eyes closed and her body went limp. As her head sagged to the table, her hair matted in her own pool of blood. "She's dead!" cried Lincoln.

"She's not dead," said Jenny, trying to remain calm. "Hang onto her, Lincoln."

"It didn't work Jenny!" ranted Lincoln. Lincoln coughed and struggled to breathe in enough air. But her rage spurred her on. "You people caused this! She believed in Barry. Now she's dead!"

Jenny ignored Lincoln. She gently rocked Barry, urging him to hang on.

Lincoln's eyes remained riveted to the gory scenario. Was the blood flow actually stopping? It was hard to tell because Barry's clenched hand and Prinity's arm were soaked with blood. The blood dripped from Barry's grasp onto the table. Then the blood stopped coming. The blood-draw units stopped and the vials were full. Prinity's limp body slid to the right and Lincoln, still holding her, laid her onto the floor.

Barry slumped forward and Jenny took the blood-draw unit out of his arm.

Barry seemed to have aged ten years, if that was even possible. "Never again," croaked Barry. "Never again."

"Call 911! Call 911!" screamed Lincoln.

At that moment Rick burst through the front door with his gun drawn. "Criminy!" he yelled. Rick quickly scanned the dining room, his gun following his eyes. It looked like a murder scene. Blood covered everyone. Lincoln sat on the floor, cradling Prinity's head in her lap. Barry slumped in his chair half unconscious with his head down on his crossed arms.

Jenny held him. A scalpel lay on the table in the middle of the blood puddle.

"What the - ?" said Rick.

"It's okay, Rick," said Jenny.

"How can any of this be okay?" said Rick. "I heard screams. What the hell happened here?"

"Rick, check on Prinity," said Jenny.

After canvassing the room for intruders, Rick scrambled to his knees and checked Prinity's pulse. "She's alive!" said Rick, his voice filling the room.

Lincoln couldn't believe it. There was so much of Prinity's blood not in her body.

"Star! Are you all right?" said Rick.

"Yeah, Dad, I think so," said Lincoln. She adjusted her oxyboost and did her best to fill her lungs.

Prinity's eyes snapped open as if she was rebooted. She grabbed the full vial of blood still tethered to her arm. "The vial from Barry's arm," she said. "Where is it?"

Lincoln didn't respond. Instead she picked up Prinity's arm and looked closely at where the scalpel incision had been made. It was not bleeding anymore. Lincoln spit into her hand and used the moistness to wipe away the crust of blood where the cut had been made. As she did so there appeared a neatly cauterized scar – a scar just like the one made on her dad's neck when Barry mended him from Leatherhead's gunshot.

Lincoln's thoughts were interrupted by Prinity who was now sitting upright.

"Barry, you did it!" said Prinity. "I knew you could mend me"

Rick's face reddened and his eyes made the squintiest squint. His fury turned towards Prinity who was dazed from the trauma.

"You had no right!" he growled. Rick still brandished his glock and waved it like an extension of his pointer finger.

"Do you realize what you've done?" Rick shouted at Prinity. "This mending was meant for my girl. It was to save her very life, not for your pie in the sky science project!" Then Rick's rage shuddered into anguish, his shouting yielding to a grieving moan. "That was her last chance, her last chance."

Lincoln had never seen her father so upset. In a flash she put two and two together: Rick had put her onto the trail of Barry in the first place so that she and Barry would form a relationship, a relationship in which Lincoln would trust Barry to put her in his mending grip despite the fantastical claim that Barry was for real. His words from their drive back from St. Pete came back to her: *I wanted you to get to know Barry so that he could help you!* No wonder her dad was acting like a lunatic. Prinity's caper meant that Lincoln's one and only opportunity to be mended… was gone.

Weak from blood loss, Prinity leaned against the wall. "Detective Rick, save the many instead of the one. My team will isolate the special mending compounds and determine how to reproduce them for the good of all. Including your daughter."

Rick looked like he had just been socked in the stomach. He removed his glare from Prinity and focused instead his crestfallen face to Lincoln. "Star, my baby girl, you don't have time for all that. It could be years before they get to where they can help you."

Lincoln tried to lower the temperature in the room. "Dad, it'll be all right. We have proof! Prinity was right all along!" The notion that Barry's mending powers were real briefly took her breath away. Her eyebrows zigged and zagged as she processed the ramifications of what just happened. The 'Mender's Paradox' was not just ramblings of an old DNA freak. The holopod episodes really were true stories based on real life! Back in the day Leatherhead left Barry alone because Barry's DNA would not have shown any healing powers. But now, if Leatherhead got wind of the holopod, then they would all be in grave danger.

Lincoln's holoband lit up and projected Windy's face. She cried, "Lincoln, Rick, you know that Chetola disaster story I've been working on? It's not environmental. I've got confirmation that those people were intentionally poisoned!"

"How do you know?" asked Lincoln.

"I have an inside source," said Windy. "He's agreed to a face-to-face, but it has to be within the hour."

"Copy that Windy." Lincoln's eyes met Rick's before she spoke again, relieved to see he was starting to calm down, with his gun held at his side. "We'll pick you up in twenty. Where does he want to meet?"

"He insists that we meet at a secure location," said Windy. "Someplace secret."

"I know just the place," said Rick. "Tell your contact to meet us behind the Third Dock. We'll see if we can save some lives instead of throwing them away." Rick threw a menacing glare at Dr. Walker before holstering his gun and storming out the front door.

CHAPTER 27

Whistle Blower

Lincoln searched her mind shack for all she knew about Chetola as she and Rick raced to Full Sail University to collect Windy and Jamie. One, radiation sickness ravaged the residents of the Phase I community. Two, Orange, New Jersey was also the former site of the U.S. Radium Company which dumped radium effluent with impunity. Three, the EPA had detected spotty traces of radium in the Chetola soil as part of the radiation sickness investigation. Four, Professor Erlenmeyer had been tricked into obtaining a gram of radium which was now in the hands of some unknown bad guy.

And five, Windy had taken the bullet train to New Jersey to investigate the story. Had she really discovered the truth about what happened to Chetola?

Lincoln's thoughts hurled through the windshield as Rick screeched the Roach Coach to a halt in front of the dormitory where Windy and Jamie waited. Windy shrieked as soon as she climbed into the idling van. "Lincoln! You're hurt!"

Lincoln beheld her arms and hands smeared with dried blood. "No, No! I'm okay. It's not my blood."

Jamie squeezed into the volume-challenged vehicle right behind Windy. "Then whose blood is it?"

"It's my doc's blood," said Lincoln.

"Oh my God!" said Windy. "Is she hurt bad?"

"Yes! I mean no!" Lincoln attempted to illustrate with her crimson stained hands as if this would help explain the situation.

"She was hurt but now she's totally fine. Guys, we have to focus on the task at hand. I promise I'll explain later."

"This is rich," said Jamie. "We're going to meet Windy's contact on the Chetola poisoning and L.J. looks like the Butcher of Boca Raton. That should make him feel nice and comfortable."

"Butcher of Boca Raton? That's not a thing, Hon," said Windy, handing Lincoln a travel pack of sanitary wipes.

"Knock it off you two," said Rick as the van rounded a corner, losing a hubcap. "Windy, what's your case for deliberate poisoning?"

"Okay. As you know, authorities attributed the radiation sickness to the fact that the Chetola community was built on toxic ground," Windy began. "After all, it wouldn't have been the first time that radium from those days turned up in that general area. A baseball field in neighboring Glendale became a Superfund Site because of radium found there."

"But there was something off about the situation. The Phase II of Chetola right across the street from Phase I remained unscathed by any radioactive contamination. And the children of Phase I were completely healthy, while the parents and some teens were very sick. I also learned that the victims had radium in their bones. That's where radium goes if you *ingest* it. I got to talk to some of them and they said that their spines actually glow in the dark!"

Lincoln nodded. "That would explain the severe cases. How would they have ingested radium?"

"I looked for patterns. You know, something that everyone living there would have access to. The water supply checked out negative. I mean, that makes sense since it goes to Phase II as well, and those people did not have radium contamination. Then, get this — whenever a family moves into a Chetola community they become a member of the Wine of the Month Club, courtesy of the Chetola Real Estate proprietors."

Lincoln's eyebrows were a-pumping. "So everyone gets a bottle of wine every month."

"Right," Windy said. "That's what made it so hard to uncover. People got sick gradually because of the wine, just like what happens from environmental poisoning. It fooled everyone... for a while," she said, smiling.

Lincoln nodded. "Until you came along! I take it you checked on who was delivering this free wine?"

"Exactly! I got access to the video surveillance at the front office where the wine was delivered every month. The delivery man was the same guy every time, but he wore a New York Yankees baseball cap so I couldn't get a good look at his face. I interviewed the front desk people to get a description of this guy."

Windy had uncharacteristically worked herself up into a lather. Lincoln wondered what it would feel like to have such a breakthrough in her own dead doctor's case.

"The guy was caucasian, described as 'creepy pale.' He wore dark glasses and the ball hat every time so they couldn't see much of his face. But he did have what looked like burn scarring protruding down to his left eye on the side of his face."

Lincoln's spine turned to ice at the thought of this all too familiar description. "I get it, Windy. The authorities assumed that the radiation sickness was due to contamination from the old U.S. Radium factory. But *you're* saying that this delivery man has been poisoning the Chetola residents with radium-laced wine."

"Yes," said Windy. "I *so* wanted this to be an environmental issue. But maybe I can write an environmental disaster story on this carbon burning, pollution spewing, greenhouse effects machine we're riding in."

"I can hear you," said Rick. "And I have a gun." Rick patted the dashboard and softly said, "Don't listen to her, baby. She's just a twisted tree-hugger."

"The poisoning explains a lot," said Lincoln. "Like why kids didn't have any radiation sickness."

"And why some people had severe radiation sickness while others had mild cases," said Windy. "The more wine they drank, the more radium accumulated in their bones. The worst part is that the radium in their bodies will continue to do damage their entire lives. There's no getting rid of it."

"They're the walking dead," said Jamie.

"I figure you are trying to I.D. the poison-wine-of-the-month delivery man," said Lincoln.

"Yes, I placed a reward request on the holosphere," said Windy. "I included a still-frame from the video of the delivery guy along with a description. I then ran all responses through a filter."

"And?" said Lincoln.

"And there was one response that caught my eye, from a concerned citizen who claims he saw this delivery guy at his workplace last week. Check this out...our new friend works with radioactive materials! I'm betting this isn't mere coincidence."

Rick emitted a low whistle.

Windy spoke so fast now the words ran together. "My source goes by the name Taj. I've been communicating with him online for the past couple of weeks while I was in Orange, and it turns out he works here in Orlando. Now all of a sudden he wants to meet us in person right away, which is why I came back."

"Great, but why the urgency?" asked Lincoln.

"Something about leaving the country."

"Great work, Windy!" said Rick.

"That's not all," said Windy. "Taj says he has evidence that his company has a top secret plan to make a killing in the market — literally!"

"Wow!" said Lincoln. "What a scoop! A real, live whistle-blower!"

CHAPTER 28

Goliath

The Roach Coach lurched into the parking lot of The Third Dock, a Fine Family Dining Establishment in Winter Park. The exterior of the restaurant resembled a fishing pier. A cat-walk led to the entrance going over a small pond stocked with live alligators. The sign in front read:

'Come on in. Dock's got a roof!'

Rick drove around to the back of the building and parked. Windy turned to the others. "Okay guys, my contact just texted me. He's almost here. Just a quick warning — he can be a little extra."

"How do you mean?" asked Lincoln.

Windy let out a deep breath. "It's hard to describe, but he can really get under your skin. You'll see. Just be cool."

As if on cue, a robo-taxi pulled up next to the van. A short brown man with salt and pepper hair stepped out of the taxi.

Windy came out from the van side door and greeted the whistleblower. "Taj? I'm Windy."

Taj clasped her hand with both of his. "Yes, Yes, I am he."

"What's the deal with the duct tape wrapped around your holoband?" asked Rick, pointing to Taj's wrist.

"It needs charging and the tape is a reminder for me to get it fixed," said Taj tapping his temple with his index finger.

"I see," said Rick, "but not really."

"Another use for duct tape," said Lincoln.

Rick produced his detective badge. "Detective Jade. I spent my career as a Homeland Special Agent."

Taj turned to Windy, his face full of alarm. "Windy, my holosphere friend, it may not be a good idea to involve the police." The urgency in his voice and the frantic way he waved his hands for emphasis reminded Lincoln of Captain James T. Kirk from when she used to watch *Star Trek* with her dad as a kid. Windy gave Lincoln a "See what I mean?" look.

Lincoln stepped in. "Lincoln Jade. The detective does not trust the police authorities either. You're safe with us, Taj."

Throwing looks over his shoulders, Jamie said, "Man, are we going to stand around all day like sitting ducks?"

Rick unlocked the back door of the restaurant. "All right, everyone come on in."

"A public place is not a wise location to discuss the situation," said Taj in his heavy accent.

"Don't sweat it pal," said Rick. "We'll soon have very private accommodations."

Rick held the door open and Taj peered inside the room stocked with shelves of restaurant supplies. "Windy, tell your policeman that this is not sufficient."

Rick ignored him. He walked to the back corner where two shiny walk-in freezers stood . Rick entered a code onto a keypad on the side of one of the freezers. The freezer door opened with a swish. "Everyone in," he said.

"We will freeze to death in there! What kind of people are you?" said Taj.

Jamie quickly ducked inside. His eyes widened. "It's not even cold in here!"

"A little cramped and dark for a pow-wow," said Lincoln.

"Looks like an elevator," said Windy.

After everyone sardined into the walk-in freezer, the door slid closed. "Hit the button marked 'G'," said Rick.

Jamie pushed the button. Lincoln's gut plummeted to her pelvis as the box dropped.

"Cool, it really is an elevator," said Jamie.

"Thank you Captain Obvious," said Lincoln.

The door slid open and Jamie bounded out first into a cavernous room with no windows. "Amaze-balls! Who knew all this was under a restaurant?"

An office occupied a corner with a sign on the door that said 'Private. Keep out!' Couches, cots, and a teak table with padded chairs furnished the underground space. Atlanta Braves baseball memorabilia covered one wall.

"Ah," said Taj. "Very clever. Here we will have our privacy."

"Dad, what gives?" asked Lincoln.

"Yes 'dad'," said Taj. "What does give?"

"Everyone take a seat and I'll tell you," said Rick, gesturing towards the table.

Once everyone sat down Rick explained their accommodations. "You know my old pal Mr. Steve... ."

"Sure," said Lincoln. "You two have been friends practically your whole lives."

"Right," said Rick. "Mr. Steve and I were dishwashers here back in high school when this place was a Steak n' Shake. He vowed to someday tear this place down. I always thought that he was blowin' off steam. But he turned out to be a savvy businessman, building a restaurant empire. He not only tore down this old Steak n' Shake, but replaced every Steak n' Shake in the country with a Third Dock Restaurant. This one here is the first one that he built. He wanted a secret yet comfortable bomb shelter in case of a nuclear bomb fallout."

"On any other day I would have considered this the wildest thing I've ever seen," said Jamie, "but here we are in a bomb shelter being all like, yeah, this is normal. By the way, totally obsolete, since there are no nukes any more."

"Anyway," continued Rick, ignoring Jamie, "he lets me use it as a safe house."

Taj looked around. "Very nice, but I would have done things differently."

"I love the gator burgers and cat-tail-slaw here," said Windy.

"Well, we're not here to eat. Let's get started," said Rick.

"Dad, we haven't patched in Barry yet," said Lincoln.

Rick picked up a remote control and a virtual TV slid up out of the end of the table. A few seconds later Barry's face appeared in eerie 3-D.

"Barry, wake up!" said Rick.

"I am awake, old bean," said Barry in a British accent, which emanated from his audio signer as he mouthed the words. "I always look like this."

"Hey Barry," said Lincoln. "We have the whole gang here, plus our new friend, Taj, who has been cooperating with Windy on the Chetola investigation."

Taj removed his lab glasses, complete with detachable side shields, revealing huge eyebrows like wooly caterpillars. He leaned forward, locking eyes one by one with everyone around the table. Only then did he address them. "Taj is not my real name. You see, my friends, I am having a pickle."

"In a pickle," said Windy. "You are in quite a pickle."

"Yes, yes, as you say," said Taj. "I am afraid that I have stumbled upon a disturbing plot involving people I work with. I cannot risk going to the television stations or police, because I too am involved in the situation. I fear for my very life. In fact, believe it or not, I have taken the precaution of having my family moved out of the country."

Taj clammed up for a moment and fidgeted with his safety glasses. "I have spoken to no one except you, Windy."

Windy coaxed Taj, her serene sincerity evident. "Taj, it's okay. You can trust them. These are my friends."

"Please forgive my hesitation," said Taj, "but I need to hear it from your comrades."

Rick pounced on this invitation. "Look Taj, or whatever your name is, don't flake out on us."

Lincoln quickly smoothed over Rick's roughness. "Taj, we're in the same boat as you, as we may have a common foe. Why do you think we're in this secret hiding place? We need to get the bad guys before they get us."

Taj's furry eyebrows came together and almost touched. "Such a web of malevolence has been spun. Where shall I start?"

"Why don't you start by telling them what you do for a living," said Windy.

"Yes, very good," said Taj. He emphasized practically every other word and spoke using his hands as if he was directing traffic. "I am a biochemist. You see, I work in a radio lab - "

"Really?" said Barry's head from the virtual TV. "That's great because I have an old radio in need of repair."

"No, no, my disembodied friend," said Taj. "What I am talking about is a laboratory where radioactive materials are used. I make drug compounds that are tested on animals."

"Just trying to lighten the mood, old chap. Okay, let me guess," said Barry. "You are using radioactive isotopes to study how your drug compounds are being metabolized by the body."

"Correct," said Taj. "You are right by the money."

"On the money," mumbled Windy. "*On* the money."

"We call these compounds tracers, because they determine what part of the body receives the drug compounds," said Taj.

"Is everybody understanding this so far? I hope so because I cannot make it any more simple."

A collective eyeroll did the wave around the table.

"Now I have to tell you about my most brilliant discovery. This is where you must listen very closely. One of the radioactive isotope compounds that I made was for treating Hashimoto's disease, which is an autoimmune disease of the thyroid. When this new tracer was used on animals, we could not trace it!" Taj paused for dramatic effect. Lincoln pinched the bridge of her nose and ran her hand down her face. 'Jeez, this guy really loves the sound of his own voice,' she surmised.

Barry's head jumped in. "You are saying that you serendipitously discovered a drug that neutralizes ionizing radiation."

"Yes! Yes, my virtual friend!" said Taj. "We successfully did the tests over and over, exposing animals to up to one sievert of gamma radiation. What we found was that our new drug worked synergistically with certain proteins in the body to mitigate the effects of gamma radiation."

"Gamma rays!" said Jamie. "The same rays that made the Incredible Hulk?"

"That was pretend science. This is real science," said Barry. "Gamma radiation is very high energy rays produced by dangerous radioactive materials. And one sievert of exposure is enough to make a person extremely sick."

"Wait a minute," said Lincoln. "Are you saying that you have a cure for radiation poisoning?"

"Not a cure," said Taj, his accent punctuating his words even more. "This drug can be taken as a preventative for radiation exposure. It can also be taken by somebody with radiation poisoning to prevent further damage to the body."

"This is for sure an important discovery," said Barry. "I imagine it's a drug that has to be taken every day to be effective."

"This is not a golden bullet, Mr. Barry," said Taj. Windy slumped in her chair and looked at the ceiling. "Would you believe that my company's new drug discovery section is directed not to investigate possible cures for disease, but to seek out solutions in which a drug must be taken every day. Every day for the rest of your life. Can you imagine?"

"I can definitely identify with that," said Lincoln. "It must cost the government a fortune to pay for the array of pills I have to take three times a day."

"Exactly!" said Taj. "The model drugs are the ones used to treat high blood pressure. Of course, they must be taken every day to prevent strokes in high blood pressure patients. Ever since drug manufacturers discovered blood pressure medication back in the 1950's, they have learned that medicines taken every day for life are very lucrative. They used to call drugs like that the rainmakers. Sadly, treatment is the business model, not cures."

Lincoln shot out of her chair and leaned forward with her hands on the table, directly across from Taj. "Let me get this straight, Taj. Instead of finding cures for diseases, you work on developing pills that string patients on for life?"

Taj put his hands up in a defensive mode. "Don't kill a messenger, Miss Lincoln. I am on your side!"

"Money drives everything," Rick grumbled.

"Is there a name for this new discovery of yours?" asked Barry.

"Gammaway," said Taj.

"I get it," said Jamie. "Gammaway keeps gamma rays away."

"Well, Gammaway certainly follows the business model. It should be a big fat cash cow," said Lincoln.

"Don't worry," said Barry. "It will never get past the FDA. After all, they would have to have a big enough set of humans exposed to significant amounts of gamma radiation...like - "

"- At Chetola!" said Lincoln, finishing Barry's sentence. "This is what the Chetola tragedy is all about."

"Show them, Taj," said Windy.

"I need the molar controller," said Taj.

"The what?" said Rick.

"I think he means the remote control for the virtual TV," said Windy, her eye twitching slightly.

Rick slid the remote control across the table to Taj, who punched some buttons; a virtual TV screen above the end of the table turned on. Jamie turned Barry's monitor around so that he could see too.

"This was broadcast late yesterday," said Taj.

A smiling woman with a microphone for show stood in front of a housing community surrounded by a fence topped with razor wire. The woman rattled away.

Behind me is the tragic site of the upscale New Jersey housing community now known as the Chetola Superfund site. A few weeks ago, the occupants of these homes were ascertained to have radiation sickness. The source of the radiation is from an illegal waste dump made by the infamous U.S. Radium Company over one hundred years ago. The former residents have been quarantined at the East Orange VA Center. Today I'm here to report that a ray of hope has been born out of this terrible tragedy. We are taking you live to the VA Center to tell you about a possible treatment for the radiation sickness.

The television scene switched to a news reporter wearing a fashionable glowing necktie, which was probably not appropriate for this particular news segment.

Good evening. I'm Mike Lions reporting from the VA Medical Center. Just beyond these steel doors is the quarantine section of the building where Chetola victims have been living for the past few months. Up until recently, the patients with radiation sickness have exhibited an array of symptoms that have steadily been getting worse. But today, I'm happy to report on what may be the 'feel-good story of the year.'

The camera pulled back to reveal another man standing next to the news reporter. This man had a pumpkin-sized head on his big frame. A patch of wavy grey hair sat atop his red face.

With me today is the president and CEO of Goliath Industries, Jackson Paluski. Goliath is the reason that the Chetola victims have experienced a remission from their symptoms. Mr. Paluski, can you please elaborate? The face of Jackson Paluski filled the screen so that it appeared that his head was coming through the virtual TV into the room. His tiny pointed nose accentuated his bulging face.

My fellow Americans...Goliath Industries is proud to have the opportunity to come to the aid of the Chetola victims. We have been developing a new medication that thwarts the effects of radiation poisoning. The Food and Drug administration has graciously allowed Goliath to offer this medication to the people for free for the rest of their lives. So far, Gammaway has prevented the patients from getting any worse. Together, Goliath and America have overcome this horrific tragedy.

The camera pulled back to frame up the reporter for his closing. *As a side note, the Gammaway medication has also been given to volunteers in Chetola Phase II to determine the effects of the drug on individuals that have not been exposed to radiation.*

Taj cut the TV off.

"Holy human guinea pigs!" said Jamie.

"Well put, young ward," said Barry, whose screen had been flipped around to face his cohorts.

"Yeah," said Windy. "Goliath has their Gammaway human trials going, complete with a control set in Chetola Phase II.

The government has announced they're going to fast-track the drug through the approval process, thanks to this incident and the live testing trials taking place. I hate to admit, it's a brilliant shortcut, but why the big hurry and the extreme course of action?"

"Agreed," said Rick. "There's something bigger going on here, I can feel it." Turning to Taj, he said, "I'm going to take a wild guess and say that you work at Goliath."

"Whoa!" said Jamie. "You work at that crazy building that looks like a giant mailbox, the eyesore on I-4?"

"Yes. Its nickname is regrettable, but it is going to be torn down soon," said Taj. He cleared his throat to focus the attention on the seriousness of his upcoming words. "You can now begin to understand my paranoia. It's too much of a coincidence for Goliath to have this Chetola situation appear soon after I discovered Gammaway."

"We don't believe in coincidence around here," said Rick. "Keep talking, pal."

Taj raised his hands like an orchestra conductor. "My friends, I wholeheartedly am telling you that when the Chetola news came out, I felt truly alone. For I, an honest man, knew too much."

'This guy ought to have his own one-man show on Broadway,' thought Lincoln.

Taj went on. "First let me tell you something about Goliath that you must understand. Decades ago, there was no Goliath. There were many, many pharmaceutical companies all over the United States gobbling each other up. For example, there was Glaxo-Smith-Kline, then Burroughs-Welcome- Glaxo-Smith-Kline, and so on. Finally, around the time of the Health Care Revolution, the government consolidated U.S. pharmaceutical companies into Goliath. The Paluski family owned Goliath, the whole waxball."

"Ball of wax," said Windy to nobody in particular.

"So basically, there was one customer and one supplier," said Barry. "The U.S. government was the customer because it paid for everyone's medications and Goliath became the sole supplier for the government's prescription plan."

"True, true my television friend," said Taj. His hands began to conduct his symphony of words, "What you must also comprehend is that Goliath has been in a major sales slump. The government has capped prices for what they will pay for medications in order to be able to meet the growing needs of the people. The government has also become quite stingy as to what they will pay for, resulting in a black market that undercuts Goliath."

"Looks like Goliath needs a blockbuster drug," said Lincoln. "I'll bet they're looking for Gammaway to fill that order."

Windy turned to Taj seated next to her. "Taj, correct me if I'm wrong...but there doesn't seem to be much of a market for Gammaway, unless there is an imminent nuclear threat."

Taj took in a deep breath and then let it out all at once through pursed lips, making a sound like a motorboat. "Yes, that is a good assumption, Windy. But I fear that a market is about to be created for Gammaway."

"What?" said Rick. "How can that be? The chance of nuclear war is pretty scarce since no one has nuclear weapons anymore."

"That may be, detective," said Taj. "That may be. However, there are other ways to strike with radioactive destruction. Just look at the current Chetola situation."

"We are. We're pretty sure it was intentional radiation poisoning," said Rick. "What makes you think Goliath is behind it?"

Taj scooted his chair back and took off his shoe. From his shoe he pulled out a folded piece of paper. He unfolded it and put it on the table in front of him. "This, my friends, is a Goliath inner-circle memo. It is regarding Gammaway sales projections. I was accidently copied on it, probably because I am the technical project manager for Gammaway."

Taj slid the memo across the table to Lincoln and Rick. The memo was from Jackson and his Chief Financial Officer. They read the memo and passed it around.

Subject: Operation Fire Sale

'The Gammaway trials have been successful so far. Projected U.S. sales for the first year are forecasted to be higher than any drug in history. Operation Fire Sale is a go.'

Sales projections in the hundreds of billions were included in a bar chart at the bottom of the memo.

As the document was passed back to Taj, the questions flew around the table.

Windy shushed everyone and turned to Taj, "Why didn't you tell me about this memo?"

"Yes, it is true. I have kept it a secret, a secret that I have been carrying around like a mill stone upon my neck. First, I had to get my family out of the country for their own protection. But I am telling you about it now!" said Taj.

Barry weighed in. "The 'trials' in the Operation Fire Sale memo must be referring to the Chetola victims being treated with Gammaway. Right?" said Barry.

"Yes," said Taj. "I believe so, my British comrade."

"Operation Fire sale!" said Jamie. "What the hell is that supposed to mean?"

Rick put his hands up. "All right everyone, calm down and let him talk." Rick turned to Taj. "Go ahead."

Taj furrowed his Marx Brother-ish eyebrows. "It gets worse."

Jamie jumped away from the table like there was a rattlesnake coiled on it. "We're hiding out in the bat cave from radioactive bad guys. How could it possibly be worse?"

"I will tell you," said Taj. "The day after I received this ominous Fire Sale Memo, Wilson Paluski visited me in my office. He is Jackson's brother and right hand man. His title is vice president of some sort...Vice President of Scariness perhaps. He looks like his brother but is about a foot shorter. With him was another man that I had never seen before. He wore shaded glasses and a Yankees baseball hat, the same hat worn by the man in Windy's holosphere ad. He also had the telltale scarring on the left side of his head. That is why I got in touch with Windy on my international communication center."

Rick looked at Windy with a questioning raised eyebrow.

"His desktop computer," said Windy. "This is how we have been communicating. He did not want to expose his face to the wrong person."

"This visit in your office Taj doesn't sound like a social call. What did they want?" asked Rick.

Taj's voice grew louder. "Wilson wanted to know if I received the Fire Sale Memo. I told them, 'Memo? What memo?' I was trying to play stupid, but I am a not a good liar."

"Dumb," said Windy.

"No, no, playing stupid was a reasonable thing to do under the circumstances," said Taj. Windy let her head drop into her hands. "However, I'm afraid he could look right through me. Wilson drew close to my face and told me that I was a very valued employee. I can tell you, that did not reassure me at all. I was instructed to reveal the conversation to no one."

"Did the man with Wilson say anything to you?" asked Rick.

"No, " said Taj. "Not a word."

Rick handed Taj the photograph that Mrs. Kuby had given him. "Take a close look. Was this the other man who visited you? He would be thirty years older now."

Taj produced a magnifying glass that popped out of its holder like a switchblade. He studied the photograph. "Perhaps... Let's see, I noticed that he was completely hairless and had a dark pigmentation coming down over his eye from under his hat. Yes, the man in my office could very well be the same as in this photograph."

Lincoln and her dad looked at each other in an 'ah-ha' moment. The key to their quest crystallized in Lincoln's brain. "Leatherhead has not been acting on his own. He works for Goliath! This is the connection we've been looking for!"

"Yep, that's Leatherhead," said Rick. "I'm sure the brothers compensate him very well for his unique skill set. You better grow eyes in the back of your head, my Taj-Mahal friend."

"Why is that?" asked Taj.

"Because Leatherhead is a sociopath, a serial killer who has murdered untold hundreds of people, over a span of three decades," said Lincoln. "And he's the one that fried Professor Erlenmeyer, murdered my mom and messed up my life." Lincoln sneered and gritted her teeth.

Rick looked sternly around the table. "I can tell you that this demon lives to kill. Highly intelligent, military trained, completely remorseless." Rick passed around the picture that he had procured from Leatherhead's parents. "This alabaster bastard is a killing machine. He uses a different M.O. every time, making it very difficult to determine where and when he'll strike next." Rick paused to let his profile of Leatherhead sink in.

"Thank you for telling me," Taj said with a quavery uncertainty in his voice.

"Riddle me this," said Jamie. "Why would the dead doctors' case be caused by Goliath?"

Lincoln's eyebrows danced a jig. "Look, Taj has told us that Goliath makes its billions on treatments, not cures. Anyone who comes up with cures for disease is a threat to Goliath. Dr. Langley's work was all about finding a way to help the body to heal itself. The doc murdered in Miami was Langley's proponent and broadcasting cheerleader. My mom died because my dad pushed hard to solve those cases."

"What about Professor Erlenmeyer's murder?" asked Windy.

Lincoln gripped the edge of the table where she sat with both hands. "Goliath needed radium so that they could create a human test situation for Gammaway at Chetola. Professor Erlenmeyer was tricked into using his connections to get it for them. He thought he was doing work for the U.S. government, and... " Her eyes began to water.

" - and Erlenmeyer became a loose end for Goliath," said Rick.

"So they sent Leatherhead to snip it," said Jamie. "And by 'snip it,' I mean blow him up."

"We followed the analogy just fine, Hon," Windy said. "Why did Goliath have to use radium?"

Barry did not hesitate to answer the chemical question. "Radium is extremely radioactive, emitting high energy gamma-rays. In fact, it was radium that killed Marie Curie, the discoverer of radium. The uniqueness of Goliath's Gammaway drug is that it can treat people that have been exposed to gamma radiation. It's very hard to come by radium metal, so they needed Erlenmeyer to procure it without it being traced back to them."

Taj watched the exchange like a tennis match, swiveling his head back and forth. "It crushes my very heart that my discovery has been used in such a vile, wicked, and evil way." Taj wrung his hands. He gazed upon the group and said, "You have shone a light into the darkness. Now you must bring the darkness to light."

Lincoln looked around the table at confused faces. "Ummm... what Taj is saying is that we need to expose the Paluski brothers and Leatherhead for their heinous crimes."

"How in the world are we going to do that?" asked Jamie

"We need to catch Leatherhead red-handed," said Rick. He's bound to surface soon."

"Oh, Leatherhead will surface soon all right," said Jamie pacing back and forth. "He'll surface like Moby Dick! Call me Ishmael."

Lincoln winced. That would make her dad Captain Ahab. Geez. Was he so obsessed with Leatherhead that he would put himself or anyone else in harm's way?

Jamie stopped pacing. "This is where we turn this case over to the cops."

"Negative Rodriguez," said Rick. "Too risky. The police are tainted. Goliath is the big money that's been paying off the authorities all along, from here to Jersey."

"I really must be going," said Taj, getting up from his chair. "I have told you what I know."

Windy put her hand on Taj's arm. "Taj, you should stay here for your own safety."

"She's right," said Rick.

"No, no, no," said Taj. "I don't want to impose myself. And I have an early flight tomorrow that I must be on. I am leaving on a jet plane to rejoin my family."

"Fair enough," said Rick. "But I will call you in the morning to check on you. Remember to charge your holo-band." He escorted Taj into the fake freezer elevator and took him up top.

"Guys?" said Lincoln. "There's something incredible I have to tell you. The podcast episodes are all true."

Stunned silence registered from Jamie and Windy.

"Barry really can mend people," said Lincoln. "I've seen it with my own eyes. He saved Dr. Walker's life yesterday. Tell them Barry."

"Zzzzz." Barry was fast asleep on the monitor.

"Man, I'd have to see that for myself to believe it," said Jamie.

"Listen, ya' wing-nut. I'm not playin'," said Lincoln.

"Hey, cool your jets, L.J," said Jamie. "You can't expect us to believe something whack like that."

"Sweetie, what you're saying is impossible," said Windy.

"Guys," said Lincoln, "I'm tellin' you, I was there when he mended her. I got the whole thing on my holo-recorder." Nobody said anything for a long time.

Lincoln didn't blame her friends for not believing her. After all, she didn't even believe her dad when he told her that Barry had saved his life. Her friends probably thought that she wanted Barry's story to be for real so much that she went off the deep end. Poor, poor sickly Lincoln. Now she's had a nervous breakdown or some sort of psychotic episode. How pitiful she must seem to them. Lincoln wanted to tell them everything she had learned the past few days. how Leatherhead almost killed her dad to get Barry's blood, how Barry saved her dad's life, and how the great Crab Lady hoax that wasn't a hoax thrust Barry into the spotlight. In that moment she felt like such a jerk for treating Barry like a delusional fool.

"I have some good news," said Lincoln, openly changing the subject. "I have material for several more podcast episodes documented on my holo-recorder. It's great stuff and the episodes may bring Leatherhead out in the open."

Jamie said, "Have any of you *read* Moby Dick? I say we let sleeping whales lie."

Windy thrust a fist into the air. "I say let's do it."

The meeting was over. Rick had returned and took everyone back up top via the freezer elevator. They got some gator burgers to-go and hauled butt back to the Station at Full Sail. Once there, Rick stood guard, while Lincoln, Windy, and Jamie produced podcast after podcast, readying them for immediate daily launches. That evening they cruised back to the safety of the 'Third Dock' bunker and settled in for the evening. As Lincoln lay down, the weight of the long day sat on her chest like a cinder block.

The next morning Lincoln awoke to Rick pacing the floor.

"What's up, Dad?" she asked.

"I just called our friend Taj to check on him. It went straight to holo-mail. I'm going over there," said Rick.

"You know I'm going with you!" said Lincoln. Rick didn't bother to argue.

The Roach coach arrived at Taj's Winter Park home in the pouring rain. Rick buzzed the doorbell. No answer. Lincoln knocked on the door and called for Taj.

"Maybe he left town already," said Lincoln.

"Criminy!" said Rick. In his frustration he pounded on the door.

Whump! To Lincoln's surprise the entire door fell into the house. Rick had his gun drawn before the door hit the floor. "Stay right behind me, Star," he said.

They stepped over the door into the foyer. Rick swept the area with his gun, then pressed Lincoln and his body against the nearest interior wall. Darkness enveloped the house as all the shades had been drawn. The staccato sound of rain pattered the tin covered roof.

They edged themselves along the wall. Lincoln strained to hold in a cough. Her mind raced. 'Where was Taj? Was there a bad guy lying in ambush around the corner?'

They came to a hallway. Rick slipped into the darkened corridor with his gun leading the way. Lincoln chanced a look around the corner. The hallway led into a family room. A figure in the room floated just inches above the floor.

Rick entered the room, then lowered his gun. "It's Taj. He's not gonna make his flight."

CHAPTER 29

New Target

Lincoln fought the urge to dash out of the house. When she woke up this morning, her agenda did not include finding a dead person. Professor Erlenmeyer's words echoed in her brain — 'Be careful what you wish for, intrepid reporter.' Had she stumbled onto a big story? Now was not the time to chicken out. As Lincoln forced herself down the hallway, the stench emanating from the family room assaulted her senses.

"I'm pretty sure he crapped himself," said Rick. "It happens when a person croaks — the bowels just let loose."

Rick had turned on the light in the family room. She recoiled at the sight of a body hanging in the middle of the room and turned away. "Ugh!" It really was Taj. Lincoln concentrated on her breathing. She would try to forget what was now the gray pallor of death on Taj's once animated face. Summoning courage that comes from sheer will power, she engaged herself in the crime scene.

"Dad, we need to figure out what happened here."

"Agreed," said Rick. "Lincoln, don't touch anything. I already called the police, so let's walk the crime scene before they get here."

"What am I looking for?" asked Lincoln.

"Clues. Like on the detective show you watch."

"You mean The Newest Sherlock Holmes?"

"I suppose. Try to notice things, really take things in." Rick strode back up the hall towards the front door lying in the entrance way. "Star, look at this door. What do you see?"

Lincoln stooped down and ran her fingers across the charred door hinges. "It looks like this door was blown right off its hinges. Deadbolt too."

"Correct," said Rick. "This was a shock-and-awe break-in. The perp likely used HIPE, high-intensity-plastic-explosives, on the hinges and deadbolt. Then kicked the door down. A little dab'll do ya' with that HIPE stuff. And from here on out, try not to touch any more evidence."

Rick winked and went back down the hall, turning on the hall lights as he did so. "Here you can see the bathroom door was kicked in. What does that tell us?"

Lincoln had not even noticed that there was a bathroom door on the left side of the hall. In the darkness she had been totally focused on Taj. "The perp kicked in the bathroom door... because Taj was in there!"

"Yeah, I'd say Taj had five, maybe ten seconds between hearing the front door come down and Leatherhead grabbing him out of this bathroom," said Rick.

"Why didn't he call for help?"

"Good question," said Rick.

Inspecting the family room, they observed the ghastly sight of Taj hanging about an inch from the floor wearing the same clothes as when he left the Third Dock hideout. His swollen and burnt barefeet signalled that Taj didn't die an easy death. The blood encrusted hangman's noose around his neck laid the skin raw. The noose rope stretched taut over a ceiling beam with the end tied to the stairway banister.

"What's missing?" asked Rick.

"I dunno — a pulse?" Lincoln replied, hotly. "Sorry, Dad, this is freaking me out a little."

"That's okay, Star," Rick reassured, "That's normal. Just don't look at his face. Focus on the rest of him and tell me what you see."

Lincoln closed her eyes and willed herself to calm. Opening her eyes, she scanned the body, starting with the blackened feet and working her way up to the bloody collar. She was about to give up when she took a second look at his forearms. "Where's his holoband, with the duct tape?"

"Good eye!" beamed Rick. "It's over on the end table, on the charger. When Leatherhead busted in, Taj didn't have a chance to grab it when he ran for the bathroom."

Lincoln snapped her fingers. "And that's why he didn't call for help. His holoband was out here!"

"Not too shabby, Sherlock. Now check out the knot on the banister," said Rick. "It's a slip-knot, easily adjustable. Leatherhead must've tied it that way so that he could raise and lower Taj. I tell you Star, this is like no other murder scene I've ever seen. I mean, what gives with a special knot and the toasted feet?"

Down on one knee, Lincoln inspected the charred feet up close. The tips of the toe bones protruded through the black, blistered skin. "Eew! Dad, these look like cryogenic burns… like severe frostbite."

"Frostbite in Florida?" said Rick.

Lincoln nodded. "I saw a Mount Everest documentary about a mission gone bad. The frostbite wounds looked like this here."

Rick came over to get a better look at the remains of the feet. "I've got Barry on the line." Rick held his holoband so that Barry had a close-up of the feet. "Barry, you getting this?"

Barry's 3-D face spoke from Rick's holoband. "Right-o, I caught a glimpse. Nasty business!" his lip reader chirped in sterling British. "I'm thinking he was forced to stand on frozen carbon dioxide, also known as dry ice. At minus 109 degrees Fahrenheit, that would produce these severe burns."

"Okay, but where did the dry ice go?" asked Rick. "There's no wet spot."

"Dry ice doesn't melt, old bean. It sublimes, going directly to the gaseous state."

Lincoln looked straight up past Taj's hanging body to the rope going over the ceiling beam and then tied onto the stairway rail. "Guys, Taj was lynched over and over by being forced to stand on the block of dry ice. He would instinctively support himself with his feet, then he would choke to death. Every time he relieved himself from being strangled by the noose, he would endure burning of his feet on the dry ice. As the dry ice sublimed, Leatherhead lowered Taj by adjusting the slip knot so that Taj could barely reach the dry ice block. Lincoln grimaced as she imagined Taj alternating between being lynched and searing his feet, over and over.

Rick nodded. "Barry, how long would that dry ice last?"

"I'd say a twelve inch by twelve inch block of ice would last a few hours."

"Poor bastard," said Rick.

"But why would Leatherhead do this?" said Lincoln.

"Taj was a loose end for the Paluski brothers," said Rick. "They must've worried that he knew enough to bring down the entire Goliath organization. They sent Leatherhead to find out if Taj had gone to the authorities or the media. He made darn sure that he had extracted all the information from Taj." Rick rubbed his chin thoughtfully, his eyes narrowing to slits. "And they wanted to know who else Taj may have gone to."

"Meaning..." said Lincoln.

"We're next. I'm sure Taj eventually told him everything about us," said Rick.

Lincoln gulped. She felt her chest get tight. She heard the whine of approaching police sirens. Absorbing the shock of Taj's brutal death gave her a glimpse into Leatherhead's world…a world where this was just another paid task for the psychopath. For Leatherhead, killing Taj probably registered the same emotion as making a sandwich.

A police sergeant and a forensic team swarmed into the house. "I'm Sergeant Shultz — are you the guy who called this in?"

Rick produced his old Homeland badge and went over to talk with them while the techs scanned the family room and bathroom for fingerprints.

Rick finished and came over to Lincoln. "How ya' doin' Star? I know this is hard to take in."

"I'm all right, but I wanna get out of here."

"Agreed," said Rick.

One of the forensic guys shouted from the bathroom. "Hey Sarge, you're gonna wanna see this."

Shultz stepped inside the bathroom. "What the…? Detective, does this mean anything to you?"

Rick and Lincoln crammed into the bathroom along with Shultz and the tech who was holding up a fingerprint scanner to the mirror. "Look what shows up when I scan the mirror for fingerprints," he said.

Scrawled on the mirror were the words: "New Target".

"New Target?" said Shultz. "What was the old target?"

"Not sure," said Rick. "It doesn't make any sense."

"Dad, it's super important because that's the last thing Taj did before—"

Rick grabbed Lincoln by the arm and pulled her out of the crowded bathroom. "Or maybe it means nothing at all." He flashed her a quick wink and continued. "Star, the first rule of investigating is to collect clues without leaping to fanciful conclusions."

As they walked down the hallway Shultz barked, "Don't go anywhere. I've got questions for you."

"We'll be right over here, sergeant," Rick said, smiling and waving.

Lincoln's eyebrows furrowed. "What's with all the weirdness?"

"We need to get out of here," Rick said, ushering her toward the back door.

"But the sergeant—"

Rick stopped and placed his face close to Lincoln's. "We don't know if any of these guys are on the Paluski payroll, Star," he whispered. "I've run into too many bought-off cops and judges covering up Leatherhead's tracks to trust the authorities. Besides, our story is pretty shaky, and even an honest cop would want to hold us for a couple days as persons of interest."

"Let me get that door," Lincoln said, unlatching and opening the door to the back yard. They walked around the side of the house, sticking to the shadows and managing to avoid any police in the front of the house. Thankfully Rick had parked the Roach Coach in the street, and they were able to slip inside, fire it up without attracting any attention, and make their getaway.

"Now where was I before I was so rudely interrupted?" Lincoln said. "Oh, yes, we were in the bathroom reconstructing Taj's final moments. We know he couldn't call 911, with his holoband on the charger in the next room."

Rick nodded. "That message was the last thing he did before Leatherhead busted in and grabbed him. Smart to write it on the mirror with his finger — it would be invisible to Leatherhead. It's gotta be key to the Paluski scheme."

Lincoln stared out the side window as she thought. "New Target. Hmm. Hey, remember that 'Operation Fire Sale' memo that Taj intercepted and showed us? It referred to expectations of record sales once they hit the 'New Target'. What if that statement isn't referring to a technical or financial goal? What if - "

" – it's about a planned terrorist attack on American soil," finished Rick. "The last target was Chetola. Something tells me this is going to be bigger, the next phase of their plan."

"Right!" said Lincoln. "Leatherhead works for Goliath. Goliath has a new drug that treats radiation sickness, and a plan to skyrocket its sales. Chetola was a test run for the effectiveness of Gammaway. And now Leatherhead is going to cause some kind of a disaster. Taj must have figured it out just before the home invasion but didn't have time to tell anybody."

"Well, he got the message to us," Rick said grimly. "Now we gotta figure out what Leatherhead is up to before it's too late."

Soon they arrived at the Third Dock hideout and took the freezer-elevator down below. Windy and Jamie greeted them.

"Where have you guys been? What's happening?"

Rick, blunt as ever, got to the point. "Leatherhead greased Taj. Lynched to death in his own family room."

"It can't be true!" said Windy.

"It's true," said Lincoln. "He's another victim to the Goliath agenda."

"Ugh! Sounds horrible, man!" said Jamie.

"You have no idea," said Lincoln.

"Taj didn't deserve this," said Windy.

"Agreed," said Rick.

A pall of silence permeated the hideout, mostly from fear and shock rather than reverence for the dead.

"It's gonna be curtains for us and I don't mean drapes," said Jamie, his voice cracking. "What the hell are we gonna do now?"

"Taj left us a secret message," said Rick. "Let's sit down and pow wow with Barry."

They gathered around the table. Lincoln slumped in her chair, tired out already from the stressful morning. The virtual TV screen popped up at the end of the table and Barry was conferenced in.

"So what's this secret message?" asked Windy.

"Taj wrote with his finger on the bathroom mirror. The fingerprint scan revealed the message to us. It said: 'New Target'."

Jamie doubled over and slapped his knee. "No way!"

Windy covered her mouth. "Oh…my…gosh!"

"What is it with you two?" asked Lincoln.

"We know what that means!" said Windy.

"Totally," said Jamie. "The New Target store's grand opening has been all over the news today!"

CHAPTER 30

Operation Fire Sale

Jamie switched on the remote control and the virtual TV beamed into the middle of the table. The news station blinked on, with the news anchor wearing a tie featuring the Target red circles on it. He stood in front of the shiny monolithic doors of Target, which had a huge red ribbon draped across them.

This is Mike Lions reporting to you live in front of the new Target Grand opening for dignitaries and VIPs. Today the top officials from the great state of Florida will be touring the first shopping experience of its kind with their families. This mega Target is not your grandmother's store. It is the anchor for a theme park shopping extravaganza for the entire family. Here the Target shopper will glide through the world of Target, viewing virtual holograms of their families outfitted with store products. Interactive android assistants will bring your dreams to reality, picking out products that are your heart's desire based on your shopping profile.

Lincoln sat up in her chair and smacked her forehead with her palm. "Duh! We've been such idiots. Operation Fire Sale is the New Target store!"

"Leatherhead is going to blow it up!" said Windy.

"Actually, I expect this attack to be a dirty bomb," said Barry from his conference monitor, in his trademark British voice coming from the audio signer.

"A dirty bomb?" asked Jamie.

"Think Chernobyl in the 1980's. When the nuclear fission reactor melted down, the fallout was radioactive isotopes of uranium, like strontium 90. A dirty bomb is a device designed to disperse such radioactive isotopes so that when they get into a body the result is ARS, acute radiation sickness."

"Criminy! You're right!" said Rick. "Once they expose these bigshots to gamma radiation then that will force the FDA's hand to approve Gammaway."

"People will be buying it for the rest of their lives. Geez, Goliath will make a killing," said Lincoln.

"Not only that, this will terrorize the surrounding population to stock up on Gammaway," said Windy.

"I'm already terrorized," said Jamie.

"Exactly what time is this Grand Opening?" asked Lincoln.

"It's at noon today," said Windy. "We have to assume the bomb is set to go off at noon or just after."

"It's 11:00 AM now," said Rick. "That's not much time to work with."

"We need to call the cops," shouted Windy. "They need to stop this!"

"And what are we going to tell them?" asked Rick. "We have no proof, just a crazy sounding conspiracy theory. They'd laugh us right off the phone."

"They wouldn't laugh at a bomb threat," said Jamie. "Don't worry — I've reconfigured my phone so that calls can't be traced."

"Hon!" snapped Windy.

Rick scratched his head. "Actually, that's not a terrible idea, Rodriguez. Do it!"

Jamie had 911 on the line. "Hello, I'd like to call in a bomb threat please. Yes, this is totally serious. Where? The New Target at uh…"

The entire table participants mouthed 'noon'.

"Um, noon. The bomb will go off at noon today. Okay, thank you...bye-bye."

"I'm guessing this is your first bomb threat, Rodriguez," said Rick.

"Hopefully it will at least keep people from going into the building when the bomb goes off," said Windy.

"Keeping people out of Target is a good start, but ultimately, it won't save them," said Barry.

"Why not?" asked Windy.

Barry spoke again, and everyone leaned in to hear him. "The key to a dirty bomb is dispersal. If I was the bad guy, I'd put it on the roof. When it goes off the radioactive isotope material would contaminate anyone within at least a quarter mile radius. Gamma rays would go right through anything not lined with lead...clothes, cars, you name it."

"Then we need to get those people completely out of the vicinity," said Rick. "Where is this material-girl theme park?"

Windy had her holo-pad lit up on Google earth. The hologram depicted a white oval shaped structure with the Target logo on the roof. The hologram zoomed out to show the surrounding area, including highways and towns. "The Target is located twenty miles east of Orlando on Colonial," said Windy. "It says here that it's built on the thousands of acres that the Mormons own."

"Too bad that land will be radioactive for decades if that bomb goes off," said Barry.

"Man, I hate to be a bummer, but it's already 11:05 a.m.," said Jamie. "We'd never make it over there in time to warn them, especially with O-town traffic."

Lincoln's face lit up, her eyebrows pumping. "Dad, we can make it in time with the Mud Skipper."

"Mud Skipper?" asked Jamie.

As soon as Lincoln said the word Mud Skipper, an almost-forgotten childhood memory jabbed her with a pang of regret. She had only flown in that vomit comet once, but once was enough.

"It's my dad's hydro-plane on the lake," said Lincoln.

Jamie gulped. All eyes were on Rick.

"We may be the only shot those people have," pleaded Windy.

Rick glanced at his holoband for the current time and then squinted like the sun was in his eyes. "Okay, let's do it!"

The gang of four bounded into the fridge elevator and ascended up top. They scampered into the Roach Coach parked out back of the Third Dock Fine Family Dining Establishment. Rick shouted "Hang on!" This was not a rhetorical statement as the Roach Coach didn't have automatic seat belts like modern cars did. Peeling out of the parking lot, Rick slapped a siren on top of the van over his driver position. The van careened north on Orlando Avenue with the siren blaring.

Twelve minutes and several run stop lights later, the environmentally vile vehicle pulled into the Marina at Lake of the Woods parking lot. The van, however, did not stop there. Instead Rick plowed it through the chain linked gate. "No time for keys!" said Rick. He stopped the Roach Coach at the marina airplane hangar which bordered the edge of the lake.

Rick barked orders. "Star, grab the binoculars. Rodriguez, help me unmoor the plane."

"I'll handle video," said Windy, grabbing a telescopic lens.

Once inside the marina Lincoln turned on her oxy-boost. Her lungs constricted as her anxiety about the takeoff was building.

The yellow craft buoyed in the water on pontoon struts between two catwalks. The sleek wings folded back like a butterfly that had just emerged from a cocoon so that the plane would fit into its docking station.

They all squeezed into the floating yellow dart with Lincoln in the co-pilot position and Jamie and Windy behind them. Rick cranked the propeller. The engine coughed and then began a low rumbling cadence that became a steady whir.

"Strap into your harnesses everyone!" said Rick. Rick maneuvered the rumbling machine out of the marina. Then he worked the console and the wings extended fully to flying position. The pontoon struts extended and the Mud Skipper rose out of the water, ready for take-off.

As Rick pointed the plane south towards the glassy runway, the elongated lake stretched out before them. Lincoln forced her eyes shut as the plane glided across the water and then rose into the air. She opened her eyes and could see the horizon tilt when the plane veered south east towards their destination. The plane kept a low altitude, flying under the radar.

"Time!" said Rick in a loud enough voice to be heard over the droning engine.

"11:46" replied Windy from the back seat.

Rick gunned it and soon they came upon the Mega Target Theme Park in a huge clearing amongst the stands of pine trees below. In the middle of the clearing a white oval structure that looked like a covered football stadium shimmered against the green landscape. Lincoln knew they were at the right place since on top of the roof proudly sported the famous red target logo.

Barry's image projected from Lincoln's holoband. "Barry, we're coming up on the Target. What are we looking for?" she asked.

"Look for anything that doesn't belong. It will probably be camouflaged."

"Agreed," said Rick and he beelined the plane directly over the length of the Target roof.

A throng of a few hundred people pushed towards the store entrance. Police had formed a barricade to keep people from getting closer to the store. High above the news helicopters huddled.

Windy peered through her telescopic holo-lens, documenting the entire flight. The Target logo loomed ahead of them. "Guys, look at the Target dot!" she hollered.

Jamie and Lincoln both trained their binoculars on the logo, which dwarfed the Mud Skipper in size. "There's a red bump on the logo dot!" said Jamie as they passed directly over it.

"I saw it too!" said Lincoln. "A red backpack."

"Time!" said Rick.

"It's 11:57!" said Windy.

"Those people are just standing there, looking at us," said Jamie.

"Let's move those people back!" said Rick. He banked the plane around for another pass. This time the Mud Skipper gained some altitude. Once it had turned back around towards the mega store, the mystery plane began a dive bomb trajectory. The straps of the seat harness dug into Lincoln's shoulders as her body lurch forward.

As the plane descended it passed right between the crowd and the entrance to the store about fifty feet off the ground. The VIPs scattered, taking to their cars as fast as they could. The police, however, stood their ground. Lincoln heard a metallic 'thunk' penetrate the howling of the engine.

"We're taking fire!" yelled Rick and he pulled up hard on the plane. Lincoln slammed back into her seat as the plane rolled upwards. She labored to breathe from the resulting G-force.

"Dad, the helicopters!" said Lincoln pointing back towards her left. The news helicopters still bunched about a hundred feet above the store entrance.

"I see 'em Star," said Rick. The plane climbed and did almost a full backwards loop. The brief sensation of weightlessness at the top of the loop caused Lincoln's internal organs to play musical chairs. Then the plane rolled to a horizontal and upright position which aimed straight towards the news vultures. They got the message and took off.

"Detective Rick!" shouted Windy. "11:59! We gotta go!"

Rick cranked the Mud Skipper to its equivalent of Star Trek warp speed in an effort to outrace the impending blast.

Jamie coped by working the controls of his own invisible cockpit, his hands pulling back on an imaginary throttle.

"Twelve noon!" said Windy.

Lincoln looked back at the Target through her binoculars. One lone news-copter remained buzzing over the Target logo. What happened next played out in a slow-motion sequence in her mind. After a thud like major league fireworks, the roof logo blew upwards in a black cloud. A split second later a sea of flame flashed across the Target roof. The shock wave from the blast flipped the news-copter causing it to crash into the roof. White flames engulfed the craft. Meanwhile concentric rings of black dust went up and outwards, mirroring what used to be the Target emblem.

Barry's image still emanated from Lincoln's holoband. "Lincoln, I heard the boom. Tell me you made it clear of the blast zone."

"I'm looking down on rings of dark smoke billowing across the theme park and surrounding areas. But, yes, yes, we made it!" said Lincoln.

"The dark rings of smoke would be the dirty bomb's radioactive particles," said Barry. "That area will be no-man's land for decades."

"Barry, this is Windy. The Target roof is on fire, a burning yellow glob!"

Jamie had ceased piloting his imaginary plane to safety. "Yeah, and a helicopter is burning through the roof. It's melting like when you put airplane glue on a model plane and light it up. You know what I'm sayin'!"

Lincoln just looked at him.

"Sounds like they detonated a secondary incendiary bomb using white phosphorus. Goliath went for the all-out terrorist effect," said Barry.

"No doubt Goliath will achieve its goal of mass panic," said Rick. "Sales of Gammaway will surely sky-rocket just as Taj's memo forecast.

"Now I know why they called it Operation Fire Sale," said Jamie.

"Yeah, but guys, we did it!" said Windy. "We saved those people!"

Lincoln shuddered at the sight of liquid pools of white phosphorus fire on the ground where droves of dignitaries and reporters had been standing before the dive bomb drove them away. The molten mass of the helicopter plunged through the theme park roof. 'Hopefully the police took the bomb threat seriously and cleared employees out of the store,' she thought. Some of the cars appeared to be out of the radioactive zone. Some had not escaped, caught in their own traffic snarl.

Rick took the plane down low to escape radar detection. They headed north west back to the marina.

Barry came on the line. "Rick, you do realize that we have a problem."

Rick did not answer.

Lincoln flinched. 'Problem? What problem?' She searched her dad's face for a clue, but his expression remained steady. They had dodged police gunfire and narrowly missed being blown up.

"They'll be looking for you," said Barry.

'Of course!' thought Lincoln. 'The authorities could assume that their dive bomb warning had something to do with the dirty fire-bomb.' A wave of panic rolled over Lincoln.

Rick winked at Lincoln. "They'll be looking for a yellow plane."

Lincoln glanced out the window and blinked hard. "Hey, the Mud Skipper is gray now!"

Rick grinned. "I'd say that color-command on this plane was a worthwhile upgrade. You know, it's the same technology used on your dorm walls."

Windy and Jamie exchanged a hug of celebration, despite their harness restraints. Lincoln felt their relief.

"I had no idea that you were such a desperado, Mr. Rick," said Windy.

"Whoo-Wee!" hollered Jamie. "We've got it made in the shade!"

But Rick was no longer smiling, his eyes riveted on the instrument gauges. "Uh-oh," he said.

"Uh-oh?" said Jamie. "'Uh-oh' is the LAST thing you want to hear on a plane!"

"We're losing fuel. And fast!" said Rick. "We must have taken a couple of rounds in the gas tank."

"You've got to make it back," said Barry. "Otherwise, you'll be sitting ducks for the authorities."

"Agreed."

Lincoln's brain told her to have confidence in her dad's aviation skill. However, her body was tense as if it were stretched on a medieval rack. The saw-palmettos and sagebrush rushing below them soon gave way to a blur of roof tops.

"I'm going to gain some altitude in case we have to glide in," said Rick.

The plane climbed, expanding Lincoln's panoramic view. She pointed to her eleven o'clock. "I see our lake!"

The Lake of the Woods stretched out before them with the marina at the far end. Lincoln's hope enkindled, suddenly finding it peaceful to be flying high above their destination.

"That's it! We're out of fuel!" said Rick.

"I stand corrected," said Jamie. "That's definitely worse than 'Uh-oh'."

It dawned on Lincoln that her moment of tranquility in the wild blue yonder was the sound of the engine not working. The plane tilted into a silent dive, with just the eerie sound of rushing wind to accompany them.

"Hang on everyone!" shouted Rick. "Your seat cushions or your neighbor can be used as a strap-on float."

Lincoln white-knuckled her seat, willing the wounded duck of a plane to glide as close to the marina as possible. The lake appeared to rise up to meet them until the plane's pontoons smacked into the water. The impact rattled every bone in her body, including her teeth. Then the plane lifted for a couple of seconds, only to pound into the water again. Although the plane slowed, it still jerked off the surface of the lake again like a bucking bronco. Finally, the Mud Skipper plowed into the water a third time, frothing a flock of anhinga water birds. The craft spun sharply to the left, snapping off the tail.

"Everybody out! Now!" hollered Rick. The pontoon landing gear had snapped off and the plane began taking on water.

Lincoln looked through the front windshield and saw the dock, so close. Then she realized that they weren't just sinking — they were sinking fast. Terror hit her like a sledgehammer when her harness would not unbuckle. Water had risen to her chin already. "Dad! Help! My harness!"

Rick leaned over and Lincoln could feel tugging at her harness like a sawing motion. Lincoln tilted her head all the way back so that her nose could stay above the water line like an alligator's snout. In a few seconds she was completely submerged, and the tugging had stopped. In the murky darkness of the cabin, Lincoln couldn't see her dad. She reached out with her arms but he wasn't there. Where did everyone go? How could her father leave her there, trapped? The irony of drowning in 10 feet of water within a stone's throw of the dock flashed through her oxygen-starved brain. She held her breath, the escaping bubbles counting down the last seconds of her life. Suddenly she felt a strong hand clasp her shoulder, a hard tug on her harness, and she was free! That same strong hand grabbed her collar and pulled her through the cabin door and propelled her to the surface.

As soon as she burst through the surface of the lake, Lincoln gulped deeply for air. Rick popped up next to her, and his right hand surfaced with an eight inch bowie knife. "Sorry to leave you, Star," he said. "Had to grab ol' Betty here from my kit," he said, turning the knife back and forth. "Not the first time she's been there when I needed her!"

The plane's tail pitched out of the water slightly and the nose-heavy cabin tilted down, bobbed a moment, and disappeared. In her haste she had forgotten to grab her seat flotation device. As close as she was to shore, in her weakened state she'd never make it without help. She flailed wildly as she struggled to tread water. Then red ropes rained down around her. She grabbed one of the ropes and then was dragged through the water. Her dad's arms embraced her and his hands had a death grip on the rope for the both of them. As the rope hauled them to the dock, a carp the size of a Boston terrier bumped into her, nearly giving her a heart attack. The lake, like any in Florida, was no stranger to alligators.

When Lincoln reached the beach, she still clung to the rope, her eyes rolling around in her head. "She's shivering!" someone said. "Get her a blanket." A large towel was draped around her. Lincoln looked around and saw the "Kayak Rescue Team" logos on the jackets of the men and women around her. Lucky for Lincoln the team had been practicing their skills near the marina when the Mud Skipper crash landed. However, Lincoln didn't feel so lucky. She coughed so hard she labored to breathe. Windy sat Lincoln upright and said, "We made it! What an adventure!"

Lincoln glanced over at Jamie kissing the ground, thinking she would have done the same if she had the strength. "Rodriguez! Stop that!" said Rick. "Help me get Lincoln to the van."

They helped Lincoln into the Roach Coach parked behind the marina and headed back in silence to the Third Dock hideout. Jamie passed the time inventing a new form of post-traumatic stress syndrome while Windy comforted him.

Lincoln's breathing gradually became less labored, despite her waterlogged oxy-boost not working. She turned toward her dad, and his tight face told her that he was really worried about her. "Dad, I'll be fine."

"Once we get back to The Third Dock, I'm getting you in to see Dr. Walker," Rick replied.

Twenty minutes later, Rick pulled the Roach Coach behind the restaurant as usual and let everyone in the back door. As they were about to enter the secret freezer-elevator, Lincoln stopped short. "My meds! I left them in the van." She grabbed the keys from Rick and headed back.

"Be careful, Star," Rick called after her.

"Thanks, Dad. I think I can manage," Lincoln replied as she reached the door.

Once outside, Lincoln went around to the side of the van, opened the door, and searched under her seat. Her hand quickly found the familiar bag and pulled it out. "Gotcha," she said. Then everything went black.

CHAPTER 31

Demolition

The first thing Lincoln noticed was the steady beep, beep, beeping of a heart monitor machine. It was a familiar enough sound from the other times when she had wound up in the hospital because of her cystic fibrosis. She lay at an incline in a bed, with a plastic oxygen nose piece taped to her face. Her lungs took in the precious gas, while she coughed intermittently.

Cracking her eyes open, she observed that she was in a big room, much bigger than Dr. Walker's exam room. A TV hung on the wall opposite her. The room lacked the usual obnoxious surveillance cameras that monitored the examination rooms she'd been in. She turned her head one way, then slowly back the other way. She was the only patient.

Lincoln closed her eyes. Her limbs felt like lead. She couldn't even move them. 'Geez, I must be super sedated.' She imagined herself on a giant planet with immense gravity holding her down.

Trying to clear her head, she stared at the ceiling while racking her brains. The last thing she remembered was reaching for her meds under the seat of the Roach Coach. She must have passed out. Her brain fought to shake off the cobwebs of drowsiness as she untangled her thoughts. 'How long have I been here? Where is everyone? Geez, It's so quiet here.'

The door creaked open. A blurry figure appeared at her bedside, then sat down on a stool next to her. He did not speak a word. Instead he began to fiddle with the instruments next to her that were monitoring her vitals. He wore the standard white medical garb, including a medical mask and surgeon's cap.

Lincoln heard the beeping rate of her heart monitor slightly increase. "Where's my dad – Detective Jade?" she heard her voice say.

"Oh, I'm sure he's on his way," said the blurry man in a tenor timber.

Through the fuzziness she said, "What kind of meds did you give me?"

Ignoring her questions, he leaned over, his eyes looking through her but not really at her. "I am a huge fan of 'The Mender's Paradox. You might even say that I am a student of your podcast."

Lincoln did a double take inside her head. "Why isn't Dr. Walker talking to me about my medical condition?"

"Dr. Walker?" he said. "Hmmm…He's not on call."

Lincoln squinted as she examined the laughing eyes on the masked face before her. He? Nobody would mistake the striking Prinity Walker as a he! Then her new podcast fan leaned in closer to her. "Tell me, Miss Jade, does Barry Blue Hawkins really have the power to heal?"

Even through her brain fog, she instinctively answered to protect Barry. "No. It's not true. It's just a way to ramp up interest in the show," she said as calmly as she could.

Beep! Beep! Beep! The sounds of the machine monitoring her vitals accelerated to an alarming rate.

Her interrogator sucked in air that indented his mask inwards. "Hmmmm…it is true!" he said. "My employers thank you."

"Wait, what?" said Lincoln. "I told you the truth — Barry is a fraud!"

"This lie detector says otherwise, Ms. Jade," the stranger grinned, tapping on the machine next to Lincoln. "We appreciate you confirming our suspicions about the man's... talents." A short wheezy giggle like an asthmatic cobra escaped from behind the mask.

Adrenaline coursed through Lincoln's veins. She snapped out of her sedated haze. Her eyes could now focus. The imposter's name tag said 'Dr. Killem'. The imposter pulled down his medical mask to reveal a face that was a whiter shade of pale.

"Leatherhead!" she said. "You murdered my mother!" She lunged at him, only to realize that her arms and legs were bound with straps, tying her body to the bed. She struggled like a trapped animal to free herself.

"Did I? The mother... in the orange Prius... outside the hospital, with the forklift... Oh my, it so sounds like a game of Clue, doesn't it?" He stroked his chin in thought. "Hmmm... Yes, yes she was job number fifty-eight. Orange Crush."

The image of her mom's orange Prius pancaked by a forklift enraged Lincoln. Her fear flipped to fury. If her eyes were lasers she would have drilled through Leatherhead's eyeballs and blasted his brains out through the back of his head. "She had a name. My mom was Rachel Jade, you creep. My dad will find me and when he does —"

Leatherhead held up his hand, cutting Lincoln off. "I'm counting on it, Miss Jade." He bent over her, his vile face inches from hers. "Absolutely counting on it." Then he stood and turned the TV on. "Enjoy the show," he said, laughing in a nauseating nasal tone. He left the room, leaving the door wide open.

Lincoln couldn't believe it. She had faced Leatherhead and was still alive. "Help! I'm in here! Hey, is anybody out there?"

No answer. It was as if the building was deserted. She willed herself to gather her wits. Tied to the bed, she never before felt so helpless. Surely someone was on the way. The TV directly across from her on the wall drew her attention. The morning news blared.

Mike Lions here, Central Florida, crashing your demolition party. Millions of people around the local area are celebrating the impending demolition this morning of the iconic Goliath building, also known as the I-4 Eyesore...

Behind the talking head was a towering structure that looked like a giant U.S. mailbox, the kind that used to populate the streets. A half dome capped the square-based building. The dome had an indentation like a mail slot waiting for a gigantic letter to be deposited. Blue tinted glass covered the outside, reflecting the sun as it moved across the sky. Something about this building set off an alarm bell with Lincoln. Her cartoon self was running around in her brain frantically looking through her memory file cabinets trying to figure it out.

The newsman on the TV babbled on.

Locals endured its stop-and-start construction over three recessions and three decades, its unfinished frame and unloveable shape looming over the tens of thousands of daily commuters on Interstate 4. Finally, Goliath Industries bought the behemoth building and transformed it into its headquarters.

"Of course!" said Lincoln out loud. "That Goliath building is the same building where Taj worked. So why am I even watching this?"

The talking head grew louder. *And I will be hangin' in there with you through the final countdown which will start in less than thirty minutes.*

Lincoln had a bad vibe about this TV news show. Worse than when Leatherhead was in the room. She thought she heard voices through the doorway. "I'm in here! Help!"

The voices became louder. It was Jamie and Windy calling. "Lincoln, keep calling!"

Lincoln hollered back. The voices grew fainter for a moment. Lincoln kept yelling even louder. "I'm here!"

Then she heard her friends' voices loud and clear. She called out again. "Here! In here, you guys!"

Jamie and Windy tore through the door looking like they had seen the end of the world. "Lincoln!" they both shouted. They ran to her. "Get up! We've got to get out of here! Now!" Windy hugged her and discovered the tie down straps beneath the bed sheets.

Rick appeared inside the doorway entrance with his gun drawn. "Star!" he said and let his gun hand relax to a downward position.

Two ghostly hands reached in through the darkened doorway. They grasped Rick's gun hand and banged it onto the door frame, causing Rick to drop his gun. In a flash Leatherhead had Rick in a half-Nelson choke hold from behind. Leatherhead had the physical advantage, being almost ten years younger than the sixty-one year old Rick. But Rick was skilled in the art of judo. Using his opponent's weight against him, Rick heaved back and then forward, tossing Leatherhead over his shoulder. Leatherhead landed on his back on the hard linoleum floor. In one fluid motion, Rick's momentum carried him forward, placing him squarely onto Leatherhead's chest. Now sitting on his chest, Rick pinned Leatherhead's arms down with his knees. Rick's fist pounded Leatherhead's face like a jackhammer, unleashing thirty years of rage in just a few seconds.

From across the room Lincoln was shocked at the savage beating. She had never seen her dad engaged in any violence at all. At the same time, she wanted Leatherhead to pay for the murder of her mom.

Rick's dominance was short-lived. Leatherhead suddenly bucked like a bronco, knocking Rick off balance. He got one arm free and with a grunt he shot the heel of his right hand into Rick's face. The punch caught Rick in the chin, knocking him backwards.

Leatherhead jumped up and dashed out the open door. Rick sat stunned for a second, then got unsteadily to his feet. He staggered towards the doorway to go after Leatherhead. From out of the darkness came two feet that hit him square in the breadbasket. The kick propelled Rick backwards and airborne, and he landed flat on his back. Leatherhead released his grip on the door frame and lightly landed just inside, looking pleased that his retreat ruse had lured Rick into his ambush.

Rick lay curled up on the floor. Lincoln flew to her dad's side. "Dad, Dad, are you all right?"

He gave her a shaky thumbs up and managed to grunt, "Just... got the.... wind knocked out of me, that's all."

Leatherhead placed his hand on the door knob. "Enjoy your stay, My Four Eyesores. I, however, am off to my homecoming tonight. Duty calls!" He slammed the door shut with a loud bang.

Jamie rushed to the door saying "No! No! No!" He tugged on the doorknob and then slammed his body against the unforgiving door. "We've got to get out of here now!" He frantically kicked the door over and over saying "Now!" every time he kicked it.

"Jamie, we're alive!" said Lincoln. "He could have killed us all!"

Jamie spun around towards Lincoln who was huddled with Rick on the floor.

"Wake up L.J.! He *is* going to kill us!"

"But he's gone," said Lincoln.

"Hello!" said Jamie, who was now screaming with all of his might. "We're trapped here on the twentieth floor of the Goliath building! You know, the one that is about to be blown up!"

A seismic shock surged through her body. She searched her dad's eyes.

"It's true," said Rick. He propped himself against the wall below the TV. "What's-his-head suckered us in here to save you."

Lincoln's eyes drifted upwards towards the TV set that Leatherhead had left on. She grappled with her new reality. She wasn't in a hospital. They were about to be entombed in the Goliath building.

The news reporter blathered on about the impending demolition, like a master of ceremonies to their imminent demise.

And here's another fun fact about our big event. It will take only one-hundred pounds of strategically placed explosives to bring down this hundred-million ton colossus. Stayed tuned, Central Florida. With a smug twinkle in his eye, the reporter delivered his carefully crafted sound bite. *We'll soon be starting our Countdown to Trashmound for the I-4 Eyesore.*

Lincoln called 911 on her holoband. No signal. She tried again and again. "Jamie! I can't get through to 911!"

"I know!" he said. "That freakazoid must be jamming us! I tried calling before we entered the building. The whole area is a dead zone. And now there's no way out!" Jamie grabbed the metal chair that Leatherhead had been using. He did a complete 360 degree spin like a deranged discus thrower. He flung the chair as hard as he could against the window wall. The chair harmlessly bounced off the transparent sheet with a resounding 'thunk.'

Lincoln almost laughed. She always thought that she would die of her cystic fibrosis. Instead she was about to be murdered by a building.

She became aware that the overhead lights had been flickering off and on. Windy was working the wall light switch in the corner on the other side of the room. With her face pressed up against the glass wall, one hand worked the light switch. She was completely focused on her task, oblivious to the chaos around her.

Lincoln asked, "Windy, what in the world are you doing?"

Windy kept working the lights. Three long light flicks, followed by three shorter light flicks, then three more long flicks. "One of us got her boating badge from Girl Scouts."

Lincoln got up off the floor and hurried over to her. "Windy, you're using Morse code. Brilliant!"

Windy continued to flash the S.O.S. "I saw somebody down there," she said. "Then he ran away. I don't know if he saw my signal."

Lincoln pressed her face against the glass and looked out at the low canopy of heavy clouds. Windy's flashing signal had turned their high-rise window room into a beacon of hope in the dark morning. Below them sprawled a vast vacant parking lot with a few trucks and a crane.

Jamie joined them next to Lincoln with his eyeballs on the window. "I see what you're doing womens. Somebody will fo'-sure see us and stop this thing. We're on TV!"

Lincoln glanced over her shoulder at the TV on the opposite wall behind them. She didn't have the heart to tell Jamie that the live feed on the news was showing the front of the building. They, however, were on the back side, where no one could see them.

"That man!" said Windy. "Down there," she pointed. "Getting into the crane!"

Jamie leaped. "The crane is coming toward us!"

The crane arm rose outside their window until it loomed above like a steely dinosaur. The three amigos stood side-by-side, pasted to the window wall while they watched the crane.

"I think he *did* see us. But… what the heck kind of rescue is this?" said Jamie.

Lincoln didn't respond. She looked back at the TV on the wall. A countdown clock in the corner of the live building picture ticked away the seconds. 'Eleven minutes 'til demolition. Whatever this crane guy is doing, he'd better do it fast.'

The Jurassic crane arm swung directly away from their window. After finally stopping, the crane arm immediately started to swing back straight towards them, moving faster and faster.

Windy kept up the flashing S.O.S. signal with the concentration of a surgeon in the middle of brain surgery. "Guys! I see something in the sky straight out in front of us. Maybe it's a drone!"

"It's getting bigger!" said Jamie.

"It's coming right at us and fast!" said Windy.

"It's a really big bowling ball!" said Jamie.

"And we're the pins! Run!" said Lincoln.

The window wall exploded inwards sounding like the crash of shattering chandeliers. The tinkling of residual glass breaking filled the room, providing a soundtrack to accompany the mini-quake caused when the wrecking ball clipped the floor structure. Suddenly everything tilted, and Lincoln started sliding into a large crack in the floor. Her flailing arm caught a protruding girder, stopping her descent but leaving her legs dangling into the room below.

Rick grabbed her by the armpit. "I got you, Star!" said Rick.

She caught a glimpse of fear in her dad's face, something she hadn't seen before.

"Hang on!" he shouted into her face.

Though half shell-shocked, Lincoln kept her wits about her. "Dad, you always say 'hang on' at the most obvious times."

Rick heaved her to safety. "I appreciate the levity," he said. "Lets me know you're okay."

In the middle of the room was a black ball about five feet in diameter, attached to a chain that went out of the gaping hole where the window wall used to be. The humid air blew into the room, punctuating their precarious predicament. Their only exit was twenty stories straight down.

The force of the impact had flipped Lincoln's 'hospital' bed, pinning Jamie and Windy up against the far wall. The mattress had protected them from serious harm.

"We're okay! We're okay!" said Windy.

"Okay? Okay?" said Jamie. "Leather Butt just tried to kill us with a wrecking ball!"

Lincoln calculated their situation, eyebrows a-twitching. "No! To Leatherhead's twisted brain, we're already dead when this building blows. This really was a rescue. Somebody else is giving us a way out."

"Like who? King Kong?" cried Jamie.

The chain on the wrecking ball became taunt, dragging the ball along the floor towards the edge of the building. It scraped along until it went over the edge and was gone.

"Now what?" asked Windy. The TV countdown clock showed that there were less than five minutes left.

"Great!" said Jamie, throwing his hands up. "So far this 'rescue' nearly killed all of us. And we still don't know how we're getting out of here!"

As if on cue the end of the crane boom lowered into view and pushed into the room like an alien probe invading their broken refuge. Lincoln and her dad scrambled out of the way.

When it hit the back wall of the room it stopped. They stared at the crane arm.

Lincoln noticed the lattice work frame of the crane arm. "This is our only chance!" she said. "Get on!"

"Agreed" said Rick and in one swift motion he hoisted Lincoln onto the crane boom.

Windy hopped on so fast that her foot kicked Lincoln in the face.

"Now you," said Rick pointing to Jamie.

"Are you guys pranking me?" said Jamie.

"Think of it as a long extension ladder Hon," said Windy.

"More like an extinction ladder," said Jamie. "No way!"

"Man up, Rodriguez," said Rick. "Get on now."

With the face of a man about to walk the plank, Jamie slung his long body onto the crane ahead of Windy. He lent an arm to Rick who clambered onto the boom.

Lincoln spotted her holo-recorder caught in the mattress box spring. Geez, she had to retrieve her recorder, right? She had not come this far to lose the graphic documentation for her story. Amid instant protests from everyone she dropped to the floor and rolled towards the crumpled mattress. She pried the precious recorder from the steel mesh.

As Lincoln turned around to get back on, the boom gave a jolt. It started backing out of the room. 'Red alert! Red alert!' sounded in Lincoln's brain. "Don't leave me!" she said as she followed the retreating crane arm.

As the crane arm crossed the threshold of the window hole, the tip of the boom had lowered to floor level.

Lincoln chased the retreating boom to the edge of the window hole. She stood at the precipice dominated by the grey expanse of clouds pregnant with rain. A bolt of lightning danced in the distance. The cries of her dad and friends seemed far away.

"Get on, Lincoln! Now! Now! Now!"

Her lungs labored like twin Hoover vacuum cleaners. Yet she could not seem to suck in enough air. 'I can't… it's too much.'

"Dive, Lincoln! Dive!" screamed Jamie.

Arms outstretched, Lincoln let herself fall forward just as the tip of the boom cleared the building. She imagined herself waking up in a place where she didn't have to think about breathing.

With a smack she landed face down on the tip of the crane. Jamie grabbed her by the arms. "I've got ya' L.J.!"

Her legs dangled off the tip of the boom. Jamie yanked her towards himself so hard that their foreheads conked together like a couple of coconuts.

Lincoln was nearly upside down on the boom. She hooked the tops of her shoe toes over the tip of the boom to keep herself from sliding into Jamie's face. Blood rushed to her head. Her head felt like a bowling ball. 'Don't pass out…breathe… breathe…,' she chanted to herself.

The crane began to move, swinging the boom away from the building. The parking lot rotated far, far below.

"Hang on!" said Rick.

Lincoln's hands already ached from her vice-like grip on the boom grating. "Another timely tip from dad."

"This would be a nightmare of a theme park ride!" said Windy.

"Yeah, The Goliath Tower of Terror meets the Boom of Doom!" Jamie said through chattering teeth.

The crane rotated ninety degrees putting the boom parallel with the Goliath building, no more than forty feet away. Lincoln wondered who was operating the crane. 'Was it really such a great idea to jump out of the Goliath building onto this boom?'

The answer to Lincoln's question was swift and undeniable.

The initial explosion burst from the base of the Goliath building. It sounded like a thunder-clap that was way too close. A cascade of detonations rippled upwards through the building. Floor by floor the building collapsed bringing the building straight down.

The shock waves emanating upwards from the multiple blasts pulsed into the boom, rattling Lincoln's bones and slamming her forehead against the boom grating. The boom rocked up and down as if it were a live tentacle trying to shake them off.

Lincoln screamed as the mail-box shaped top of the building fell toward them by priority mail. As she braced herself for certain death, she drew in what must surely be her last breath. She peeped out of one eye as the I-4 eye-sore went right past them! With a degree of relief she exhaled through pursed lips. The architectural menace disappeared into the dust devil below.

With that, the explosions ceased and the rumbling of the crumbling debris subsided. The boom that they were still perched on stopped rocking. The Goliath building was no more.

Jamie broke the stillness. "We're alive!" he said. "We're still here!"

Lincoln's head was smashed up against Jamie's. "Hey whiz kid, quit using my ear for a megaphone!"

"What now?" said Windy. "I don't feel very rescued!"

"Star, are you all right?" asked Rick who was furthest away from Lincoln on the boom.

Lincoln did not answer. She was not all right. She began to lose her toe grip at the tip of the boom and gravity pulled her in a slow slide into Jamie's chest. Jamie clamped down extra hard on Lincoln's shoulders, pressing her into the hard metal boom.

"Star! Daughter!" shouted Rick with a trace of panic in his voice.

Without warning, the crane rumbled to life again, this time moving downward. "Hang on!" counseled Rick with characteristic sagacity.

Through the dust cloud, Lincoln saw a neat shiny mound that looked like a gravel pyramid where the Goliath building had once stood. She shuddered at what would have indeed been their tomb had they not escaped the building.

The crane boom stopped moving when they were suspended a little over the ground. Rick and Jamie dropped down and helped the women off.

Lincoln lay flat on her back as if painted onto the parking lot blacktop. Jamie kissed the ground for the second time in as many days. Windy huddled over Lincoln, holding her hand.

"Lincoln, we did it!" said Windy. "We're safe now."

"Uh…then why is Mr. Rick about to bash someone's skull in?" said Jamie, who froze and stopped the dramatics with Mother Earth.

Rick stood with his back to them, wielding a metal bar like a baseball bat. He was peering through the dusty mist at the crane cab about fifty yards away.

The crane operator cab jostled with movement inside. The door flung open and a dark figure stumbled out. The thing had a furry face and large shiny eyes. The hulking creature ambled straight toward them. Lincoln lifted her head to see but was too tired to panic.

Jamie, however, presented enough panic for everyone. "It's a Sasquatch! Get 'im! Get 'im, Mr. Rick!"

The furry man-beast moved faster and faster, panting and grunting, becoming louder the closer it came. Rick dropped his makeshift weapon with a clunk and put his hands on his hips. He shook his head. "Son of a gun," he said to the big man. "You are full of surprises!"

CHAPTER 32

Back from the Dead

"Professor Erlenmeyer!" exclaimed Windy. "But how?"

"Gaaaah!" said Jamie. "Even worse than a sasquatch — it's a ghost!"

Professor Erlenmeyer made it to them and stood panting with his hands on his knees. "Is everyone all right?" he asked. His face was mostly concealed by a very bushy beard and his Clark Kent glasses. He still wore a tie as if this completed a re-fined look.

"Wait just a minute!" said Jamie. "We saw Professor Erlenmeyer die in his car on fire!"

"Negative Rodriguez!" said Rick. "You saw a John Doe corpse from the morgue burn up in Erlenmeyer's car. We staged the whole thing."

"Rumors of my death have been greatly exaggerated," said Professor Erlenmeyer. He paused a beat. "Sorry, I just had to say that."

Lincoln's baffled brain raced back to that terrible night. They didn't actually see the professor get into his car. They just heard his car door slam around the corner and then the vehicle ignited. The memory of greasy burnt flesh sickened her already jostled stomach.

Erlenmeyer gushed forth with his traumatic tale. "Rick saved my foolish life. I've been secretly living like a refugee in Mr. Steve's private office in the Third Dock bunker with you guys."

Lincoln reviewed her memories, recalling the shadow that passed under Mr. Steve's office door. Her dad hid Professor

Erlenmeyer right under their noses! Sitting up on the ground she said, "Dad, why didn't you tell us that he was safe and alive? I mean, we grieved for him."

"Sorry Star, but Leatherhead would have sniffed out the truth if anyone knew. It was for everyone's protection. And I never said Erlenmeyer was dead."

Professor Erlenmeyer got down on one knee to address Lincoln. "It was my own fault. I was a chump." He wrung his hands. "I thought I was a patriot working for Homeland to procure that radium. Instead I played right into the Paluski brothers' plot." His voice volume dropped to a few decibels. "I became a loose end. Leatherhead let me know that. He called me from my own home, threatened to do terrible things to my family if I told anyone what I had done. I couldn't go to the police. So I called the only person I could trust — your dad."

Lincoln slapped her thigh. "So that's why you asked me for his phone number. Geez! That was actually Leatherhead who called you during our last meeting?"

"When the professor called me and told me what had happened, I knew Leatherhead wasn't one to trust people to keep secrets — not when they're alive, anyway," said Rick. "So to protect the professor and his family, I had to make him dead as soon as possible."

The group fell silent for a brief moment as they took it all in. Lincoln gave him a long hug around the neck. "We are SO glad to see you, professor!"

"Agreed," confirmed Rick.

Jamie grabbed the good professor by the shoulders. "Man, if your goal was to blow my mind then mission accomplished! But what's the deal with you and the crane?"

Still panting from all of the action, Professor Erlenmeyer slowly stood and explained. "I overheard the phone call from my hiding place in the bunker, when Leatherhead called after the kidnapping. You dad and friends knew it was a trap, but they had to try to save you anyway. And I couldn't just stay here and do nothing, so I followed them. When I finally arrived here, I felt so helpless. I knew that you guys were somewhere in the building trying to rescue Lincoln. I didn't follow you inside because I didn't want to be trapped or ambushed by your Letterhead."

"Leatherhead," corrected Rick.

The professor fidgeted from one foot to the other, his post traumatic stress welling up from the experience. "I knew the building was about to be blown to bits! I couldn't think. I didn't know what to do...but then I saw the S.O.S flashing from the office window."

"Yay Windy!" interjected Jamie.

Erlenmeyer continued, now bubbling over with excitement. "I made a bee-line for the tower-crane that was parked back here." He motioned with his hand towards some heavy trucks. "I hauled my butt into the crane and lined it up with your position in the building. I used to operate such a machine working my way through University. It's actually pretty easy, like playing a video game."

"Except for the part where you nearly killed us!" said an exasperated Jamie.

Professor Erlenmeyer shrugged. "It works better in the movies."

Windy hugged Professor Erlenmeyer, filthy and hairy as he was.

Rick stepped in. "I hate to break up this touching reunion but we have to get out of sight. Leatherhead thinks that we're all dead."

"Great! Let's keep it that way," said Windy.

They squished into the Roach Coach and scurried back to the Third Dock Fine Family Eating Establishment.

Windy waved good-bye at the Goliath ruins disappearing in the distance. "So how were we able to get into a building that was cleared for imminent demolition? And with the power still on?"

Rick answered, "Leatherhead told us that Lincoln was on the twentieth floor. He specifically instructed us to go around back. There were no cops there. It was a set up to make sure we got in to meet our doom."

Jamie kicked in. "The Paluski brothers kept the power on for the TV torture countdown to demolition. Owner's prerogative, I suppose."

"Good point, Rodriguez," said Rick. "They staged the whole thing!"

As soon as Lincoln entered the secret underground bunker of the Third Dock she collapsed onto her cot.

She awoke to a heated discussion. Jamie, Windy, and Professor Erlenmeyer sat at the long table, while Rick stood, too agitated to join them. "I'm telling you," said Rick, "the Paluski brothers aren't finished. The dirty bomb destruction of the new Target Theme store was just a warm up act for their grand finale!"

"How so?" asked Professor Erlenmeyer.

Windy jumped all over that question as if the answer was completely obvious. "Massive dirty bomb attacks! Check it out — the Paluski brothers own Goliath. They have the only treatment for radiation poisoning…that Gammaway stuff…"

"Agreed," cut in Rick. "And if they incite world wide panic using Leatherhead to strike at key targets, then they stand to make huge amounts of money with their Gammaway."

"So it's like they will be holding the world hostage for the antidote ransom," said Professor Erlenmeyer, straightening his dirty tie.

Lincoln shivered in her cot, cocooning herself in her blanket. A cough welled up inside her. She suppressed it so as not to interrupt the conversation at the big table.

Jamie kicked his feet up onto the table and leaned back in his chair. "Well, the lead lining in this mess is that Leather-butt thinks we're all dead. Staying down here... we're safe."

Windy shot Jamie a look like a lawn dart. "Brilliant. So, what's your plan, Hon? Live underground like a wild potato? That may be on-brand for you, but somebody needs to stop Leatherhead and expose the Paluski brothers!"

"Easy babe, easy! What the heck are we supposed to do?" asked Jamie.

Rick stood with his hands on the back of his chair. He peered into some unseen light. "After that psycho knocked me senseless, he said something. That's the first time I ever heard him speak in thirty years. It must have been important."

"Yeah, yeah," said Jamie. "Bad guys always have to say something clever before leaving you to die. He said something about going to his shindig."

"Actually," said Windy, "he said that he was going to his homecoming tonight."

"Homecoming? Ah... Where is this leather person originally from?" asked Professor Erlenmeyer as he stroked his bushy beard.

"His early years were in a Bavarian orphanage," said Rick.

"Germany?" said Jamie. "That doesn't make any sense."

Rick heaved a sigh and repeated the line. "'I am off to my homecoming tonight. Duty calls.' What does it mean?"

At that point Lincoln sprang up in her cot like a jack-in-the-box. "I'll tell you what it means…but you're not gonna like it. Leatherhead is going to bomb Disney World tonight!"

CHAPTER 33

Sinkhole City

The discussion at the teak table ceased. Silence filled the subterranean hideout. All eyes locked on Lincoln. Until now, they had not realized that she had awakened.

"Say what?" asked Jamie.

Lincoln started to reply but interrupted herself with a coughing fit. Windy sped to her side with a glass of water. "You've been asleep all afternoon.

Rick took a knee next to Lincoln's cot. "Welcome back, Star. That coughing didn't sound like a good thing."

"I'm okay, Dad. Don't worry." Lincoln's lungs burned as though she had swallowed a lit cigarette.

"Hey L.J.!" said Jamie. "How does Leatherhead's homecoming riff make you pop up from the land of the dead and say 'Disney go boom'?"

"The Mad King of Prussia," she sputtered between gulps of water. Her brain had zipped from point A to point D. Noticing the blank stares pointed at her, she started over.

"There was this guy, King Ludwig II of Prussia, back in the nineteenth century. He put all his wealth towards building three beautiful castles. He grew so obsessed with them that he became known as the Mad King and it cost him his throne. Fun fact…Walt Disney modeled Cinderella's Castle on the Mad King's castle Neuschwanstein. It had a white exterior with blue spires. Sound familiar?"

"Yeah, super fun fact," said Windy. "But what points you to Disney World and not Germany?"

Lincoln smiled. "Two words: 'Duty calls.' He works for the Paluskis, and so far all his 'duties' have been committed stateside. Also, an attack at Disney World would be much huger than an isolated castle in Europe."

Professor Erlenmeyer looked over the top of his glasses. "Putting aside Ms. Jade's use of 'huger,' I agree with her theory that The Leatherman is *figuratively* going to his Bavarian Homecoming at Disney World."

Lincoln nodded.

"And given that his last 'duty' was a dirty bomb at mega-Target, that means that Leatherhead is going to place a large radioactive fire-bomb somewhere on the top of Cinderella's Castle," said Rick. "A million people will get radiation poisoning!"

"I betcha that the bomb goes off during the fireworks display they do every night at nine," said Jamie. "That way people would think it's part of the show and not evacuate immediately."

Windy popped a fist into her hand. "I can see how Cinderella's Castle would be the perfect target. Those tourists are from all over the globe. This attack would be an international incident and cause world-wide panic. The government has already approved distribution of Gammaway. Sales would sky-rocket, making the Paluski brothers super rich."

"Super richer," Lincoln mumbled. "It's never enough for people like that." She pulled her blanket over her shoulders. "Geez, they're using Taj's discovery, something so good, to do so much bad."

Rick stood up. "They had Leatherhead poison the Chetola residents with radium so that they could try out Gammaway like a controlled experiment, using the victims as guinea pigs *and* get immediate FDA approval for their drug."

"Then they had him attack the Target Theme Park with a dirty bomb that poisoned the VIPs there for the grand opening."

Windy put it together. "That was the practice run. This attack will be much bigger and will have everyone demanding Gammaway. Tonight is the pay-off."

Lincoln laid back down on the cot. "So much suffering for the greed of a few."

Windy, monitoring her news feed on her holopad, sprung up from Lincoln's cot. "Hey guys, we made the news!" She dashed over to the head of the table, turned on the virtual screen, and flipped to the news feed. Voice-over accompanied B-roll footage of their plane in the distance dive-bombing the mega-Target entry.

'... and hospitals have been flooded with radiation poisoning victims, but reports are optimistic for their survival thanks to the availability of the new Gammaway drug treatment. Police are still searching for the pilot of the yellow float plane that appeared to participate in the attack. Authorities say the toll could have been worse had there not been a bomb threat called in that prompted the evacuation of employees and had the crowd not been fleeing the building to avoid the attacking plane.'

A photo replaced the footage on the TV, showing a younger version of a face that Lincoln had recently seen. A face that made her cringe and cover her eyes. Below the photo was the name Robert Kuby. The newscaster's audio filled the room.

Breaking news! Robert Kuby is wanted in connection with the bombing of the Target Theme Park Mega Store in Orlando, Florida, which is being called the worst terrorist attack ever on American soil. An aerial video showed a black oval spot where the structure once stood. This person is armed and considered extremely dangerous. For more on the story we go to Mike Lions.

The familiar reporter with his microphone appeared on the TV screen standing next to an older man in an expensive suit.

The talking head of the reporter boomed. *Today I'm with Jackson Paluski, CEO of Goliath Industries. Mr. Paluski has just divulged to the authorities that one of their employees is responsible for the Target bombing. He – .*

Paluski grabbed the microphone from the reporter and pushed his bulbous head into the forefront. *We discovered that a large amount of our radioactive isotope stock was missing. This is very dangerous material used for our research. Video surveillance revealed that it was one of our employees, Robert Kuby, who broke in and took the supply. He is a very troubled man. He has military training and is an expert marksman. I encourage authorities to use all means at their disposal to bring this man to justice, even the use of deadly force, to prevent further innocent loss of life.* Paluski looked truly distraught, his red face quivering as he wiped his eyes with a handkerchief.

"Wowzer!" said Jamie. "Leatherhead has been fired."

"Before the final event?" asked Windy. "Why would the Paluskis throw Leatherhead under the bus now?"

"Because," said Rick, "Leatherhead has become a liability for them." Rick glanced around the room. "This turn of events gives us a clue."

"Aha!" exclaimed Professor Erlenmeyer, pointing his index finger upwards. "The bomb has already been placed on top of the Cinderella Castle roof. Otherwise, the Leather Man's employer would not have turned him in."

"Well, geez," moaned Lincoln. "So much for figuring out where Leatherhead is gonna be."

"Oh, he'll be at Disney World, all right," replied Rick. "I know this guy. Tonight really is a special night for him, his masterpiece, the culmination of his career. He's gonna want to be right there when it happens."

"Why would he be anywhere near a dirty bomb?" asked Windy. "He doesn't strike me as someone looking to end his life now."

"I'll bet my Second Amendment rights he'll be in the fallout bunker," said Rick. When he noticed the blank stares around him, he added, "It's a Disney secret. They have a nuclear fallout shelter under Cinderella's castle, with a mini-monorail escape system leading directly to Jacksonville 100 miles away, a decent emergence point far from any major targets."

"And how would you know this?" asked Jamie.

"I was Homeland, dammit," said Rick. "I had clearance."

"Hey guys," Lincoln interjected. "Shouldn't we get Barry in on this?"

Silence engulfed the room.

"What?" asked Lincoln. "What is it?"

"Star," said Rick gently, "Barry has gone radio silent since the Goliath building came down. We haven't heard from him all day."

Lincoln buried her head in her hands. "It's all my fault!"

"Take it easy, Linc," cooed Windy. "We don't know what, if anything, has happened to the man."

"I have to tell you guys something." Lincoln lifted her head. "When Leatherhead kidnapped me to make a trap for you guys, he also interrogated me. He had me strapped to a hospital bed and hooked up to some kind of lie detector. He knows. *He knows* that Barry's healing power is for real."

"That's no longer relevant, at least to Leatherhead," said Rick. "He got fired, remember? He wasn't after Barry for his healing abilities. He simply had an assignment, and now all assignments are off."

"But what if Leatherhead went after Barry before he got fired? What if he went straight from the Goliath building to Barry's house!"

"Man, he's a goner," said Jamie.

"Hon!" said Windy.

"Barry has known for a long time that this day would come," said Rick. "I'm sure he had a plan to deal with Leatherhead."

"But Dad-"

Rick held up his hands. "I know, I know, Star…but there's nothing we can do now, unless you can travel back in time. Right now we have to deal with the immediate threat. I'm going to Disney World right now. I'm going to finally get this guy, no matter what."

Lincoln got up off her cot awkwardly like a gumby girl. "I'm ready."

"Hold on, Star," said Rick. "I have a call in for Dr. Walker to meet you at the hospital. I know you're in a downward spiral with all you've been through."

In a downward spiral? Her dad didn't know how bad off she really was. Her downward spiral already deposited her in a deep dark hole. Still she persisted. "Dad, you need all the eyes you can muster to look for that bomb. And for Leatherhead, if he pops his head out of his hole. Handing out 20-year-old photos of Barry Kuby to Disney security is a waste of time. *We're* the only ones who have seen him recently, how he looks today. You need us, Dad." She paused. "I need this. I need to do it for Barry. And for myself."

To Lincoln's surprise, Rick said, "Agreed. But after our little trip to Disney you are going straight to the hospital."

"Agreed," said Lincoln.

"Right on, Lincoln! After Chetola and mega-Target, I want to stop a disaster for a change, instead of investigating it afterwards. Not to mention how badly I want to reveal the Paluski brothers for the environmental terrorists that they are!"

Windy lasered her gaze at Jamie.

"Whoa, hey, of course I'm going, babe," said Jamie. "Who's going to look after you and protect you from danger? Don't answer that. I'll bring my camera and do a live episode right there at the castle for the Mender's Paradox. Might come in handy for clearing our names if the cops ever find out who was in the yellow float plane."

"Professor," said Rick, "You can return to your family."

"But isn't the Leather-headed one still out there?" said Professor Erlenmeyer, tugging at his overgrown beard.

"That psycho-killer has no reason to come after you, now that he's been betrayed," said Rick.

Rick walked over to the virtual TV and kicked the wall below. A drawer popped out, from which he retrieved a thin block of wood. Giving the object a cracking motion, a gun barrel flipped switchblade style from the stock, revealing a miniature rifle. "It's already 7:00. We don't have much time if Rodriguez is right about the 9 p.m. fireworks show from hell."

"What the heck is that?" asked Jamie, pointing at the gun Rick held.

"It's called a Peace-Monger," said Rick. "Metal detectors won't pick it up because it's made of a non-metallic polymer composite." Rick took aim down the barrel of the fun-size rifle. "If that punk Leatherhead shows up, I'm bringing him in, dead or hurt real bad."

Jamie cranked a fist pump and mocked, "I'm going to Disney World!"

Lincoln could barely walk, let alone survive a trip to the most magical place on earth to hunt down a killer and avert a radioactive disaster. With the others distracted, she slipped a hand into her purse, pulled out one of the adrenaline boosters that Dr. Walker had given her, and injected herself. Seconds later she could start to feel the effects. She straightened her back and walked to the elevator door. "So what are we waiting for?"

Ten minutes later, the Roach Coach charged down the Interstate-4 corridor. The contraband siren on top of the van and its disco flashing light cleared a path as they sped towards Disney World.

"So, uh, Dad..." said Lincoln. "How are we going to get into Disney World? I'm pretty sure a siren won't be enough to bluff our way in, especially in this rig. Do you have $10,000 for our day passes?"

"Negative, Star," answered Rick. "I plan to call in a favor." He meant it literally as he tapped his holoband.

Lincoln's first instinct was doubt, but her dad had proven to be remarkably resourceful as of late. She heard a man answer her dad's call, but her attention inevitably was drawn back to her fear over the fate of Barry Blue Hawkins. Was he alive or dead? If Leatherhead went after him before the Paluskis' betrayal, then Barry must be dead by now. Sure, he knew that this day was coming, but how could bed-bound Barry possibly elude Leatherhead?

What started out as humoring an old man led to the discovery of cold-case murders, the Chetola radiation poisoning, and the Goliath Gammaway scandal, all of which have been captured on the podcast. The Mender's Paradox gave purpose to her driving ambition. She was sitting on the investigative story of a lifetime. Her dream come true, yes, but bittersweet knowing it put Barry in harm's way.

The Roach rocketed past downtown Orlando as the highway lights flickered on. They were getting into theme park territory. She pressed the side of her face against the passenger window.

Holographic billboards flashed in her eyes advertising the same tourist attraction.

DISNEY'S SINKHOLE CITY OPENING SOON!

A family car weaved down Mainstreet USA while buildings disappeared into the earth. A bus plummeted through the words, DARE TO ESCAPE SINKHOLE CITY!

She groaned at the next holoboard. HOLESOME FUN FOR THE HOLE FAMILY!

Radiant pixie dust swept it clean. A GENUINE FLORIDA EXPERIENCE … WITH THE DISNEY MAGIC TOUCH!

"Sinkhole City!" said Jamie. "What a gas! I'll be first in line!"

"Really, Hon?" said Windy. "Isn't our real-life disaster enough thrills for you?"

"At least with Sinkhole City I can enjoy the experience without worrying about being killed!" said Jamie.

Lincoln almost enjoyed their banter. It dulled her anguish regarding Barry. She would join in their conversation if she wasn't so wiped. Sinkhole City. What a gas indeed.

Windy read from her holopad. "'Sinkholes are not uncommon in Florida. They are caused by underground erosion. Acidic water dissolves limestone forming underground caverns that eventually cave in. A classic Florida sinkhole occurred in 1978 when a Porsche dealership in downtown Winter Park was devoured over the course of a day. The world's largest sinkhole is in Venezuela and measures almost a quarter a mile across and a quarter of a mile deep and could easily hold the Empire State Building'."

She skipped ahead. "Here's the Sinkhole City connection. 'In 2045 a massive sinkhole swallowed the monorail station at the front entrance of the Magic Kingdom'."

Lincoln recalled how Disney Imagineers sprinkled Tinkerbell's fairy powder to make a natural disaster into marketing gold. They turned the sinkhole into a theme park ride that would have no rival on the planet – Sinkhole City was born.

"This ride will be the most awesome ever!" Jamie could hardly contain himself. He snatched the holopad from Windy's hands. "Let me lay it on you guys." He read from the holopad. "'The premise of Sinkhole City is that you are on a tour bus. As your bus enters the town, a lamp post disappears into the ground right before your eyes. A tree on the other side of the street does the same. As the bus rounds a corner a house is sucked into the earth. The bus speeds up to get out of town. Going through downtown, buildings are going down on either side of you. The road becomes impassable and the bus hops the sidewalk, falling headlong into the sinkhole chasm. You become weightless in the free fall as people and cars fall all around you. Out of nowhere a hovercraft clamps onto the bus with mechanical talons. As it pulls the bus to the surface, a tall building falls in front of the bus almost ruining your escape. The bus reaches the surface and is gently set down on solid ground. Congratulations! You have survived Sinkhole City!'"

Lincoln grinned at Jamie's infectious enthusiasm, then turned to her dad. "So, Dad, who did you call? A park employee friend to get us in through a back door?" asked Lincoln.

"Not exactly, Star," replied Rick. "A few years before I retired, I was assigned to look after Stu Chaplain, a Disney bigwig working on some kind of big secret project, something about a roller coaster in a hole. It rankled me that this was considered a national asset, but he turned out to be a good guy and we got along. He said if I ever needed anything… well, he's getting us in through the front door."

"Sinkhole City was his baby?" yelped Jamie. "Detective Jade, you *are* a rock star!"

Minutes later the Roach Coach squealed to a stop at a ticket booth. "Detective Rick Jade," Rick nearly shouted at the attendant, thrusting his old Homeland Badge in the young man's face. "I have to…"

"We've been expecting you, Detective," replied the attendant with a welcoming smile. "Mr. Chaplain has instructed us to send you to meet the security team at the main entrance. Simply follow the lane with the yellow stripe and 'Be our gues….'"

Rick did not wait, peeling rubber as he veered onto the service road, which bypassed the monorail and shuttle systems. It was already 8:15. "Thank you!" yelled Jamie, a futile gesture at politeness seeing as how they were too far away for the attendant to hear.

Sinkhole City loomed in front of them. It was hard to miss. A stadium-sized dome was being built over the sinkhole. Construction had been underway for nearly five years and the unfinished section straddled the old park entrance. Jamie and Windy gathered up the mobile broadcasting equipment and night-time binoculars, conking heads in the cramped quarters. Lincoln, conserving every calorie for the Podcast, laid back in her seat.

Within minutes they arrived at the front gate, where a pair of uniformed security personnel met them.

"Are you Homeland Special Agent Rick Jade?" asked the woman.

"Affirmative," Rick answered. "We believe there is a radioactive detonation device on the castle. Put men on the castle roof ASAP. Take me to the fallout bunker. The perp may be hiding out there. And have your control room people scan the video feeds in and around the castle for any large objects that don't belong."

"Follow us," she said. She and her partner led them in a side gate and directed them through the zero-tolerance metal detector. The state-of-the-art machine remained silent.

"Geez," Lincoln could not help saying aloud. It hit Lincoln that Rick was a man obsessed. He had zoomed down I-4 using an illegal siren, convinced a Disney heavy hitter to get them in, flashed an expired Homeland badge, and walked successfully through a metal detector packing his switchblade Peacemonger rifle.

"Are you gonna make it, Star?" asked Rick.

"You bet, Dad." Lincoln gritted a smile to mask the wooziness she felt as the adrenaline booster started to wear off. She still had energy, but probably not for long.

"I'll meet you kids fifty yards in front of the castle in about twenty minutes," said Rick. With that, Rick hustled away with his two security escorts, pulling them by their arms to make them keep up with him.

Lincoln felt winded just walking through the turnstiles. Seeing her gasp for breath, Windy elbowed through the tourists milling about like a herd of bison at Yellowstone National Park and rented a scooter.

"All right!" said Jamie. "Let's ramble on."

The trio took a right turn onto Main Street and headed towards the castle. The multitude of people were clearing the streets to make way for the parade that accompanied the upcoming fireworks. Though not a far walk, the scooter rental proved to be a lifesaver for Lincoln.

When they reached their rendezvous point in front of the castle, Jamie transformed from knucklehead to production engineer. He picked out a spot on the right-hand side of the castle sidewalk. "I'll set up here," and he plunked down his knapsack of supplies. He fished three necklaces with a shiny bead on them from his pocket and handed one to both Lincoln and Windy. "Put these Eye-Spy cameras around your necks. I'll record your audio-video view of whatever happens." Pointing at a lamppost, he directed, "L.J., scoot over there so that we'll have an angle of the castle rising up from behind you." The White Castle with the turquoise blue turrets shone like a thousand Christmas trees.

Windy did her best to untangle Lincoln's hair. "You got this?"

"Yeah," said Lincoln, nodding. Actually, Lincoln had no idea what she was going to say. Instead, the movie screen in her head featured an image of Barry impaled to his family room floor with a pitchfork, courtesy of a Leatherhead Special.

Windy grabbed the binoculars and scanned the castle roof. "I'll holler if I see any activity up there."

The gleaming castle captivated Lincoln. Beneath its lofty archway a team of white horses hitched to Cinderella's carriage waited for the parade and fireworks to start. Herds of tourists packed both sides of Main Street. The evening breeze fluttered the turret flags.

About to break the story of the year, Lincoln had long anticipated the glory she would reap. Yet in this moment, she was humbled. Her friends, her dad, her teacher, and Barry had put their lives on the line because of her. But not for her, exactly. Professor Erlenmeyer was right. It wasn't all about her. They were trying to do the right thing. In that moment she took on a tremendous obligation and duty to the public good.

Jamie shouted, "Tick-tock my peeps! We are going live in five, four, three, two...." Jamie stood in front of the camera and played 'Heroes', the podcast theme song.

He flashed his billion-dollar smile and looked directly into the camera. "Hello out there, fellow heroes! J-Rod of the holo-pod here, your master of ceremonies for a special live edition of 'The Mender's Paradox.' Our courageous crew is on location at Walt Disney World in Orlando, Florida. Cast your eyeballs into this stream, frothing fans, for danger is afoot. We are here to save the Magic Kingdom from becoming the Tragic Kingdom. And now I turn you over to the brightest jewel in any kingdom, Lincoln Jade."

Lincoln winced and made a mental note: write own intros. The corniness she could live with, but 'brightest jewel?' She stepped off her scooter and turned to face the camera. Oh geez, her head felt warm like a toaster, though the night air was crisp. She didn't know if she was going to make it through this shoot. Her body was rebelling against her iron will. If she couldn't do it for herself, maybe she could find the strength to do it for those she loved. For her dad, Windy, Jamie, Professor Erlenmeyer, and Barry. And for the multitudes of people that were immediately in harm's way.

Lincoln steadied herself and looked into the camera. Behind it, Jamie gesticulated like a performing monkey urging her to say something, as they were still recording live.

Lincoln reviewed the flurry of recent events that popped into her head. "Lincoln Jade reporting to you for The Mender's Paradox in front of Cinderella's Castle. Would you believe that in the past twenty-four hours I've been kidnapped, interrogated by a psychopath, left to die in the Goliath demolition, and then rescued by my dead professor?"

She paused to catch her breath. "We will be sure to catch you up on what's been happening. But right now, we are here to foil corporate greed at the highest level. The Paluski brothers, who own Goliath Industries, plan to put thousands of people in harm's way to enrich themselves with their new Gammaway product. They used a contract killer to plant a dirty bomb on top of the castle roof directly behind me."

Lincoln panted like a Mississippi hound, her breathing becoming more labored. "Unless we figure out a way to stop it, the bomb will turn the Magic Kingdom and surrounding theme parks into a radioactive wasteland. The ensuing explosion would make the Mega-Target Store bombing look like a campfire. You are witnessing a terrorist act on American soil that could cause international panic and —"

Windy stepped into the camera frame. "I've got something on the roof." She jumped around, waving her arms, and pointed to the blue castle roof. The huge night-time binoculars dangled from her neck. "There is an architectural inconsistency on the tallest turret…something like a large hump projecting near the back of the dominating spire." Windy's voice leaped an octave higher. "We've got movement on the roof! Somebody's up there!"

Rick burst into the camera frame. He grabbed the binoculars without removing them from Windy's neck, causing her forehead to knock into Rick's chin. "I see him!" said Rick. "It looks like Disney security, in a blue uniform. Holy smokes, those guys are on the ball!"

With a tremendous effort, Windy snagged the binoculars from Rick. She trained them on the loftiest spire, which at one hundred and eighty-nine feet towered above the other castle blue turrets. "There's a large white bundle moving down the side of the tallest spire! It appears that the Disney security guy up on the roof is hoisting it down with a rope and pulley. Hon, are you getting this? Tell me that you are getting this!"

"Oh yeah babe, I am totally zoomed in on that roof action."

"Give that man a cigar!" said Rick, waving his hands in the air. "That thing has to be the bomb. He's got to bring it down fast so it can be disarmed."

The bomb package had been camouflaged on the back side of the spire, but was now in the spotlights as it was being lowered. The park parcour hero brought the bundle from the spire to his position on the roof. He heaved the Dumbo-sized bundle onto his back.

Lincoln stood in front of the camera. "It appears that a large package, presumably the bomb, has been located on the tallest spire of the castle and has been brought down to the roof."

By now the standing audience had seen the roof action and everyone was pointing to it. Without wasting any time, the man rappelled down the castle façade towards the arch.

"Geez, this guy is incredibly strong," thought Lincoln. She grabbed the binoculars from Windy and focused on the courageous security man in blue. As the hero twisted on the rappelling line, Lincoln locked onto his face. She gasped. "I knew it! That's no Disney cop. That's Leatherhead!"

"No way!" shouted Windy. "Why would Leatherhead take his bomb?"

Rick ripped the binoculars out of Lincoln's hands. Like a gargoyle coming to life, Leatherhead dropped down the castle wall. "Criminy! It's him all right!" Rick lowered the binocs. "Your ass is grass, dirtbag, and I'm the lawnmower. I finally got you!"

The crowd noise became louder as everyone watched the unfolding drama directly above the castle arch. The horses pawed the ground and bucked their decorated manes.

Leatherhead landed on top of the lead horse. He manhandled the bomb across the mighty steed's back. Then he cut the reins, freeing the horse from the rest of the team and carriage.

Fireworks shot up from the back of the castle in colors of red, white, and blue. The crowd oohed and aahed. Hidden loud-speakers serenaded, 'When you Wish Upon a Star'.

Leatherhead swatted the horse's rump and the stallion reared up, while a burst of fireworks serendipitously framed the image. The crowd clapped and cheered, Leatherhead became part of the Disney magic. As soon as the steed came down on all fours, it took off down Main Street. Hunched over the steed's neck, Leatherhead held onto the blob of the bomb bouncing on the horse's back with one hand and clung to the mane with the other.

"He's coming right towards us!" cried Windy.

"Ohhh yeah! TMZ Holopod of the Year is in the bag!" said Jamie as he tracked the action with his camera.

Rick whipped out his jack-knife Peace-monger rifle. "He'll pass right by us. Hello, Leatherhead. I got your homecoming right here!"

The fireworks painted the sky with an intricate depiction of Cinderella's pumpkin carriage. The Disney theme song thrummed over the din of the cheering tourists. Leatherhead's horse pounded the cobblestone, rushing toward Lincoln's position on the sidewalk.

Windy's question troubled Lincoln. Why *would* Leatherhead take the bomb? It didn't feel right.

Rick took one step off the curb and into the street. He raised his wee rifle and took aim. "Time to die, Leatherdead. Die die die die die!"

As Leatherhead passed, Lincoln swatted the barrel of Rick's rifle upward with the last of her strength. It discharged into the night sky.

"Star!" Rick shouted, looking at Lincoln with a combination of confusion and rage at Leatherhead's escape.

"I've got to see where he's going!" Lincoln gasped. "Trust me, Dad. No time to explain." However, she was completely spent. Then she remembered the second booster shot in her bag. "I shouldn't, but I gotta," she thought, ripping the needle from its package and sending a second dose of Dr. Walker's adrenaline mix into her weakened system.

She hopped onto her scooter and chased Leatherhead. Her peripheral vision picked up on the shapeless masses of people still lining the streets, thoroughly enjoying the 'show'. Though she had her scooter at full throttle, Leatherhead easily pulled away, the bomb package jostling across the back of the horse.

"That's it, you mangled maniac," Lincoln said through gritted teeth. "Take that bomb out of here."

At the end of Main Street stood a tall cement construction wall where the street took a sharp right bend. Leatherhead did not veer or slow. Instead, he pulled out a short tube, extended it into a long tube, and put it on his shoulder. The back of the tube flashed and the wall exploded.

"Geez!" Lincoln shouted. "He just used a bazooka to blast a hole into the wall!" She watched the Lone Stranger jump his horse through the freshly created gap.

Lincoln made it to the hole in the wall but could not go any further. She realized that she was still shooting live with her Eye-Spy camera on her head. "Lincoln Jade is still here," she said as she tried to catch her breath. "Leatherhead has acquired one of Cinderella's horses and bolted down Main Street carrying what we presume to be the sum of all fears bomb."

As the smoke cleared from the explosion of the wall Lincoln could see that Leatherhead was headed straight towards the Sinkhole City project. The synthetic sky of the partially completed dome shone daytime blue against the night sky. "Leatherhead is galloping towards the exposed chasm of

Sinkhole City," she said as she did her best to steady herself and broadcast the action unfolding before her eyes. The ghost-rider dressed in blue did not slow down. Was he going to commit suicide? Lincoln peered through the bazooka blast smoke. The last she saw of the spectacle was the back of the horse's hooves as they disappeared over the edge of the big black hole.

"Unbelievably, Leatherhead, horse, and bomb have gone into the sinkhole!" Lincoln shouted. For the sake of her podcast audience she panned upwards towards the fake blue sky of the Sinkhole City dome. They saw a surreal scene of a man-made blue sky with real night sky cracking through it. She panned to the frighteningly silent hole. It had been over a minute since the galloping gremlin leapt into the abyss.

Lincoln felt energized and woozy at the same time. She let her head drop. Her Eye Spy gave her viewing audience the exciting view of her feet. Then something extraordinary happened. The concrete crumbs from the destroyed wall appeared to be dancing at her feet. A rumbling noise emanated from the sinkhole. The ground vibrated through her feet. The reverberating roar increased until it seemed like a close encounter with a SpaceX rocket launch.

Lincoln's camera recorded the vastness of the great hole getting bigger. The edges of the hole caved inwards. The dome's blue sky twisted back and forth making a head-splitting sound of fingernails on a cosmic chalkboard. It cracked down the middle and folded in half as it crashed into the expanding sinkhole.

"This is Lincoln Jade for the Mender's Paradox signing off!" she gasped.

Rick's voice commanded, "Star! We are getting the hell out of here now! Meet us at the van!"

"Copy that," she said to her holoband. "I'm on my way!"

Lincoln whipped her scooter around and snaked her way through the confused crowd to the exit gate. When she arrived at the Roach Coach, her dad and friends helped her crawl through the back door of the van where she plopped on the floor. Rick put the hammer down and squealed out of the Disney parking lot. Soon the courageous crew was headed back west on I-4, siren wailing.

"Whooooo-EEEEE!" shouted Jamie. "We nailed every bit of that action! Way to stick with it, L.J.. Your Eye Spy footage was the best part."

"That Leatherhead appearance was one thing, but for him to take the bomb from the castle to the sinkhole blew my mind," said Windy.

"Yeah, that was a one-way trip for Leatherhead!" said Jamie. "The bomb must have gone off at the very bottom of the hole. Sinkhole City caved in upon itself. I can see tomorrow's headline: 'Florida Man on Horseback Blows Up Sinkhole City'. RIP in pieces, Leatherhead!"

"Better for it to go off deep inside the earth instead of on top of the Disney castle," said Windy.

Her crew's loud voices filling the small space of the Roach Coach hammered Lincoln's aching head. She squeezed her eyes shut and then opened them. Hundreds of bobby pins held up the headliner on the van ceiling. The pinheads lit by the roadside lights twinkled like the stars that had peeked through the dome's blue sky. The ceiling darkened as her vision blurred. Her breathing grew shallow.

"Who would have thought that Leatherhead would turn out to be the hero and save all of those people?" said Windy.

"He's no hero," retorted Rick. "Leatherhead doesn't exactly have a track record of rescuing people. Anything he does, he does for himself."

"Do you think it was some kind of public suicide?" asked Jamie.

"Negative," said Rick. "Leatherhead is a survivalist. He's spent his career evading the likes of me."

"Ooooooooooo!" said Windy. "What if Leatherhead saw the evening news report where the Paluski brothers set him up as the disgruntled employee -turned-terrorist?"

"So he goes back to doublecross the doublecrossers?" said Jamie.

Windy cut in. "You bet, Hon! The Paluskis betrayed Leatherhead. He wouldn't want them to profit from his work. He crawled out of whatever hole he was hangin' out in and returned to the castle to stop the bomb."

"That's the most likely scenario," said Rick. "It must have been too late to disarm the bomb, so he dumped it into the bottomless Sinkhole City." He paused. "I have to admit, it's a good thing Lincoln deflected my gunshot away from Leatherhead to let him pass. Otherwise, the Paluskis would have won. Yeah, Leatherhead did everyone a favor tonight."

"Good thing for those Paluskis that Leatherhead went with the bomb into the sinkhole," said Windy with a shudder. "I wouldn't want to be on that guy's naughty list if I had doublecrossed him and he was still around."

"You know," said Jamie, letting his words play out slowly. "On camera I couldn't clearly see when the horse went over the edge. There was so much smoke from when Leatherhead bazooka-ed the wall. L.J., you think your spy cam got a good shot of Leatherhead falling to his doom? It would be the perfect closing video."

No response.

"Star?" said Rick, his voice registering alarm.

Windy bent over Lincoln on the van floor. She put her ear close to Lincoln's mouth, then felt her forehead. "She's burning up!" said Windy.

"Rodriguez! Get the oxygen on her," said Rick. "There's a canister under the back seat."

Lincoln was scared. Sure she had covered Leatherhead's grand finale. But at what cost? She didn't want to end up like one of those guys who climb to the top of Mount Everest but don't make it off the mountain. She focused her attention on getting air in and out of her lungs. The fever meant she had a bad infection. The damage to her lungs over time had so reduced her lung capacity that she fought for each breath. On top of that, her heart was racing from the double dose of boosters. Thank goodness for the plastic nose and mouth mask that Jamie clamped onto her face.

Rick took the hospital exit without slowing. "How's she doing?" His voice ramped up to a panicking yell.

"Not good!" said Windy. "We've got to get her to a hospital now!"

"One step ahead of you. I've already talked to Dr. Walker," said Rick as he ran a red light as if it weren't there.

"Hey!" said Jamie pointing out the window. "We've just passed the hospital!"

"We're not going to the hospital," said Rick leaning into the steering wheel. "We're going to Barry Blue Hawkins' house."

CHAPTER 34

The Good Fight

The fearless four roared into Barry's driveway. "Rodriguez, get Lincoln," Rick ordered as he vaulted to the doorstep. Jamie scooped Lincoln out of the back of the van while Rick pounded on the door.

"Barry! Barry!" He tried the doorknob and found it unlocked. Leading with his Peace-monger rifle, he entered the house.

"Barry! It's Rick."

No answer.

Rick rushed into the living room where he found Moon Dog walking in circles with a red dart in his shoulder. Jamie gently laid Lincoln on the big red couch. Windy entered the room with Prinity right behind her. Dr. Walker sat on the couch with her bag and checked Lincoln's vitals.

"Rick, your daughter's oxygen uptake is only thirty percent. This is bad, really bad," said Prinity, her voice wavering.

Lincoln had no breath to talk or move. Coldness gripped her body. Coldness like she was trapped in water just below the ice. She could see Dr. Walker and Rick above her through this sheet of ice separating her from the world.

Rick turned his attention to the old people's Christmas tree in the far corner. He stared. The angel on top of the tree softly glowed, then dimmed, over and over. He strode to the tree and pulled it away from the wall, revealing an air conditioning grate. Rick opened it and removed the filter. He stooped down and spoke into the dark two-foot by two-foot square hole. "Barry! Jenny! It's Rick. All clear."

Moments later, Barry poked his head out of the hole like a prairie dog making sure that it was safe to come out.

Rick pulled Barry by the shoulders and stood him up. They were face to face, inches apart with Rick holding Barry up by his armpits.

"Barry." Locking eyes, Rick said, "It's Lincoln."

Without a word, Barry nodded.

Rick hauled Barry to the big red couch. Lincoln's skin and face were as pale as a waning moon. "She's past my help," said Prinity, as she relinquished to Barry her spot and knelt next to Lincoln.

Jenny clung to Barry on the couch. "It's okay," said Jenny, a tear rolling down her cheek. "You were born to do this."

Barry turned to her and raised his right hand. All of his fingers were extended except for the third and fourth fingers.

Jenny put her lips to Barrys' and said, "I love you, too, Bear."

Barry turned towards Lincoln and grabbed her wrists. Grimacing, he bowed his head. He let go of her and moaned. "I don't have the juice, there's nothing left of me," he said.

"She's stopped breathing," busted in Prinity. She stood and began CPR.

Jenny put her hands on Barry's head. "Try again, Bear." Barry took Lincoln's hands in his. As one, the others put their hands on Barry. Barry's arms shook, his breathing lurching like a locomotive. Lincoln was as still as a stone even as his body quaked. Time turned into eternity. No one moved.

Suddenly Lincoln gulped. Her chest heaved.

Barry held on even as the quivering in his arms died away. He let go of Lincoln's hands and slumped backwards into Jenny's lap. His eyes closed as he said, "I have finished the race."

Lincoln's eyes popped open and everyone swarmed around her. Color returned to her face. Her chest rose and fell in an even tempo.

"Star! It's Dad," said Rick as he caressed her head.

"L.J. Sista-Gal!" said Jamie. "You're alive!"

"Oxygen uptake is up to seventy percent," said Prinity, as she hovered over Lincoln. "Fever is going down."

"Oh Lincoln, I'm not sure what just happened but I'm glad it did!" said Windy.

Mass hugging ensued at Lincoln's end of the big red couch. Jenny sat alone with Barry at the other end.

"Jenny, you and Barry beat Leatherhead!" said Rick in a triumphant voice. "You beat him and the Paluskis, forever and ever."

"Amen!" said Jamie.

Jenny's eyes were wet and red, her face firm.

Windy sat on the floor next to Jenny. "Miss Jenny, we are so grateful for what you've done for us and for Lincoln. I don't know what we could…."

"Windy, you young people have done so much for us. Barry wanted his story to be told. It has, thanks to the Mender's Paradox," said Jenny.

Prinity reached over and took Jenny's hand. "Jenny…I don't know if this is the right time or place to tell you this, but medicine will forever be turned on it's pointy head thanks to Barry. We've been working with the blood samples I took when Barry mended my slashed wrists. We've identified several novel compounds from those samples and we're working on synthesizing them in our labs. Someday soon there will be medicine that helps people's bodies heal themselves. Put them on the mend, as Barry would say."

"Thank you for that, Dr. Walker," said Jenny, stroking Barry's bald head. "Putting people on the mend will be Barry's legacy."

Lincoln propped herself up on her elbows and looked around. "I feel better." Her eyes fell upon Barry and Jenny. "Jenny, how's Barry?"

"He's fallen into his final sleep, dear," she sobbed.

Lincoln plopped her head back down. "Sleep. Yeah, sleep sounds good." And Lincoln conked out like a tuckered toddler.

Two days later Lincoln woke up in her old room in her dad's house. She shielded her eyes from the sun pouring through her window. As she stretched she savored a deeply satisfying breath and then exhaled. She sprang up to a sitting position. Geez! She had never experienced a full lung capacity. Then she was hit with a notion to do jumping jacks. After a minute or so of bouncing all over her room, she did not feel winded at all. She stood still. It dawned on her what Barry had given her. Yes, he had endowed her with his final mending, giving his final breath. Barry, oh Barry…she would always remember him. And with a smile, for the old codger had worked his way into her heart. As for Jenny, well, gratitude filled Lincoln's being for the sacrifice Jenny had made. Lincoln wanted to pay it forward to infinity.

Ooooooo yeah! A tsunami of joy swept over Lincoln's body. So this was what it was like to breathe without trying. No longer shackled by grueling fatigue and pain, she felt like a superhero, like she could do anything. The world could use some superheros, so why not her? After all, who had x-ray vision to see the people struggling with invisible illness. She did. Bam! She airboxed an uppercut. She had the power to adapt and persevere, no matter what the storm. Bop! A right hook. She possessed a heart on fire, burning to will the good of others. Ka-chop! A flying karate kick.

Yeah, she could be a superhero. After all, she learned from the best...Prinity, Jenny, her friends, Barry, her Dad of course, and even Professor Erlenmeyer. She could fight the good fight. And she would start with doing her part to make sure that the Paluski brothers went to Maximum Retro-Prison.

The podcast theme song "Heroes" played in her head. She pictured two dolphins frolicking towards the horizon. Her dark hair fell about her face, her head bobbing as she grooved to the music.

Lincoln felt like she could accomplish anything. She had so much work to do now that she had her health. But was this for real? Her body had failed her before. Was there some way that she could be sure that her body was ready?

When she had asked Barry what he would do if he could do anything, he said that he would swim in the ocean.

Yes, she knew how to give her body a proper test drive. She was going to the beach today. She would swim like the dolphins, like the dolphins can swim.

Epilogue

Jackson Paluski dreamt he was at one of his beach houses listening to the soothing sound of the surf pounding the shore. Dank cold permeated his bones. Perhaps this was his Cape Cod beach mansion. He heard a voice calling him.

"Jackson!" came the urgent cry. "Jackson! Help, help me!" It was Wilson, his little brother, whose frenzied voice penetrated Jackson's dream. "Jackson! Jackson! Wake up!"

Jackson opened his eyes to see a head on the beach about twenty feet straight in front of him. Behind the head the menacing ocean churned while the orange glob of sun crawled over the horizon. Waves smacked the back of the head and then receded into the face of his brother. They were not on Cape Cod.

Jackson recognized the stretch of pristine beach. Cape Kennedy National Wildlife Preserve protected the sea turtle sanctuary. Humans were not allowed on the beach except for special nighttime ranger tours when the sea turtles came ashore to lay their eggs. He did not recall any tours at dawn.

"Wilson, I see you!" yelled Jackson. "Hang on, I'm coming." Jackson had always looked out for his little brother. However he would be no help today. Buried up to his chin, he was just another head perched on the sand. The tide rolled in as the sun rose. Jackson helplessly watched the waves batter his brother's head.

Jackson couldn't believe their situation. How could this happen? Who was doing this to them?

Jackson watched in horror as a white ribbon of foam snaked its way towards him and nearly reached his own head. He gulped as his brother struggled to keep his nose above the water line, what would soon be his own fate if he couldn't get out of this.

Yet another wave crashed over Wilson and receded. "Jackson, your Frankenstein assassin is standing right next to you."

Jackson knew only one assassin. He was unable to look up, but he could rotate his head a few inches. A pair of brown boots stood just off his shoulder. Good gravy, it was him! Impossible! He was dead. He had plunged over the edge of Sinkhole City on the horse with that bomb. Right? But only that psychopath would think of burying them up to their chins on a beach.

"You maniac!" said Jackson, squirming his head as much as he could. "I know it's you! We get your point. We know you're upset. But this is not acceptable. Dig us out immediately!"

No response.

Wilson thrashed his head, drowning over and over every time a wave reached him and then returned to the ocean. He didn't have long before the tide covered him.

The water pooled around Jackson's chin as the tide continued to rise and sloshed around the boots standing next to him. "You're pushing it really close. You're killing him. That's enough. Enough I say!"

No response.

The sun cleared the horizon, revealing a clear blue sky. Wilson's head, now almost completely submerged, no longer thrashing about anymore. The very top of the head bobbed like a beachball between waves.

Jackson shrieked. He cried. He didn't know if it was because his brother was dead or because the same thing was about to happen to him. "You killed my brother, you know. This will be duly noted! Duly noted!" A one-foot tall wave rudely slapped him in the face. His breathing accelerated. The sand that entombed his body was crushing his lungs. He couldn't get enough air. It was such a helpless feeling. The water creeped over his mouth. The deadly liquid might as well have been molten lava.

"Look, I get it, '' said Jackson, spurting water out of his mouth and gulping in air. "We had to tell the media and police about you to throw them off our trail. We were trying to save the whole operation. We were going to cut you in for a third of what we would have made from the Gammaway profits."

No response.

"Please, dig me out of here and I will cut you in as an equal Goliath partner, split fifty-fifty!

No response.

This time a wave so big engulfed Jackson that he had to hold his breath as long as he could.

"You owe it to me to let me go!" Jackson swallowed a hunk of sea water. The extreme saltiness made his stomach queasy. His lungs labored like twin Hoover vacuum cleaners.

Jackson tried his antagonizer one more time. "Listen to me, boy! I made you. I gave you a job. I gave you a career! I gave you…purpose!"

A shovel speared into the sand dangerously close to Jackson's face. The owner of the boots responded in an even tone. "Thanks to you…I have a new purpose."

The boots turned and walked away.

THE END

Made in the USA
Middletown, DE
15 February 2022